IF YOU COULD SEE THE SUN

IF YOU COULD SEE THE SUN

ANN LIANG

inkyard PRESS

ISBN-13: 978-1-335-91584-9

If You Could See the Sun

For questions and comments about the quality of this book, please contact us
at CustomerService@Harlequin.com.

Inkyard Press
22 Adelaide St. West, 41st Floor
Toronto, Ontario M5H 4E3, Canada
www.InkyardPress.com

Printed in U.S.A.

To my wonderful parents, who aren't allowed to read this book.

And to my little sister, Alyssa,
who would like everyone to know how awesome she is.

1

My parents only ever invite me out to eat for one of three reasons. One, someone's dead (which, given the ninety-something members in our family WeChat group alone, happens more often than you'd think). Two, it's someone's birthday. Or three, they have a life-changing announcement to make.

Sometimes it's a combination of all the above, like when my great-grandaunt passed away on the morning of my twelfth birthday, and my parents decided to inform me over a bowl of fried sauce noodles that they'd be sending me off to Airington International Boarding School.

But it's August now, the sweltering summer heat palpable even in the air-conditioned confines of the restaurant, and no one in my immediate family has a birthday this month. Which, of course, leaves only two other possibilities…

The anxious knot in my stomach tightens. It's all I can do not to run right back out through the glass double doors.

Call me weak or whatever, but I'm in no state to handle bad news of any kind.

Especially not today.

"Alice, what you look so nervous for ya?" Mama asks as an unsmiling, qipao-clad waitress leads us over to our table in the back corner.

We squeeze past a crowded table of elderly people sharing a giant pink-tinted cream cake shaped like a peach, and what appears to be a company lunch, with men sweating in their stuffy collared shirts and women dabbing white powder onto their cheeks. A few of them twist around and stare when they notice my uniform. I can't tell if it's because they recognize the tiger crest emblazoned on my blazer pocket, or because of how grossly pretentious the design looks compared to the local schools' tracksuits.

"I'm not nervous," I say, taking the seat between her and Baba. "My face just always looks like this." This isn't exactly a lie. My aunt once joked that if I were ever found at a crime scene, I'd be the first one arrested based solely on my expression and body language. *Never seen anyone as jumpy as you*, she'd said. *Must've been a mouse in your past life.*

I resented the comparison then, but I can't help feeling like a mouse now—one that's about to walk straight into a trap.

Mama moves to pass me the laminated menu. As she does, light spills onto her bony hands from the nearby window, throwing the ropey white scar running down her palm into sharp relief. A pang of all-too-familiar guilt flares up inside me like an open flame.

"Haizi," Mama calls me. "What do you want to eat?"

"Oh. Uh, anything's fine," I reply, quickly averting my gaze. Baba breaks apart his disposable wooden chopsticks with a loud snap. "Kids these days don't know how lucky they are," he says, rubbing the chopsticks together to remove any splinters before helping me do the same. "All grow up in honey jar. You know what I eat at your age? Sweet potato. Every day, sweet potato."

As he launches into a more detailed description of daily life in the rural villages of Henan, Mama waves the waitress over and lists off what sounds like enough dishes to feed the entire restaurant.

"*Ma,*" I protest, dragging the word out in Mandarin. "We don't need—"

"Yes, you do," she says firmly. "You always starve whenever school starts. Very bad for your body."

Despite myself, I suppress the urge to roll my eyes. Less than ten minutes ago, she'd been commenting on how my cheeks had grown rounder over the summer holidays; only by her logic is it possible to be too chubby and dangerously undernourished at the same time.

When Mama finally finishes ordering, she and Baba exchange a look, then turn to me with expressions so solemn I blurt out the first thing that comes to mind: "Is—is my grandpa okay?"

Mama's thin brows furrow, accentuating the stern features of her face. "Of course. Why you ask?"

"N-nothing. Never mind." I allow myself a small sigh of relief, but my muscles remain tensed, as if bracing for a blow. "Look, whatever the bad news is, can we just—can we get it over with quickly? The awards ceremony is in an hour and if I'm going to have a mental breakdown, I need at least twenty minutes to recover before I get on stage."

Baba blinks. "Awards ceremony? What ceremony?"

My concern temporarily gives way to exasperation. "*The* awards ceremony for the highest achievers in each year level."

He continues to stare at me blankly.

"Come on, Ba. I've mentioned it at least fifty times this summer."

I'm only exaggerating a little. Sad as it sounds, those fleeting moments of glory under the bright auditorium spotlight are all I've been looking forward to the past couple of months.

Even if I have to share them with Henry Li.

As always, the name fills my mouth with something sharp and bitter like poison. God, I hate him. I hate him and his flawless, porcelain skin and immaculate uniform and his composure, as untouchable and unfailing as his ever-growing list of achievements. I hate the way people look at him and *see* him, even if he's completely silent, head down and working at his desk.

I've hated him ever since he sauntered into school four years ago, brand-new and practically glowing. By the end of his first day, he'd beat me in our history unit test by a whole two-point-five marks, and everyone knew his name.

Just thinking about it now makes my fingers itch.

Baba frowns. Looks to Mama for confirmation. "Are we meant to go to this—this ceremony thing?"

"It's students only," I remind him, even though it wasn't always this way. The school decided to make it a more private event after my classmate's very famous mother, Krystal Lam, showed up to the ceremony and accidentally brought the paparazzi in with her. There were photos of our auditorium floating around all over Weibo for days afterward.

"Anyway, that's not the point. The *point* is that they're handing out awards and—"

"Yes, yes, all you talk about is award," Mama interrupts, impatient. "Where your priorities, hmm? Does that school of yours not teach you right values? It should go family first, then health, then saving for retirement, then—are you even listening?"

I'm spared from having to lie when our food arrives.

In the fancier Peking duck restaurants like Quanjude, the kind of restaurants my classmates go to frequently without someone having to die first, the chefs always wheel out the roast duck on a tray and carve it up beside your table. It's almost an elaborate performance; the crispy, glazed skin coming apart with every flash of the blade to reveal the tender white meat and sizzling oil underneath.

But here the waitress simply presents us with a whole duck chopped into large chunks, the head still attached and everything.

Mama must catch the look on my face because she sighs and turns the duck head away from me, muttering something about my Western sensibilities.

More dishes come, one by one: fresh cucumbers drizzled with vinegar and mixed with chopped garlic, thin-layered scallion pancakes baked to a perfect crisp, soft tofu swimming in a golden-brown sauce and sticky rice cakes dusted with a fine coat of sugar. I can already see Mama measuring out the food with her shrewd brown eyes, most likely calculating how many extra meals she and Baba can make from the leftovers.

I force myself to wait until both Mama and Baba have taken

a few bites of their food to venture, "Um. I'm pretty sure you guys were going to tell me something important...?"

In response, Baba takes a long swig from his still-steaming cup of jasmine tea and swishes the liquid around in his mouth as if he's got all the time in the world. Mama sometimes jokes that I take after Baba in every way—from his square jaw, straight brows and tan skin to his stubborn perfectionist streak. But I clearly haven't inherited any of his patience.

"Baba," I prompt, trying my best to keep my tone respectful.

He holds up a hand and drains the rest of his tea before at last opening his mouth to speak. "Ah. Yes. Well, your Mama and I were thinking... How you feel about going to different school?"

"Wait. *What?*" My voice comes out too loud and too shrill, cutting through the restaurant chatter and cracking at the end like some prepubescent boy's. The company workers from the table nearby stop midtoast to shoot me disapproving looks. "What?" I repeat in a whisper this time, my cheeks heating.

"Maybe you go to local school like your cousins," Mama says, placing a piece of perfectly wrapped Peking duck down on my plate with a smile. It's a smile that makes alarm bells go off in my head. The kind of smile dentists give you right before yanking your teeth out. "Or we let you go back to America. You know my friend, Auntie Shen? The one with the nice son—the doctor?"

I nod slowly, as if two-thirds of her friends' children aren't either working or aspiring doctors.

"She says there's very nice public school in Maine near

her house. Maybe if you help work for her restaurant, she let you stay—"

"I don't get it," I interrupt, unable to help myself. There's a sick feeling in the pit of my stomach, like that time I ran too hard in the school Sports Carnival just to beat Henry and nearly threw up all over the courtyard. "I just... What's wrong with Airington?"

Baba looks a little taken aback by my response. "I thought you hated Airington," he says, switching to Mandarin.

"I never said I *hated*—"

"You once printed out a picture of the school logo and spent an entire afternoon stabbing it with your pen."

"So, I wasn't the biggest fan in the beginning," I say, setting my chopsticks down on the plastic tablecloth. My fingers tremble slightly. "But that was five years ago. People know who I am now. I have a reputation—a good one. And the teachers like me, like *really* like me, and most of my classmates think I'm smart and—and they actually care what I have to say..." But with every word that tumbles out of my mouth, my parents' expressions grow grimmer, and the sick feeling sharpens into ice-cold dread. Still, I plow on, desperate. "And I have my scholarship, remember? The only one in the entire school. Wouldn't it be a waste if I just left—"

"You have half scholarship," Mama corrects.

"Well, that's the most they're willing to offer..." Then it hits me. It's so obvious I'm stunned by own ignorance; why else would my parents all of a sudden suggest taking me out of the school they spent years working tirelessly to get me into?

"Is this... Is this about the school fees?" I ask, keeping my voice low so no one around us can overhear.

Mama says nothing at first, just fiddles with the loose button on her dull flower-patterned blouse. It's another cheap supermarket purchase; her new favorite place to find clothes after Yaxiu Market was converted into a lifeless mall for overpriced knockoff brands.

"That's not for you to worry," she finally replies.

Which means *yes*.

I slump back in my seat, trying hard to collect my thoughts. It's not as if I didn't know that we're struggling, that we've been struggling for some time now, ever since Baba's old printing company shut down and Mama's late shifts at Xiehe Hospital were cut short. But Mama and Baba have always been good at hiding the extent of it, waving away any of my concerns with a simple "just focus on your studies" or "silly child, does it look like we'd let you starve?"

I look across the table at them now, really look at them, and what I see is the scattering of white hairs near Baba's temples, the tired creases starting to show under Mama's eyes, the long days of labor taking their toll while I stay sheltered in my little Airington bubble. Shame roils in my gut. How much easier would their lives be if they didn't have to pay that extra 165,000 RMB every year?

"What, um, were the choices again?" I hear myself say. "Local Beijing school or public school in Maine?"

Evident relief washes over Mama's face. She dips another piece of Peking duck in a platter of thick black sauce, wraps it tight in a sheet of paper-thin pancake with two slices of cucumber—no onions, just the way I like it—and lays it down on my plate. "Yes, yes. Either is good."

I gnaw on my lower lip. Actually, *neither* option is good.

Going to any local school in China means I'll have to take the gaokao, which is meant to be one of the hardest college entrance exams as it is without my primary school–level Chinese skills getting in the way. And as for Maine—all I know is that it's the least diverse state in America, my understanding of the SATs is pretty much limited to the high school dramas I've watched on Netflix, and the chances of a public school there letting me continue my IB coursework are very low.

"We don't have to decide right now," Mama adds quickly. "Your Baba and I already pay for your first semester at Airington. You can ask teachers, your friends, think about it a bit, and then we discuss again. Okay?"

"Yeah," I say, even though I feel anything but okay. "Sounds great."

Baba taps his knuckles on the table, making both of us start. "Aiya, too much talking during eating time." He jabs his chopsticks at the plates between us. "The dishes already going cold."

As I pick up my own chopsticks again, the elderly people at the table beside us start singing the Chinese version of "Happy Birthday," loud and off-key. "Zhuni shengri kuaile… Zhuni shengri kuaile…" The old nainai sitting in the middle nods and claps her hands together to the beat, smiling a wide, toothless grin.

At least someone's leaving this restaurant in higher spirits than when they came in.

Sweat beads and trickles from my brow almost the instant I step outside. The kids back in California always complained about the heat, but the summers in Beijing are stifling, merciless, with the dappled shade of wutong trees planted up and down the streets often serving as the sole source of relief.

Right now it's so hot I can barely breathe. Or maybe that's just the panic kicking in.

"Haizi, we're going," Mama calls to me. Little plastic take-out bags swing from her elbow, stuffed full with everything—and I mean *everything*—left over from today's lunch. She's even packed the duck bones.

I wave at her. Exhale. Manage to nod and smile as Mama lingers to offer me her usual parting words of advice: Don't sleep later than eleven or you die, don't drink cold water or you die, watch out for child molesters on your way to school, eat ginger, lot of ginger, remember check air quality index every day...

Then she and Baba are off to the nearest subway station, her petite figure and Baba's tall, angular frame quickly swallowed up by the crowds, and I'm left standing all alone.

A terrible pressure starts to build at the back of my throat.

No. I can't cry. Not here, not now. Not when I still have an awards ceremony to attend—maybe the last awards ceremony I'll ever go to.

I force myself to move, to focus on my surroundings, anything to pull my thoughts from the black hole of worry swirling inside my head.

An array of skyscrapers rises up in the distance, all glass and steel and unabashed luxury, their tapered tips scraping the watery-blue sky. If I squint, I can even make out the famous silhouette of the CCTV headquarters. Everyone calls it The Giant Underpants because of its shape, though Mina Huang—

whose dad is apparently the one who designed it—has been trying and failing for the past five years to make people stop.

My phone buzzes in my skirt pocket, and I know without looking that it's not a text (it never is) but an alarm: only twenty minutes left until assembly begins. I make myself walk faster, past the winding alleys clogged with rickshaws and vendors and little yellow bikes, the clusters of convenience stores and noodle shops and calligraphed Chinese characters blinking across neon signs all blurring by.

The traffic and crowds thicken as I get closer toward the Third Ring Road. There are all kinds of people everywhere: balding uncles cooling themselves with straw fans, cigarettes dangling out of mouths, shirts yanked halfway up to expose their sunburned bellies, the perfect picture of *I-don't-give-a-shit*; old aunties strutting down the sidewalks with purpose, dragging their floral shopping trolleys behind them as they head for the open markets; a group of local school students sharing large cups of bubble tea and roasted sweet potatoes outside a mini snack stall, stacks of homework booklets spread out on a stool between them, gridded pages fluttering in the breeze.

As I stride past, I hear one of the students ask in a dramatic whisper, their words swollen with a thick Beijing accent, "Dude, did you see that?"

"See what?" a girl replies.

I keep walking, face forward, doing my best to act like I can't hear what they're saying. Then again, they probably assume I don't understand Chinese anyway; I've been told time and time again by locals that I have a foreigner's air, or qizhi, whatever the hell that's supposed to mean.

"She goes to *that school.* That's where that Hong Kong

singer—what's her name again? Krystal Lam?—sends her daughter, and the CEO of SYS as well... Wait, let me just Baidu it to check..."

"*Wokao!*" the girl swears a few seconds later. I can practically *feel* her gaping at the back of my head. My face burns. "*330,000 RMB* for just one year? What are they teaching, how to seduce royalty?" Then she pauses. "But isn't it an international school? I thought those were only for white people."

"What do you know?" the first student scoffs. "Most international students just have foreign passports. It's easy if you're rich enough to be born overseas."

This isn't true at all: I was born right here in Beijing and didn't move to California with my parents until I was seven. And as for being rich... No. Whatever. It's not like I'm going to turn back and correct him. Besides, I've had to recount my entire life story to strangers enough times to know that sometimes it's easier to just let them assume what they want.

Without waiting for the traffic lights to turn—no one here really follows them anyway—I cross the road, glad to put some distance between me and the rest of their conversation. Then I make a quick to-do list in my head.

It's what works best whenever I'm overwhelmed or frustrated. Short-term goals. Small hurdles. Things within my control. Like:

One, make it through entire awards ceremony without pushing Henry Li off the stage.

Two, turn in Chinese essay early (last chance to get in Wei Laoshi's good graces).

Three, read history course syllabus before lunch.

Four, research Maine and closest public schools in Beijing

and figure out which place offers highest probability of future success—if any—without breaking down and/or hitting something.

See? All completely doable.

"Are you sure you're a student here?"

The security guard furrows his bushy eyebrows and stares me down from the other side of the wrought iron school gates.

I swallow my exasperation. We go through this every single time, never mind that I'm wearing the school uniform or that I checked in only earlier this morning to move my stuff back into my dorm. Maybe it wouldn't bother me so much if I hadn't personally witnessed the guard waving Henry Li inside with a broad grin, no questions asked. People like Henry probably don't even need to carry an ID around; his face and name alone are verification enough.

"*Yes*, I'm sure," I say, wiping at the sweat coating my forehead with my blazer sleeve. "If you could please let me in, shushu—"

"Name?" he interrupts, now taking out some kind of expensive-looking tablet to record my details. Ever since our school decided to go completely paper-free a few years back, there's been no end to the amount of unnecessary technology they've brought in. Even the menus at our cafeteria are all digital now.

"Chinese name is Sun Yan. English name is Alice Sun."

"Year level?"

"Year Twelve."

"Student ID?" He must catch the look on my face, because

his frown deepens. "Xiao pengyou, if you don't have your student ID—"

"N-no, no, it's not that—okay, look, I'm getting it," I grumble, fishing my card out and holding it up for him to see. We took our student ID photos during exam season last year, and as a result, I look like something that just crawled out of a gutter in mine: my usually sleek black ponytail is an oily mess from a week of skipping hair washing to revise, my face is covered with stress blemishes, and there are giant dark circles sagging under my eyes.

I swear I see the security guard raise his eyebrows slightly at my photo, but at least the gates heave open a few moments later, creaking to a stop beside the two guardian stone lions facing the streets. Scooping up the last of my dignity, I thank him and hurry inside.

Whoever designed the Airington school campus clearly intended to create an artistic blend of Eastern and Western, old and modern architectural elements. It's why the main entrance is paved with flat, wide tiles like those in the Forbidden City, and farther down are artificial Chinese gardens with koi ponds and tiered pagodas with slanting vermillion roofs, but the actual school buildings are built with polished floor-to-ceiling windows and glass bridges stretching over slices of green lawn.

If I'm being honest though, it looks more like someone started filming one of those ancient Chinese costume dramas here and forgot to clean up the set.

It doesn't help that everything is so spread out. It takes me almost ten minutes to run across the courtyard, around the science building, and into the auditorium, and by then, the vast, brightly lit space is already packed with students.

Excited voices bounce off the walls like waves off a shore. The volume is even louder than usual as people launch into monologues on everything they did over the summer. I don't even need to listen to know the details; it was all over Instagram, from Rainie Lam's bikini pics at some villa the Kardashians once stayed in, to Chanel Cao's many filtered selfies on her parents' new yacht.

As the noise reaches a crescendo, I scan the auditorium for a place to sit—or, to be more accurate, people I can sit beside. I'm friendly enough with everybody, but the social divisions are still there, shaped by everything from your first language (English and Mandarin are most common, followed by Korean, Japanese, and Canto) to how many times you've achieved something impressive enough to be featured in the school's monthly newsletter. I guess it's the closest thing to a meritocracy you could expect to get in a place like this, except Henry Li's been featured fifteen times in his four years here.

Not that I'm counting or anything.

"Alice!"

I glance up to see my roommate, Chanel, waving at me from the middle row. She's pretty in that Taobao model kind of way: pointed chin, pale glass skin, air bangs kept deliberately messy, a waist the size of my thigh, and double eyelids that definitely weren't there two summers ago. Her mum, Coco Cao, actually *is* a model—she did a shoot with *Vogue China* just last year, and you could spot her face on pretty much every magazine stand in the city—and her dad owns a chain of upscale nightclubs all over Beijing and Shanghai.

But that's more or less the extent of everything I know about her. When we first moved into our dorms at the start of Year Seven, part of me had hoped we'd grow to become best friends. And for a while, it seemed like we would—we went to the cafeteria together for breakfast every morning and waited for each other at our lockers after class. But then she started asking me to go out shopping with her and her rich fuerdai friends at places like Sanlitun Village and Guomao, where the designer bags sold probably cost more than my parents' entire flat. After I turned her down the third time with some vague, stammered excuse, she simply stopped asking.

Even so, it's not like we're on bad terms or anything, and there's an empty seat right beside her...

I motion toward it, hoping I don't look as awkward as I feel. "Can I sit here?"

She blinks at me, clearly a little taken aback. Her waving at me was out of politeness, not an invitation. But then, to my relief, she smiles, her perfect porcelain veneer teeth almost glowing as the auditorium lights begin to dim. "Yeah, sure."

No sooner than I've sat down, our senior coordinator and history teacher, Mr. Murphy, strolls out onto the stage, microphone in hand. He's one of the many American expats at our school: English degree from decent but non–Ivy League university, Chinese wife, two kids, probably came to China because of a semi midlife crisis but stayed because of the pay.

He taps the microphone twice, creating an awful screeching sound that makes everyone wince.

"Hello, hello," he says into the resulting silence. "Welcome to our first assembly of the academic year—a very special assembly too, if you might recall..."

I sit up a little straighter in my seat, though I know the awards are coming only at the very end.

First, we have to get through a whole round of self-promotion.

Mr. Murphy makes a signal with his hand and the projector comes on, filling the screen behind him with familiar names and numbers and easily recognizable school logos. Acceptance rates.

According to the PowerPoint, over 50 percent of last year's graduating class were accepted into Ivy Leagues or Oxbridge.

A few students in the audience murmur in amazement—most likely this year's newcomers. Everyone else is used to this already, impressed enough but not in awe. Besides, the graduating class from the year before had an even higher rate.

Mr. Murphy drones on and on about *success in all areas* and *a commitment to excellence* for what feels like years. Then he announces our performers for the day, and everyone's alert at once when Rainie Lam's name comes up. Somebody even cheers.

Rainie sashays her way up to the stage to deafening applause, and I can't help the slight tug in my chest, half admiration and half envy. It's like kindergarten all over again, when a kid shows up at school with the shiny new toy you've secretly been eyeing for weeks.

As Rainie sits down at the piano, the spotlight spilling over her in a bright golden halo, she looks just like her mother, Krystal Lam. Like a legitimate Hong Kong star who's toured all around the world. She must know it, too, because she flips her glossy mahogany hair as if she's in a Pantene commercial and winks at the crowd. Technically, we're not even allowed to dye our hair, but Rainie's been strategic about it. Over the past year, she's been dying her hair a subtle shade lighter every two weeks to stop teachers from noticing the change. It's almost impressive, her dedication. Then again, I guess it's easy to be strategic when you have the time and money.

Once all the cheers finally die down, Rainie opens her mouth and starts singing, and of course it's one of JJ Lin's newest singles. A shameless nod to the fact that he was a guest at her mum's concert last November.

After her, Peter Oh comes up and performs one of his original raps. If it were anyone else, people would probably be cringing and giggling in their seats, but Peter's good. *Really* good. There are rumors he's already got a deal lined up with some Asian hip-hop company, though it's just as likely he'll inherit his dad's position at Longfeng Oil.

More people take their turn on the stage: a violin prodigy from the year level below, a professionally trained Asian-Australian opera singer who's performed at the Sydney Opera House before, and a guzheng player dressed in traditional Chinese robes.

Then at last, at long last, it's my turn.

The piano is wheeled away to some dark corner behind the curtains and the presentation slides change. The words *Top Achiever Award* flash across the screen in bold. My heart sings a little.

There's really not much suspense when it comes to these award ceremonies. We're all notified through email if we're up for an award months in advance, and aside from Year Eight, when I underperformed in my Chinese exam because I came down with a severe case of food poisoning, Henry and I have tied for Top Achiever every single year since he got here. You'd think I would've grown used to it by now, maybe started to care a bit less, but the opposite is true. Now that I have an established streak of success, a reputation to uphold, the stakes are even higher, and the thrill of winning greater than ever before.

It's sort of like what they say about kissing the person you love (not that I would really know): each time is like the very first.

"Alice Sun," Mr. Murphy booms into the microphone.

All eyes swivel to me as I rise slowly from my seat. There aren't any wild cheers, not like with Rainie, but at least they're looking. At least they can see me.

I smooth out my uniform and head toward the stage, careful not to trip along the way. Then Mr. Murphy is in front of me, shaking my hand, guiding me into the spotlight, and people start clapping.

See, I could shrivel up and die on the spot if I ever thought people were judging me or talking shit behind my back, but this, this kind of positive attention, with my full name on display as applause pounds through the room like a drumbeat—I wouldn't mind bathing in this moment forever.

But the moment barely lasts a few seconds, because then Mr. Murphy calls out Henry Li's name, and just like that, everyone's attention shifts. Refocuses. The applause grows noticeably, painfully louder.

I follow their gazes, and my stomach clenches when I spot him standing up in the front row.

It's truly one of life's greatest injustices—aside from youth unemployment and taxes and all that, of course—that Henry Li gets to look the way he does. Unlike the rest of us, he seems to have skipped that awkward midpuberty stage altogether, shedding his cute, Kumon-poster-boy image almost overnight near the end of last year. Now, with his sharp profile, lean build and thick, black waves of hair that somehow always fall perfectly over his dark brows, he could just as easily pass for an idol trainee as the heir to China's second biggest tech start-up.

His movements are smooth and purposeful as he steps onto the stage in a single stride, that look of mild interest I hate so much carefully arranged on his beautiful, terrible face.

As if he can hear my thoughts, his eyes cut to mine. The twisting, burning sensation in my stomach sharpens to a knife.

Mr. Murphy steps out in front of me. "Congratulations, Henry," he says, then releases a loud chuckle. "Must be getting tired of all these awards by now, eh?"

Henry merely offers him a small, polite smile in response.

I force myself to smile too, even as I clench my teeth so hard my jaw hurts. Even as Henry takes his place beside me, leaving only two terrible, maddening inches of space between us. Even as my muscles tense as they always do in his presence, as he leans over, crossing the unspoken boundary, and whispers so only I can hear—

"Congratulations, Alice. I was afraid you wouldn't make it this year."

Most international schoolkids end up with some watereddown version of an American accent, but Henry's accent has a distinct British lilt to it. At first I thought he was just following a step-by-step tutorial on how to become the most pretentious person alive, but after some stalking—no, *researching*—I found out he'd actually spent a couple years of primary school in England. And not just any primary school, but the same school as the prime minister's son. There's even a photo of the two of them together by the school stables, all wide smiles and ruddy cheeks, while someone's cleaning out horse manure in the background.

Henry's accent is so distracting it takes me a full minute to register his insult.

I know he's talking about our most recent chemistry finals. He'd gotten full marks as usual, and I'd lost a mark just because I rushed through a particularly difficult redox equation. If not for the two extra-credit questions I aced at the end, my whole rank would've slipped.

For a moment, I can't decide which I hate more—redox equations, or him.

Then I see the smug smile now playing at the corners of his lips, and remember, with a new spike of resentment, the first time we stood on the stage together like this. I'd tried my best to be civil, had even *complimented* him on doing better than me in that history test. But he'd simply worn the exact same smug, infuriating expression on his face, shrugged a little, and said, *It was an easy test.*

I clench my teeth harder.

It's all I can do to remind myself of the goal I made earlier: refrain from pushing Henry off the stage. Even if it'd be very, *very* satisfying. Even if he's been the bane of my existence for pretty much half a decade, and totally deserves it, and is still looking at me with that ridiculous smirk—

No. Refrain.

We're forced to stay in place anyway as a photographer hurries forward to take our photo for the annual yearbook.

Then realization washes over me like ice-cold water: by the time the yearbook's out, I won't be a student here anymore. No, not just that—I won't be graduating in this auditorium, won't have my name listed under the Ivy League acceptances, won't be walking out these school gates with a bright future laid out at my feet.

I feel the smile on my face freeze, threaten to dissolve at the edges. I'm blinking too quickly. In my peripheral vision, I see the school slogan, Airington is Home, printed out in giant letters on a strung-up banner. But Airington isn't home, or isn't *just* a home for someone like me; Airington is a ladder. The only ladder that could lift my parents out of their dingy flat on the outskirts of Beijing, that could close the distance between me and a seven-figure salary, that could ever allow me to stand as equals with someone like Henry Li on a large polished stage like this.

How the hell am I meant to climb my way to the top without it?

This is the question that gnaws at my nerves like a starved rat as I return to my seat in a daze, barely registering Mr. Chen's special little nod of approval or Chanel's smile or my other classmates' whispered congratulations.

The rest of the ceremony crawls by at a snail's pace, and I sit for so long, my body frozen to the spot while my mind works in overdrive, that I start to feel cold all over, despite the stifling summer heat.

I'm actually shivering by the time Mr. Murphy dismisses us for the day, and as I join the tides of students pushing out through the doors, a small part of my brain entertains the idea that maybe this chill isn't normal.

Before I can check if I have a fever or anything, someone behind me clears his throat. The sound is oddly formal, like a person readying themselves to deliver a speech.

I spin around. It's Henry.

Of course it is.

For a long moment he just stares at me, cocks his head, considering. It's impossible to tell what he's thinking. Then he steps forward and says in that infuriating British accent of his: "You don't look very good."

Anger spikes inside me.

That's it.

"Are we insulting my looks now?" I demand. My voice sounds shrill even to my own ears, and more than a few students pushing past us turn to shoot us curious looks.

"What?" Henry's eyes widen slightly, the faintest trace of confusion disrupting the precise symmetry of his features. "No, I just meant..." Then he seems to catch something on my face—something cruel and tightly wound—because his own expression shutters closed. He shoves his hands into his pockets. Looks away. "You know what? Never mind."

The bottom of my stomach dips at the sudden flatness in his tone, and I hate him for it, hate myself even more for my reaction. I have at least twenty thousand better things to worry about than what Henry Li thinks of me.

Things like the cold still spreading under my skin.

I whirl back around and run out through the doors, onto the grass courtyard. I expect to feel better in the sunlight, but my trembling only grows more violent, the chill running down to my very toes.

Definitely not normal.

Then, without warning, something slams straight into my back.

I don't even have time to cry out; I crash hard onto my knees. Pain shoots through me, the stiff, fake grass digging into my raw palms.

Wincing, I glance up in time to see that the culprit isn't *something*, but *someone*. Someone built like a bull and twice my height.

Andrew She.

I wait for him to help me up—to apologize, at the very least—but he simply frowns as he regains his balance, his eyes passing right over me, and turns around to leave.

Confusion wars with indignation in my head. This is *Andrew She*, after all; the boy who cushions his every sentence with phrases like "sorry" and "I think" and "maybe," who can't speak up in class without his face going red, who's always the first person to greet the teachers good morning, who's been teased mercilessly by everyone in our year level for being polite to a fault.

But when I turn toward the tinted glass doors to check for any injuries, all thoughts of Andrew She and basic etiquette vanish from my head. My heart slams violently against my ribs, a loud, ragged beat of this-can't-be-happening-this-can't-be-happening—

Because the doors reflect everything like a mirror: the kids spilling out onto the basketball courts, the emerald bamboo groves planted around the science building, the flock of sparrows taking to the skies in the distance...

Everything but me.

2

My first thought is not so much a thought as a word that begins with *f.*

My second thought is: *How am I supposed to hand in my Chinese essay like this?*

I'm starting to understand what Mama meant about needing to seriously reevaluate my priorities.

As I stare at the empty space in the glass—the space where I'm supposed to be—a thousand questions and possibilities stir up a frenzy inside my mind like the wild, flapping wings of startled birds, all force and no direction. *It must be a dream,* I tell myself. But even as I repeat the words again and again, I don't believe it. My dreams are never this vivid; I can still smell the cooked spices and coconut curry from the school cafeteria, feel the cool, smooth fabric of my skirt against my thigh, the ends of my ponytail tickling my sweat-coated neck.

I push myself shakily off the ground. My knees sting like hell and I'm dimly aware of the small blood droplets oozing from my palms, but it's the last of my worries at the moment. I try to breathe, to calm myself down.

It doesn't work. There's a faint buzzing sound in my ears and my breaths come out in quick and shallow puffs.

And through the cloud of panic, annoyance spikes inside me. I *really* don't have time to be hyperventilating.

What I need are answers.

No, even better, what I need is another list. A clear course of action, like:

One, figure out why the hell I can't see my own reflection like some kind of vampire in an early 2000s movie.

Two, rearrange afternoon homework plans depending on results.

Three…

As I rummage my brain for a third point, it occurs to me that I might just be hallucinating, that maybe this is some early onset psychological condition—it would also explain the strange cold spell earlier—and I should probably go to the school nurse's office.

But on my way there, the sense of *wrongness* digs deeper into my bones. More students bump into me, their gazes gliding over my face like I'm not even there. After the fifth kid steps on my foot and reacts only by sending the ground a quizzical look, a bizarre, terrible thought enters my head.

Just to test it, I run up to the closest student in my line of view and wave a hand in front of his face.

Nothing.

Not even a blink.

My heart pounds so hard I think it might fly out of my ribcage.

I wave my hand again, hoping against hope that I'm somehow wrong about all of this, but he just stares straight ahead.

Which means either the whole school has banded together
and manipulated every surface on campus to play the most
elaborate prank of all time or—

Or I'm invisible.

This is a slightly bigger inconvenience than I'd imagined.

I twist out of the student's path before he can knock me
over and move to stand in the shelter of a nearby oak tree,
my mind reeling. There's no point going to the nurse now
if they can't even *see* me. But maybe—surely—someone else
can help. Someone who'll believe me, come up with a solution, and if not, then at least comfort me. Tell me everything's
going to be okay.

I do a quick mental scan of all the people I know, and
what I end up with is a harsh, painful truth: I'm friendly with
everybody…but I'm friends with nobody.

This sounds exactly like the sort of realization that should
inspire a good hour of careful soul-searching. Under any
other circumstance, it probably would. But the rush of fear
and adrenaline pulsing through my veins won't let me rest,
and already I'm making more calculations, trying my best to
strategize my next move.

So I don't have any close relationships to rely on during a
personal, potentially supernatural crisis. Fine. Whatever. I can
be objective about this. Treat this like an extra-credit question
on a test, where all that matters is getting the right answer.

Now, *objectively* speaking, there *is* a person here at school
who might prove useful. A certain person who reads obscure
academic journals for enjoyment and once interned at NASA

and didn't even blink that time a North Korean dignitary rocked up at our school. A certain person who might actually be calm and competent enough to figure this shit out.

And if he *doesn't* have any idea what's happening to me… Well, at least I'll have the satisfaction of knowing there's a puzzle Henry Li can't solve.

Before my pride can catch up to my logic and convince me why this is a terrible idea, I march toward the one building I never thought I'd go near, let alone seek out intentionally.

Minutes later, I'm staring up at the words painted over a set of vermillion double-doors in sweeping calligraphy:

Mencius Hall.

I take a deep breath. Check to make sure no one's watching. Then push open the doors and walk in.

All four of the dorm buildings on campus are named after ancient Chinese philosophers: Confucius, Mencius, Laozi, and Mozi. It *sounds* pretty classy and everything, until you stop and think about the number of horny teens who've hooked up in Confucius Hall.

Mencius is by far the fanciest building of them all. The corridors are wide and spotless, as if swept clean by the school ayis at hourly intervals, and the walls are a rich shade of ocean blue, decorated with framed ink paintings of birds and sprawling mountains. If it weren't for the names printed over every door, the place could probably pass for a five-star hotel.

It doesn't take long to find Henry's room. His parents were the ones who donated this building, after all, so the school decided it was more than fair to assign him the only single room at the end of the hall.

To my surprise, his door has been left half-open—I'd always pegged him as the type to be super private about his personal space. I take a tentative step forward and pause in the doorway, overcome by a sudden, inexplicable urge to smooth out my hair.

Then I remember why I'm here in the first place, and a bubble of hysterical laughter rises up inside me.

Before I can lose my nerve or comprehend the true absurdity of what I'm about to do, I slip inside.

And freeze.

I'm not sure what, exactly, I expected to see. Maybe Henry reclining on giant piles of money, or polishing one of his many shiny trophies, or exfoliating his ridiculously clear skin with crushed diamonds and the blood of migrant workers. That sort of thing.

Instead, he's seated at his desk, his dark brows furrowed slightly in concentration as he types away on his laptop. The top button of his white school shirt is undone, his sleeves rolled up to reveal the lean muscles in his arms. Soft afternoon sunlight streams through the open window beside him, bathing his perfect features in gold, and as if the whole scene isn't dramatic enough, a light breeze drifts in and runs its fingers through his hair like this is some goddamn K-pop music video.

As I watch on with a mixture of fascination and disgust, Henry reaches for the jar of White Rabbit milk candy next to his laptop. Peels off the white-and-blue wrapper with his slender fingers. Pops it in his mouth, his eyes fluttering closed for an instant.

Then a small voice in the back of my head reminds me that I did not come all the way here to watch Henry Li chew a piece of candy.

Unsure how else to proceed, I clear my throat and say, "Henry."

He doesn't respond. Doesn't even look up.

Panic floods through my veins, and I'm starting to wonder if maybe people can't *hear* me either—as if being invisible wasn't already hard enough—when I notice he's got his AirPods in. I sneak a peek at his Spotify playlist, half certain it'll be all just white noise or classic orchestral music, only to find Taylor Swift's latest album playing instead.

I'm about to make a comment on it, but then my eyes fall on the laminated photo taped to his desk, and the significance of Henry Li secretly jamming out to Tay Tay pales in comparison.

It's a photo of us.

I remember it floating around in a couple of school advertisements; it was taken at the awards ceremony three years ago, back when I still had those ridiculous side bangs that covered half my face. In it, Henry's wearing his signature expression—that look of polite interest I find so infuriating, as if he has better things to do than stand around and receive more applause and prestigious awards (what makes me angrier is the fact that he probably does). Beside him, I'm staring straight at the camera, shoulders tensed, arms held stiff at my sides. My smile looks so forced it's a wonder the photographer didn't make us retake the photo.

I have no idea why Henry would keep this lying around, other than as visible proof of my clear inability to look better than him in photos.

Suddenly Henry tenses. Tugs his AirPods out. Spins around in his seat, eyes sweeping the room. It takes me a second to realize I've leaned too far forward, accidentally brushing against his shoulder as a result.

Well, I guess that's one way to get his attention.

"Okay," I say, and he starts, swiveling his head at the sound of my voice. "Okay, please don't freak out or anything but… it's Alice. You just, um. Can't see me right now—I promise I'll explain—but I'm right here." I pinch the fabric of his left sleeve between two fingers and pull it once, lightly, just to show what I mean.

He goes completely, utterly still.

"Alice?" he repeats, and I hate how much posher my name sounds on his tongue. How elegant. "Is this a joke of some sort?"

In response, I tug at his sleeve harder, and watch the series of emotions flicker over his face like shadows: shock, uncertainty, fear, skepticism, even a hint of annoyance. A muscle spasms in his jaw.

Then, unbelievably, his usual mask of calm falls back into place.

"How…strange," he says after a long silence.

I roll my eyes at this severe understatement, then remember that of course, he can't see me.

Great. Now I can't even spite him properly.

"It's more than strange," I say aloud. "It should be—I mean, this should be *impossible*."

Henry takes a deep breath. Shakes his head. His eyes search for me again, only to end up falling on some random spot above my collarbone. "But I saw you less than half an hour ago…"

Heat spikes through me at the memory of our last exchange. I will it away. "Well, a lot can change in half an hour."

"Right," he says, drawing the word out. Then he shakes his head again. "So how exactly did"—he makes a motion in my general direction—"happen?"

To be honest, I thought he'd give me a much harder time about this—at least demand to know why I came *here*, out of all places. But he simply snaps his laptop shut, pushing it back so that, whether on purpose or by accident, it's covering the old photo of us, and waits for me to speak.

So I do.

I go over everything, from the brief cold spell to Andrew She knocking me over, careful not to leave out any detail that might serve as a clue to what the hell is going on. Well, everything except for my little meeting with my parents before the assembly; no one at school really knows about my family's situation, and I intend to keep it that way.

When I'm done, Henry suddenly leans forward, his hands clasped over his lap, dark eyes thoughtful. "You know what?"

"What?" I say, trying not to sound too hopeful. I'm expecting something profound, scientific, maybe a reference to some recent social phenomenon I haven't read about yet, but what comes out of his mouth instead is—

"This is an awful lot like *The Lord of the Rings*."

"*What?*"

"The part with the invisibility—"

"Yeah, no, I got that," I splutter. "But how—why—okay. Wait a second. Since when were you into high fantasy?"

He straightens in his seat. "In a few years," he begins, which sounds like a very long-winded way of answering a straightforward question, "I'll be the CEO of the biggest tech startup in all of China—"

"Second biggest," I correct automatically. "Don't lie. The *Wall Street Journal* said so just a week ago."

He shoots me an odd look, and it occurs to me a second too late that I definitely should not know this much about his father's company. "As of now, yes," he says after a short pause. Then the corner of his mouth lifts up in an expression so smug I have to resist the urge to punch him. "But not once I take over. *Anyway,*" he continues, as if he hasn't just made the most arrogant statement in the history of mankind, "considering the role that awaits me, it's important that I'm well-informed on a range of subjects, including commercially successful media franchises. Also makes it easier to connect with clients."

"Right," I mutter. "Forget I asked."

"But back to your new power—"

"It's not a *power,*" I cut him off. "It's an—an affliction—a difficulty, a very major inconvenience—"

"Everything's a form of power," he says simply.

"Yeah, well, power implies some level of control," I protest, even though a small part of my brain—the part not clouded by panic and my four-year grudge against him—agrees with the statement. In theory. "And I can't control anything about my current situation."

"Really?" He rests his cheek on one hand. Cocks his head

to the side, just as another lazy breeze flutters in and ruffles his hair. "Have you tried?"

"Of course I've—"

"Have you tried harder?"

There's something so patronizing about the question or the way he says it that the last thread of composure inside me—already pulled taut in his presence—snaps.

I grab the back of his chair and pull him closer toward me in one abrupt movement, an all-too-familiar rage bubbling under my skin. To my immense satisfaction, his eyes widen slightly. "Henry Li, if you're suggesting this is about a lack of willpower, I *swear to god*—"

"I was only asking—"

"As if *you* could handle this shit any better—"

"That's not what I'm saying—just calm down—"

"Do not tell me to calm—"

Two sharp raps on the half-open door make the rest of my sentence freeze in my throat. Henry goes even quieter, his entire body motionless beside me, as if carved out of ice.

Someone snorts on the other side of the door, and a second later, a lightly accented male voice drifts in through the gap—

"Dude, you got a girl in there or something?"

It takes me a moment to identify it as Jake Nguyen's: star athlete, Harvard-bound, and, if the rumors are true, the cousin of a famous male porn star. I remember seeing his name a few doors down on my way here.

"Not at all," Henry says smoothly, despite the brief delay in his response. "I'm on the phone with someone."

"With your girlfriend?" Jake persists, and I can almost imagine the smirk on his broad-jawed face as he says it.

"No." Henry pauses. "It's just my grandma."

I snap my head around and shoot him a withering glare—then, realizing the effort is wasted in my current state, hiss loud enough for only him to hear, "Seriously? Your *grandma*?"

The asshole doesn't even have the decency to look apologetic about it.

And as if everything isn't terrible enough, Jake says, "Dude. No offense or anything, but why does your grandma sound like Alice Sun? Like all shrill and aggressive and shit?"

"You think?" Henry replies, keeping his tone carefully neutral. "I never noticed."

Jake laughs his usual hyena laugh, taps the door once more, then says, "All right my man. I'll leave you to it then— Oh, and if you ever *do* get a girl or two in your room—"

"I assure you the probability is quite low," Henry interrupts.

But Jake doesn't even falter. "Just feel free to invite me in, yeah?"

Henry frowns, looking for a moment as if he's fighting himself on whether or not to answer. Then, with a sigh, he says, "What about your girlfriend?"

"What?" Jake sounds genuinely confused.

"You know. Rainie Lam?"

"Oh, *her*." Another loud laugh. "Dude, where've you been? We broke up ages ago—like, almost a whole ass *month* ago. I'm super available now."

"Right," Henry mutters. "Good to know."

Please just go, I beg Jake in my head. But the universe must really not be in a cooperative mood today, because Jake continues—

"Wait a second. You're not asking because *you're* interested in Rainie, are you? I mean, I'd be totally cool with that. Hell, I'd even set you two up if you—"

"No," Henry interrupts, with surprising force. His gaze darts to some spot near my chin, as if he's looking for me. As if I'm suddenly an important part of this conversation. "I have no interest whatsoever."

"Okay, okay," Jake says hastily. "Just putting it out there. But if you ever are—"

"I'm not."

"But *if* you ever are, we can do, like, a trade. You know what I'm saying?"

Henry makes a noncommittal sound with the back of his throat, and finally, Jake seems to take the cue to leave. I listen to the heavy thumps of Jake's footsteps echoing down the corridor—it's a humiliating testament to how loud I was talking that I didn't hear them before—and count to ten in my head to calm myself.

Or try to, at least; I haven't even reached seven when Henry turns to me.

"Er," he says, in a very un-Henry-like way. His eyes lift up to meet mine, and with the sun hitting them at just the right angle, I can almost make out the curve of every individual eyelash. It's ridiculous. "I—I can see you again."

I can see you again.

I don't think I've ever heard such beautiful words in my life.

But my relief is quickly cut short by the realization that I'm standing far too close to him. I scramble backward, nearly banging my leg on the corner of his bed.

He makes a movement as if to help me, then seems to think better of it. "Are...you all right?"

I straighten. Fold my arms tight across my chest, trying to shake the feeling that I've just woken up from some disorientating dream. "Yeah. Perfect."

There's an awkward silence. Now that the immediate issue of my invisibility is resolved, neither of us knows what to do next.

After a few more seconds, Henry rakes a hand through his hair and says, "Well, that was interesting."

I focus on the pale expanse of sky stretching beyond his window, on anything but him, and nod. "Mm-hmm."

"I'm sure it was a one-time event," he continues, now adopting that voice he always uses when answering a question in class, his accent coming in thicker and every word enunciated to make him sound smarter, more convincing. I doubt he's even aware it's something he does. "An oddity. The equivalent of a freak storm, only made possible under a very specific set of circumstances. I'm sure," he says, with all the confidence of someone who's rarely ever contradicted, who has a place in this world and knows it, "everything will go back to normal after this."

For what might be the first time in his life, Henry Li is wrong—and I can't even gloat about it.

Because despite all my prayers, everything most definitely does not go back to normal.

I'm in Chinese class when it happens again, just two days after the awards ceremony. Wei Laoshi is drinking from his giant thermos of hot tea at the front of the room while everyone around me is groaning about the in-class essay we've just been assigned: five hundred words on an animal of choice.

From what I've heard, the advanced First Language class—mostly for the mainland kids who attended local schools before coming here—have to dissect the Chinese equivalent of Shakespeare and write short stories on weirdly specific topics like "A Memorable Pair of Shoes." But my class is full of Westernized Malaysians, Singaporeans, ABCs and people like me, who can speak and understand Mandarin just fine but don't know many idioms besides *renshan renhai*: people mountain people sea.

So what we get instead are essays about animals. Sometimes seasons, too, if the teacher's feeling particularly sentimental.

I stare down at my gridded notebook, then up at the classroom walls, hoping they might offer some form of inspiration. There are the couplets we wrote up for Chinese New Year, the characters *peace* and *fortune* wobbling over the crimson banners; the intricate paper cuttings and fans pasted over the round windows; and a series of Polaroids from last year's Experiencing China trip, featuring what seems like way too many shots of Rainie and not nearly enough of the actual Terra Cotta Warriors—nor of any animals.

Frustration bubbles up inside me. It's not as if the task itself is hard; I'm willing to bet most people will just pick the panda or one of the twelve zodiacs. But that means I need to do something different.

Something better.

I rub my temples, trying to ignore the sound of Wei Laoshi's tea sipping and Henry's furious scribbling three seats away. This is to be expected—Henry's always the first to start and first to finish for all our assignments—but it still makes me want to stab a hole through the desk.

After five more torturous minutes of me racking my brain for something full-marks worthy, I finally write down the rough beginnings of a first line: *The sparrow and the eagle both can hunt, can fly, can sing, but while one soars free, the other...*

Then I pause. Stare down at my wonky Chinese handwriting. Read the line over and over again until I decide it's pretty much the worst combination of words anyone has ever come up with since the dawn of time.

A low hiss escapes my gritted teeth.

God, if this were English, I'd be flying through the second page already, all the right words pouring out of me. I'd probably be *done*.

I'm about to scrap the whole thing and make a new essay outline when that terrible, unshakeable cold I first felt in the auditorium begins to creep under my skin.

My pen freezes over the page.

Not again, I beg silently in my head. *Please not again.*

But the cold deepens, sharpens, pours into every pore of my body as if my clothes have been soaked in freezing water, and through it all my brain registers the alarming fact that either I'm running a high fever, or I'm about to turn invisible before a class of twenty-two people.

I stand up so abruptly that Wei Laoshi jumps, almost spilling his tea. Twenty-two pairs of eyes snap to me, all while the cold continues seeping, growing like some terrible rash, and any second now—

"I—um—I have to go the bathroom," I blurt out, and bolt out of the room before Wei Laoshi can even respond. Humiliation floods through me as I sprint down the corridor, my old leather shoes pounding over the gleaming floors. Now everyone in my Chinese class probably thinks I have chronic diarrhea or something.

But better that than the truth. Whatever the hell the truth is meant to be.

By the time I reach the closest bathrooms on the second floor, I've already turned invisible. There's no shadow attached to my feet, and the reflection in the floor-length mirrors doesn't change when I step in front of them, only showing the faded pink door swinging wide open on its own. If anyone else were in here, they'd likely think this place was haunted by ghosts.

I lock myself in the last stall with trembling fingers, wincing as the sharp smell of disinfectant assaults my nose. Then I sit down on the closed toilet lid. Try to think.

And all that pops into my head is:

Once is an accident. Twice is a coincidence. Thrice is a pattern.

So.

It's happened twice already; it could still mean nothing.

Or maybe it's an even more common affliction than I realize, and the people suffering from it just tend to keep it to themselves—like irritable bowel syndrome, or herpes.

On that inspiring note, I pull my phone out of my inner blazer pocket. It's an old Xiaomi, which is pretty much a smartphone for elderly people, but it works, and it's cheap, so no complaints there.

It takes a few minutes for the home page to load onto the cracked screen, and another few minutes for me to get my VPN working so I can head over to Google.

Finally, I manage to type into the search bar: *Have you ever turned invisible before?*

And wait, holding my breath.

The results show up almost immediately, and disappointment settles deep in my stomach. It's all just chicken-soup-for-the-soul advice and anecdotes about being metaphorically invisible, plus a bunch of memes I'm in no mood to scroll through.

But then a related search result catches my eye.

What would you do if you were invisible for a day?

It's got over two million views already, and thousands of answers. After I've filtered through more than a few creepy comments, I'm surprised by the range of answers, and the whiff of eagerness—even desperation—to them. There's everything from suggestions of espionage and robbery to deleting emails accidentally sent to bosses and taking back old love letters from exes, the kind of things people would normally be too embarrassed to do.

And as I read on, Henry's words drift back to me: *Everything's a form of power.*

Of course, it's hard to feel very powerful when you're hiding on top of a toilet. But maybe, just maybe…

Before I can finish the thought, I see another comment buried at the end of the thread, dated back years ago. Some anonymous user had written: *Descartes was wrong when he said "To live well, you must live unseen"; Trust me, actually being invisible isn't anywhere near as fun as y'all think.*

I stare down, unblinking, at my cracked screen until my vision blurs. Until the sentence begins to dance around in my head. *Trust me… Being invisible…*

Then I lean back against the toilet, my heart pounding.

It should be a joke. That's all. Everyone else in the forum

clearly seems to think so—the comment only got six likes, and four dislikes. Plus, the first thing we learned in history was how to separate reliable from unreliable sources, and a now-deactivated, anonymous account's comment on a website best known for its shitposts is basically the *definition* of unreliable.

But if, hypothetically speaking, they meant every word— What would that mean for me?

The bathroom door slams open, breaking through my thoughts, followed by a series of sharp, staggered breaths, like...muffled sobs. I freeze. There's a rustle of footsteps. The tap turning on. Then a voice speaking over the steady rush of water, low and choked with tears:

"...just want to fucking *kill him*. This is just—it's so bad. It's so fucking bad, and once they get out..."

My mouth falls open.

I almost don't recognize the voice at first; Rainie always sounds like she's gushing over some new sponsored hair product on Instagram—which, given her 500K followers, probably isn't too far from the truth. But there's still that distinct raspy quality to it, the very quality which made her mother rise to fame, so when she speaks again, I'm certain it's her.

"No—no—listen, I get that you're trying to comfort me, and I love you, but you...you don't understand." She draws a long, shaky breath. The taps squeak and the water pumps out louder. "This is like, a big fucking deal. If someone leaks it onto Weibo or some shit like that—it's going to be a witch hunt. It doesn't matter if it's technically illegal, they're all going to blame me anyway, you know they are, they always do and— Oh god, I'm such a fucking idiot. I don't even know what I was thinking and now—now it's all over—" Her voice cracks on the last word, and she's crying again, her sobs rising in pitch and intensity until they barely sound human anymore, more like some wounded animal's keening.

Guilt stabs at my stomach. The last thing I want is to sit here and listen in on what are clearly some pretty serious private issues, but there's no way for me to step out now. Not without giving Rainie a heart attack.

I'm still trying to figure out what to do next when I realize the bathroom has gone quiet again, save for the splash of water hitting the sink.

"Is—is someone there?" Rainie calls out.

My heart falters a beat. How could she know—?

Then I look down and see my own shadow spilling around my feet, black and firmly outlined against the light pink floor. My form must've returned some moments ago without me knowing.

I grit my teeth. This whole invisibility thing seems about as predictable as Beijing's pollution—here one second, gone the next.

"Uh, hello?" Rainie tries again, and it's clear I can't keep hiding in here any longer.

Bracing myself, I unlock the toilet door and step out.

The instant she sees me, Rainie's expression changes with unnerving speed, the crease between her long, defined brows smoothing out, the corners of her full lips lifting into an easy smile. If it weren't for the puffiness around her eyes and the faint red patches rising up to her cheeks, I might've thought I'd imagined her whole breakdown.

"Oh, hey girl!"

Rainie and I haven't had a single proper conversation since

she started school here in Year Seven—unless you count that time I helped her with her history homework—but from the way she's greeting me now, you'd think we were best friends.

As I try to come up with an appropriate response, she slides her phone into her skirt pocket, then cranes her neck toward the stall I just came out from. Frowns slightly. "Were you... in there long? I didn't see you when I came in."

"Yeah, no," I babble. "I mean—yes. A...relatively long while."

She studies me for a beat. Then she grabs my wrist, her eyes wide with sympathy. "Girl, do you have cramps or something?" Before I can protest, she continues on, "Because I just got *the* best scented heat pack to help with that—like, I know they sponsored me, but I'd never recommend anything I haven't tried myself, you feel?"

"Right. I, uh, feel you."

She smiles at me with such warmth I almost return it. "Okay well, if you want, you can just go to the link in my bio—you follow me on Instagram right?"

"Right," I repeat. I don't add that she never followed me back. Now is not the time to be petty.

"Cool cool cool," she says, bouncing her head in beat with every word. "There's also a little discount if you use my code, INTHERAINIE. It's the same as my handle—"

"Sorry," I interrupt, unable to help myself and my irrational need to care about people who very likely don't care much about me. "But it's just—earlier, I couldn't help overhearing... Are you—is everything okay?"

Rainie stills for a moment, her expression inscrutable. Then she tilts her lovely head back and laughs, long and loud and breathless. "Oh my god, *that*. Girl, I was only practicing my lines for this role I'm auditioning for. My agent wants me to like, branch out, give acting a shot—all the idols are doing it these days, you know—and it's meant to be a secret but"—she leans in and drops her voice to a conspiratorial whisper—"I hear Xiao Zhan is up for the male lead." She steps back, her grin widening. "I mean, how great would that be?"

"Oh," is all I can think to say, confusion and embarrassment swirling inside me. Could she be telling the truth? Yet her sobs earlier sounded so real—and what she said on the phone...

Maybe Rainie sees the uncertainty flicker over my expression, because she gives my arm a squeeze and says, with another laugh, "Trust me, my life is not that dramatic. You're sweet for being concerned, though. I mean, now that I think of it, it's so weird we don't hang out more, you know? I bet we'd have a great time."

And suddenly I understand why everyone at our school loves Rainie Lam so much. It's not just that she's gorgeous, since basically all the girls in my year level are pretty in one way or another (Mama always says there are no ugly women, only lazy women—but from what I've gathered, it's more like there are no ugly women, only broke women); it's how she makes you feel when you're around her, like you're someone who matters. Like you have a special bond with her even if you've never exchanged more than a few sentences before. It's a rare talent, the kind you can't acquire through sheer determination and hard work.

Jealousy wraps its cold claws around my throat and squeezes, hard. And I find myself wishing, not for the first time, that I wasn't always so acutely aware of the things I lack.

"Um, Alice?" Rainie peers at me. "You okay?"

If Rainie is a convincing actress, then I'm a terrible one. My thoughts are probably written all over my face.

"Of course," I say, forcing myself to smile. The effort is close to painful. "But anyway, yeah, that all sounds good. As long as you're—it's great." I angle my body toward the door, more than ready to leave this strange conversation and the stench of disinfectant behind me. "I should probably get back to class, though. Good luck with your auditions and everything."

"Thanks, girl." Rainie flashes me another one of her perfect Insta-model grins, then adds, almost as an afterthought, "Oh, and don't tell anyone about the auditions, yeah? Just in case I don't get the part—wouldn't want people to get excited over nothing, you know what I'm saying?"

Her voice is light and airy, but there's an odd tension simmering beneath her words, the slightest waver at the end of her sentence, like a news anchor trying to keep their cool while a volcano literally erupts behind them.

Or maybe I'm just imagining it.

Either way, I mime zipping my lips before I turn to leave, wondering what she would say if she knew of all the other secrets I'm keeping locked up inside me.

The rest of the school week passes by in a nauseating, anxiety-inducing blur.

I feel that same telltale chill on Thursday, forcing me to sprint out of history class before I've written down a word of Mr. Murphy's lecture on the Taiping Rebellion, and watch my shadow disappear halfway down the corridor. Then it happens again during Friday lunchtime, effectively snuffing out any last hopes I had about this all being some kind of spontaneous occurrence.

So when I find myself hiding in a locked bathroom stall for the third time since school started, my choked, uneven breaths audible over the sounds of the toilet flushing in the neighboring stall, I'm forced to admit the truth:

This is an issue.

For obvious reasons, involuntarily turning invisible at random is an issue, but it's an even bigger issue because of all the classes I'm missing; the very thought of the red marks on my once-perfect attendance record makes my stomach twist like those braided, deep-fried mahua snacks they sell at the school café. If this continues much longer, the teachers are surely going to start asking questions, maybe even start emailing the principal and— Oh god, what if they tell my parents?

They'll probably think I've been worrying myself sick about the whole leaving-Airington-situation. Then *they'll* be worried sick and want to have another talk about Maine and Chinese public schools and insufficient scholarships and my future...

As a fresh tide of panic sweeps over me, my phone buzzes in my pocket.

It's a WeChat message from my aunt.

I click onto the app, expecting another one of those articles about treating excessive internal heat with herbs, but instead it's just one line of text, written in simplified Chinese:

Is everything okay?

I frown at the screen, my pulse quickening. It's not the first time my aunt has sent me a perfectly timed message out of the blue; just last month, she wished me luck on a test I hadn't even told her about. I've always attributed it to one of those inexplicable sixth senses only adults develop, like how teachers somehow always manage to set important assignment deadlines on the exact same day without discussing it beforehand.

But this time it feels different, somehow.

Like a sign.

As an unwelcome chill snakes down my spine, I text back slowly, my fingers fumbling over the correct pinyin:

why wouldn't it be?

She shoots back a message within seconds:

I don't know. Just had a bad feeling—and the thread on my handkerchief snapped earlier this morning, which is never good omen in those palace dramas. You will tell me if something is wrong at school, won't you?

My heart pounds faster, the bass-like beat rattling my skull. The rational part of me wants to dismiss her messages, to simply say everything's fine and tease her for taking her Chinese soap operas way too seriously.

But instead what I type is:

can i visit you this weekend?

3

I'm greeted at my aunt's door by Buddha.

Not the Buddha himself—though it certainly wouldn't be the strangest thing to happen to me this week—but a giant poster of him, half peeling at the corners and framed with gold. Around it, there are little yellowing stickers my aunt has clearly tried and failed to scrape off, some advertising cleaning services and what may be a porn site, and others sporting nothing but a surname with a phone number printed underneath. Next to the Buddha's serene, smiling face, they look almost comically out of place.

I shake my head. It should be the local wuye's responsibility to get rid of all the spam, but in a small, rundown compound like this one, most tenants are left to fend for themselves.

"Yan Yan!"

Xiaoyi's voice drifts out to greet me before she does, and despite myself, I find my lips tugging upward at the familiar childhood nickname. It's hard for me to really feel at home anywhere with all the moving around I've done, but there's something about Xiaoyi and her little flat that always grounds me, pulls me back to simpler times when everything felt safe and warm.

Then the door swings wide open, the strong smell of cabbage dumplings and damp cloth hitting my nose, and Xiaoyi appears before me in a plastic floral apron, patches of white flour sticking to her permed hair and hollow cheeks, her resemblance to Mama striking despite the nine-year age gap between them.

She grabs my hands in her calloused ones, the cool wooden beads of her bracelet brushing my skin, and proceeds to pinch and pat my cheeks with alarming strength for her petite frame.

Once she's satisfied I haven't lost or gained too much weight, she steps back, smiling, and asks, "Have you eaten, Yan Yan?"

"Mm," I say, even though I know she'll make me sit down and eat with her anyway, that she's probably spent half the day preparing my favorite food for me with fresh produce from the morning markets. Xiaoyi doesn't have any children, but she's always doted on me like I'm one of her own.

Just as I predict, she starts ushering me into the cramped dining room, pausing only when she notices me bending down to untie my school shoes.

"Aiya, no need to take your shoes off!"

"Oh, it's fine," I say, as if we haven't had this same exact conversation every single time I've visited. "I don't want to dirty your floor—"

She speaks over me, flapping her hands in the air like wings. "No, no, make yourself at home. Really—"

"Really, Xiaoyi," I tell her, louder. "I insist—"

"No! Too inconvenient for you!"

"It's not inconvenient—"

"Just listen to me—"

"*No*—"

Ten minutes later, I'm sliding into a pair of faded Mickey Mouse slippers while my aunt hurries into the kitchen. She yells something to me about tea, but her voice is drowned out by the roar of the range hood and the loud pop and sizzle of spices heated in oil.

As I wait for her, I sit myself down on a wooden stool near the window—the only surface not littered with old jars and boxes Xiaoyi refuses to throw out.

Maybe one of the reasons why Xiaoyi's flat is so comforting is that it always seems frozen in time. The fridge is still covered with photos of me as a baby, head unevenly shaved (Mama swears it's the secret to shiny, straight black hair) and dressed in baggy split pants that give no consideration to privacy. There are photos of me as a toddler, too, from those last days before we moved to America: me making the V sign with two fingers from a crescent-shaped bridge in Beihai Park, willow trees swaying in the background, the emerald river water flowing underneath; me chewing happily on the end of a bingtang hulu at a Chinese New Year parade, the sugar-coated haw fruits glistening like jewels.

But even the unsentimental objects in the room haven't moved an inch all these years, from the butter cookie tins filled with threads and needles and the pair of strange walnut-shaped balls meant to improve blood circulation, to the jar of paper origami stars and vials of green medicine oil perched on the windowsill.

I'm distracted by the savory aroma of herbs and soy sauce wafting out of the kitchen. Seconds later, Xiaoyi emerges with two plates of steaming dumplings and a bottle of black vinegar balanced in her hands.

"Yan Yan, quick! Eat before it gets cold—the dumplings will stick!" she calls, disappearing back into the kitchen before I can even offer to help.

Soon, the small fold-out dining table has been weighed down by enough dishes to feed everyone in the building. Aside from the dumplings, Xiaoyi's also made fluffy white steamed buns with embedded red dates, sweet-and-sour pork ribs sprinkled with cut scallions, and a thick rice congee topped with delicate slices of century eggs.

My mouth waters. The cafeteria food at Airington is pretty impressive, with daily specials like xiaolongbao and fried dough sticks taken straight from the pan, but it's still nothing compared to this.

I grab one of the buns and sink my teeth into it. The warm dates melt on my tongue like honey, and I lean back, a happy sigh escaping my lips.

"Wa, Xiaoyi!" I say, ripping out another chunk of the bun with my fingers. "You could start your own restaurant!"

She beams. This is the highest praise for anyone's cooking—unless, of course, you're eating at a restaurant, in which case the highest praise is naturally to compare it to home-cooked meals.

"Now, Yan Yan," she says, helping herself to the dumplings, "what brings our busy little scholar over to see her old aunt, hmm?"

I swallow the rest of my bun, open my mouth, then hesitate. My invisibility issue is the whole reason I came here, but it hardly seems like the kind of conversation one should have over a plate of cabbage dumplings.

"Oh, it's nothing, just..." I stall, searching for another topic. "Did you know my parents were thinking of sending me to America?"

I expect Xiaoyi to look surprised, but she simply nods, clasping her hands together over the table. "Yes, your Mama told me a while ago."

My gut clenches. How long have my parents been planning this without telling me, preparing for the very worst as I prepared to return to school? I was with them all summer, laughing and chatting with them every breakfast and dinner. If they could hide so much from me so easily, what else— what other hardships and burdens and worries—have they kept to themselves?

"Why don't you look happy?" Xiaoyi asks, reaching over to smooth my hair. "I thought you would want to go back to America, no?"

Go back.

The words scratch at my throat like barbed wire. *Go back*, as if the teachers and kids at my school in California weren't always asking me the same thing: if and when I'd be *going back* to China. As if there's still a home in America for me to return to, as if America *is* home, and Beijing has been nothing more than a temporary stop in between for an outsider like me.

Yet the truth is, I remember far less about America than my relatives realize.

The memories I do have come in bursts and flashes, like

something from a dream sequence: the sun pressing down on my bare neck, a too-blue sky stretching out overhead, cloud kissed and endless, palm trees swaying on either side of a quiet, suburban road, pale hills rising in the distance.

There are other memories too: the bright, stacked aisles at Costco, the crumpled In-N-Out burger wrappers littering the back seat of our rental car, filling the tiny space with the smell of salt and grease, and Baba's voice, with its uneven inflections and stuttered pauses, reading me a bedtime story in English as I drifted off to sleep...

But simmering beneath it all was this—this tension. A tension that grew with every odd look and ill-concealed insult and racist joke tossed my way, so subtle I didn't even notice it building inside me day by day, the same way the teachers failed to notice Rainie Lam's slowly changing hair color over the years. It wasn't until I stepped out into Beijing International Airport, suddenly surrounded by people who looked like me, suddenly both seen and blended in, that I felt the full weight of that tension right as it lifted off my shoulders. The relief was dizzying. I was free to simply be a child again, to shed the role of translator-chaperone-protector, to no longer feel the need to constantly hover around my parents in case they needed something, to shield them from the worst of America's many casual cruelties.

"...you to stay, but, well, I didn't have enough to lend to your Mama at the time," Xiaoyi says, moving the dumplings around with her chopsticks to stop them from sticking.

The clink of plates pulls me from my thoughts, and it takes a moment for my brain to register the rest of Xiaoyi's sentence. My heart seizes. "Wait. Mama…came to you for money? Why?"

Xiaoyi doesn't reply right away, but deep down, I already know the answer: For my education. My school fees. My future.

Me.

But Mama is even prouder, even more stubborn than I am; she once worked a twenty-hour hospital shift with a sprained ankle just because she didn't want to ask for a break. The thought of her bowing her head to ask for money from her own little sister makes my chest ache. Mama and Baba would really do anything just to make my life easier, better, no matter the cost.

Maybe it's time I do the same for them.

"Xiaoyi," I say, and the urgency in my voice gets her attention at once.

"What is it?"

"There actually is something I came here for… Something I need to tell you." I push my bowl aside. Take a deep, steadying breath. "I can turn…" I pause, realizing I've forgotten the Chinese word for invisible. *Yin shen? Yin xing? Yin*…something.

Xiaoyi waits, patient. She's used to these abrupt gaps in conversations with me by now, sometimes even tries to fill in the words I don't know. But there's no way she could predict what I want to say next.

"People can't see me," I say instead, settling for the closest translation and hoping she'll understand.

Her tattooed brows knit together. "What?"

"I mean—no one can—my body becomes—" Frustration

boils inside me as the words jumble around in my mouth. There's no correlation between fluency and intelligence, I know that, but it's hard not to feel dumb when you can't even string together a complete sentence in your mother tongue. "No one can see me."

Understanding dawns upon Xiaoyi's face. "*Ah.* You mean you turn invisible?"

I nod once, my throat too constricted for me to speak. I'm suddenly afraid I've made the wrong decision by telling her. What if she thinks I'm hallucinating? What if she calls Mama, or the local hospital, or someone from one of her many We-Chat shopping groups?

But all she says is, "Interesting."

"*Interesting?*" I echo. "That—that's it? Xiaoyi, I just told you—"

She waves a hand in the air. "Yes, yes, I know. I can hear perfectly well." Then she falls into silence for what feels like eons, her large earth-brown eyes thoughtful, her lips moving soundlessly.

I can't help squirming in my seat as I wait for her verdict. It feels like the buns in my stomach have turned to stone, and in hindsight, I realize I probably should've told her all this *before* we started eating.

Finally, Xiaoyi glances up and points to some spot behind me. "Yan Yan, can you fetch me that statue of the Buddha over there?"

"What?" I twist around, and locate the little bronze statue sitting atop an old bookshelf. Old worn copies of classics like *Journey to the West* and *Dream of the Red Chamber* are stacked beside it. "O-Oh. Yeah, sure." I nearly trip over my chair in my haste to grab the statue for her, my fingers trembling as they close over the cool surface. I've never been the super religious type (when I was five, Mama told me that all humans are just a clump of cells waiting to decompose) but if I can lose all visible shape and form without warning, who's to say a mini bronze Buddha can't give me the answers I need?

I hand it over to Xiaoyi with both hands as you would a sacred artifact, heart hammering in my chest, watching intently as she unscrews the Buddha's foot, reaches inside and pulls out…

A toothpick.

"Um," I say, uncertain. "Is that for—"

Using one hand to cover her mouth, Xiaoyi slides the thin wooden stick between her teeth with a loud sucking sound. She snorts when she sees the expression on my face. "What, did you think this was for you?"

"No," I lie, the rush of heat to my cheeks giving the truth away. "But, I mean, I was kind of hoping you could…"

"Offer you guidance? Explain to you what's going on?" Xiaoyi offers.

"Yes." I plop back down on my chair and look pleadingly across the table at her. "That. Anything, really."

She considers this for a moment. "Hmm… Then you'll have to tell me how it first began."

"If I knew how it began, Xiaoyi, I wouldn't be having this problem right now," I point out.

"But how were you feeling at the time?" she presses. "What were you thinking?"

I frown. The first memory that surfaces is Henry's smug, disgustingly pretty face as he moved to join me onstage. I quickly shake it away. My hatred toward that boy might be all-consuming and powerful enough to keep me up at night, but it's not *so* intense as to trigger some freakish supernatural reaction.

And besides, I didn't notice anything weird until after we both got our awards and our photos taken, or after it occurred to me that...

"I would be leaving," I murmur. My hands go still on the table. "That without Airington, I'd be—"

I'd be nothing.

I can't bring myself to finish my sentence, but Xiaoyi nods sagely, as if she can read my mind.

"One of my favorite authors once said: Sometimes the universe offers us the things we think we want, but which turn out to be a curse," she says, which would probably strike me as a lot more profound if it weren't for the toothpick still sticking out of her mouth. Or the fact that I know her favorite author is a web-novelist who exclusively writes fantasy books about hot demon hunters. "And sometimes the universe grants us the things we don't know we need, which turn out to be a gift." She spits the toothpick into her palm. "Another author also said that the self and society are like the sea and the sky—a change in one reflects a change in the other."

As I listen to her speak, I get that feeling I often do when analyzing Shakespeare for Mr. Chen's English class; that the words *should* mean something, but I have no idea what. Yet unlike in English, I can't just bullshit my way through the answer with pretty prose.

"So...are you telling me this is a curse? Or a gift?"

"I think," Xiaoyi says, screwing the Buddha foot back on, "that depends on what you make of it until it goes away."

"And if it never goes away?" It's not until I've spoken the words aloud that I realize this is my greatest fear; the permanent loss of control, the rest of my life fragmented and ruined, forever at the mercy of those unpredictable flashes of invisibility. "If I'm just...stuck in my current condition? What then?"

Xiaoyi shakes her head. "Everything is temporary, Yan Yan. And all the more reason to seize whatever's in front of you while it's still there."

4

"I have a plan."

Henry jerks his head up at the sound of my voice, trying—and failing—to find me in the dim light of his dorm. Faint confusion touches the space between his brows as he sets the dumbbell in his hand down on the desk, still scanning the room for me. As he does, the clouds shift outside his window, and a stream of pure, silvery moonlight spills in around him. Sweat drips from his midnight curls, darkening the collar of his tight-fitted tank.

I feel a hot stab of irritation. Who the hell works out at four in the morning? And who looks this good while doing it?

"Alice?" he calls, his voice quiet, slightly uneven from exertion. "Are you..."

"It happened again," I say by way of explanation, as I step around his bed and stride toward him. Pat his arm to let him know where I am. His skin is warm beneath mine, the muscles underneath tensing instantly at my touch.

"Jesus Christ," he mutters. "Couldn't you at least knock before—"

"The door was open," I speak over him. "Besides, this is important." I grab the mini notebook from my blazer, flip it open to the right page, and hesitate. Just for a moment—enough for me to feel the notebook's weight in my hands, to realize the significance of what I'm about to trust him with. The risk of it. But then I remember the jagged scar running down Mama's palm, the hundreds of thousands of yuan I need and don't have, the threat of leaving Airington looming over my future like a sharpened axe, and I unfreeze. Press the opened pages into his hands.

As soon as it leaves my fingers, the notebook must become visible to Henry, because his eyes widen. Then he focuses on what's been written in my tiny scrawl, all the highlighted numbers and color-coded tables and detailed lists I spent most of my weekend working on, and his eyebrows arch.

"This looks like a business proposal," he says slowly.

"That's because it is."

"For...?"

"My invisibility services. See, I was thinking about it," I say, injecting as much confidence into my voice as possible. I imagine myself a businesswoman, like the ones you see on TV, all fresh-ironed pencil skirts and swishing ponytails and clacking stiletto heels as they sell their pitch to a table of bored executives. "And it seems like a waste not to monetize what's otherwise a pretty shitty situation, don't you agree?"

He folds his arms over his chest. "I thought you said you couldn't control it."

"I can't," I say, fighting back a small surge of annoyance as

I recall our last conversation. "But I've been tracking the instances I turn invisible, and there's a sort of pattern to it: I always get the same strange cold sensation right before—almost like my body has an inbuilt warning system—which gives me about two to three minutes to run to a deserted area. It's not ideal, of course, but it'd be enough for me to work with if—*when* we get this business running."

He glances down to study my notes again, his expression unreadable. "And this business would be…you carrying out whatever tasks people at our school want from you while invisible." He says it like a question, like he's not sure if I'm joking.

"It wouldn't be *any* task," I tell him. "I'm not down to help some creep get his hands on his crush's underwear or set the school on fire or whatever. But imagine how much money people would be willing to pay just to—I don't know, see if their exes secretly still look through old photos of them, or if their best friend's been gossiping about them behind their back. We'd turn a profit in no time."

"And where do I fit into all this?"

"I need an app," I say, pacing before him. His gaze follows the soft shuffle of my footsteps. "Something that can allow people to send their requests easily, without getting caught. Or maybe a website, some sort of device. It's your call—you're the tech guy. But once we get our communication channels sorted, I'll be doing all the dirty work."

I study his face carefully as I speak, watching for the telltale sign that he's lost interest. If you look close enough, you can always catch it: the second his eyes grow distant, cold, even as he continues smiling and nodding and saying all the right things in that polite-but-bored way of his. Years of careful observation have shown me that trying to hold Henry Li's undivided attention is like trying to hold water in your hands.

Which is why I'm so surprised to see the light in his eyes now. Feel the intensity of his gaze and focus on me, even if he can't see me, can only hear the words coming out of my mouth.

When I'm finished, he nods once and says, slowly, "That does sound like a plan…"

"But what?" I say, catching his tone.

"Well, what about the ethical implications?"

"What about them?" I challenge.

"So you think there aren't any," he says, eyebrows raised, enough sarcasm dripping from his voice to form a pool at his feet. "According to you, everything about your plan screams perfectly moral. Everything. As in, if Jesus were here, he'd be completely on board—"

I roll my eyes. "Don't drag Jesus into this. You're not even religious."

"But to capitalize on people's vulnerabilities, their darkest secrets—and our own classmates, no less, who you're going to have to sit next to and talk to every day…"

And despite myself, despite the carefully thought-out list of pros and cons I've already made addressing these exact concerns, I do feel a jolt of guilt.

But right now, my wants are bigger than my fears. This plan is a perfect win-win situation, if only I have the nerve to carry through with it; with the profit I make, I could stay here at Airington and complete my IBs instead of taking the gaokao or moving across the world, pay the 250,000 RMB needed for my school fees, maybe even my college tuition, and give all the extra money to my parents, to Xiaoyi. I could treat Baba and Mama to a real feast, at a proper Peking duck restaurant where they carve the meat right in front of us, buy Mama expensive hand creams and lotions to undo the damage from all that scrubbing and soaking around in disinfectants at the hospital, get her and Baba a car so they never have to squeeze into the subway at peak hour again...

I almost consider telling him this, justifying myself, but then I remember who I'm talking to. 250,000 RMB is just a number to Henry Li, not the difference between two lives. He would never understand.

"*You*, of all people, shouldn't get to make a speech on ethics," I snap. "SYS has enough money to basically stop global warming, but instead all you're doing is coming up with new algorithms to benefit your sponsors and contribute to the rising wealth gap—"

"Our apps do their part to benefit society," he says smoothly, readily, standing up straighter all of a sudden, and I wonder for a second if I've just stepped into a company ad. "And *for your information*, forty-three percent of our daily active users are actually from third- and fourth-tier cities, and over thirty percent—"

"—identify as being from lower-income families, yeah I know," I cut in, impatient, then realize my mistake.

God, I really need to stop talking.

Henry pauses. Stares in my direction, long and hard. If his eyebrows shoot up any higher, they'll probably disappear. "I'm sorry, do you—do you secretly work for my father's company or something?"

I make a noncommittal noise with my throat, though it

sounds more like I'm choking, and scramble to get back to the point. "Look. If you're so concerned about ethics, we can donate ten percent of the profits to charity—"

"That's not how—"

I snort. "That's exactly how all the big corps work, and I'm not even doing it to dodge taxes."

He opens his mouth to argue, then clamps it shut again. Most likely because he knows I'm right. A silence falls over us, broken only by the low rumble of snores from the neighboring rooms and the persistent chirp of cicadas outside. Then he says, "To be honest, I'm surprised you of all people would come up with something like this." Amusement curls the corners of his lips. "Weren't you the one who burst into tears in Year Eight maths because the teacher scolded you for not bringing a graphing calculator to class? Then followed up the next day with a signed ten-page letter vowing to never make the same mistake again?"

"How—how do you even remember that?" I demand, humiliation burning through me at the memory. The truth is that I *had* brought a calculator with me that day, but it was one of those old second-hand ones Mama had found in a sketchy little store down the street. It'd broken into pieces by the time I pulled it out from my bag at school, and after the teacher's scolding, I'd used up all my lunch money for the next month to buy myself the same calculator as my classmates.

But Henry definitely doesn't need to know the full story.

"I remember everything," Henry is saying. Then he clears his throat, some indecipherable emotion flickering over his face. "About everything, is what I mean. I just happen to have an excellent memory."

I don't know whether to laugh or roll my eyes. Henry's arrogance will truly never cease to amaze me.

"So? Are you in?" I ask, fighting back a swell of impatience. Every second we waste standing around here talking is a second that could be better spent getting this thing up and running.

Henry moves to sit down on the edge of his perfectly made bed, crossing one long leg over another. "What's in it for me?"

I'm more than prepared for this question; I did the calculations last night. "Forty percent of all profits," I say. It's more than he deserves, but I need to make an appealing case. Right now, he's the best—and maybe only—person who can help me.

"Fifty."

"What?"

"I'll settle for fifty percent."

I grind my teeth together so hard I half expect them to fall out. "Forty-two."

"Fifty-five."

"Wait—*what*? That—that's not how negotiations are supposed to work," I splutter, anger rising to my cheeks. "You can't just keep—"

"Fifty-six," he says, leaning back now, his gaze steady, his eyes the same ink-black shade as the night sky outside.

"Look, you asshole, forty-two is more than generous—"

"Fifty-seven—"

"Forty—"

"Fifty-eight—"

"*Fine,*" I snap. "Fifty percent."

He grins, amusement dancing in those night sky eyes, and

the effect is striking. Disarming. My stomach dips as if coming off the high of a roller coaster.

Then he says, "You're a terrible negotiator, Alice."

And I consider strangling him. I probably would, if it weren't for the fact that murder seems like a less-than-ideal way of starting a business partnership.

"Do we have a deal, then?" I press, hoping to walk away from this conversation with something concrete to hold on to, to plan around, at the very least.

But ever the experienced negotiator, all Henry says in response is, "I'll think about it."

Henry and I don't speak a single word to each other for the next three days.

Not for lack of trying on my end; every time I try to make eye contact with him from across the classroom, he's distracted, a distant, faraway look on his face, or he's busy working on something on his laptop, his long fingers flying over the keys. Then as soon as the bell rings, he's gone, striding out the doors without even a glance back. If I didn't know any better, I'd think he was the one with the invisibility problem.

Soon I'm starting to regret everything—seeking him out in his dorm, revealing the details of my plan, believing we might actually make some kind of partnership work between us—and with the regret comes a fast-brewing anger, like a gathering storm. This is my nightmare scenario; Henry Li knowing he has something I want, and having every right to withhold it from me. I imagine him mocking me in his head—*I can't believe what Alice Sun asked me to do the other day*—and resentment fills my mouth like spit.

But then Thursday rolls around, and Henry hurries into our social ethics class ten minutes late.

This is unprecedented.

Everyone turns to stare at him, whispers flying across the room as we take in his appearance. He looks—well, not *disheveled*, exactly, since Henry at his very worst still looks better than every other guy at their most polished. But his normally immaculate school shirt is creased at the sides, the top two buttons undone, exposing his sharp collarbones. His hair falls in wild waves over his brows, rumpled and uncombed, and his perfect porcelain skin is a shade paler than usual, the area under his eyes stamped with dark circles.

If he notices the stares, he doesn't show it. He simply takes off his fancy pollution mask, folds it into his blazer pocket, and makes his way over to the teacher's desk.

"Sorry I'm late, Dr. Walsh," Henry says to our social ethics teacher. Her full name is Julie Marshall Walsh, and she insists on being addressed as *Dr.*, but everyone just calls her Julie behind her back.

Julie purses her lips, her white-blond Anna Wintour bob bouncing past her ears as she shakes her head. "I must say, I expected better of you, Henry. You missed ten minutes of a *very* important lecture."

Someone makes an abrupt coughing sound that sounds suspiciously like a snort. The very important lecture in question is, in fact, a slideshow on "poor kids in Asia." We've spent the entire class looking through high-resolution photos of matchstick-boned children covered in mud or eating scorpions, all while Julie sighs and gasps—at one point, I swear I see her pale blue eyes fill with tears—and dramatically whispers things like, "Can you *imagine*?" and "Oh, it really makes you realize how very *lucky* you are, doesn't it?"

Henry's brows lift a fraction, but his voice sounds completely respectful, earnest when he says, "I won't let it happen again, Dr. Walsh."

"I certainly hope not." Julie sniffs. "You can go to your seat now."

As Henry turns around, his dark eyes search the room, then lock on mine. My mouth goes dry, a violent bolt of anger and something else I can't quite name flashing through me. *Now* he's decided to acknowledge my presence? I glare at him with all the force I can muster, and—to my surprise—he holds my gaze, as if trying to convey something meaningful without moving his hands or his lips. Clearly, this boy has overestimated my ability to read minds.

I jerk my shoulder in the universal I-have-no-idea-what-you're-saying gesture, and he frowns. Drags a hand through his messy, crow-black hair. Opens his mouth—

"Is something the matter over there?" Julie calls. It's a known fact around the school that the chirpier Julie Walsh's voice gets, the angrier she is.

And she sounds very chirpy right now.

Henry must hear it too, because he quickly slides into his usual seat at the opposite end of the room. I'm not even sure when that started happening—us sitting as far away from each other as possible in every classroom. If it was something intentional, or if perhaps we work like magnets, with some kind of invisible field automatically pushing us apart wherever we go.

But for the first time, I hate the distance between us. What was he trying to tell me? And why was he late?

I can barely keep still for the rest of class. Even as the classroom lights dim and the projector flickers on again, more images of starving, unsmiling children flashing over the screen like phantoms, I can't stop peering over at where Henry is sitting, trying to search his face for clues. And more than once, I catch him looking at me too.

The second the bell rings, Henry strides over to my desk. "Can we talk?" he asks. The dark circles under his eyes are even more prominent up close, yet there's no trace of exhaustion in the way he's carrying himself, his chin lifted and his back straight as an arrow, or the crisp inflection of his tone.

"Um. Right here?"

The thing is, I *want* to talk, I'm dying to, but I'm all too aware of the kids around us slowing their footsteps, the curious glances they're sending our way. Everyone knows Henry and I are sworn enemies, and even if we weren't, Henry has never approached anyone in class before. He doesn't need to; people have a way of gravitating toward him.

"Maybe somewhere more...private," he concedes, seeming to realize the issue. He shoots a look at Bobby Yu, who's lurking around my desk, and Bobby quickly ducks his head and hurries away, textbooks tucked under his beanpole arms.

Then, without another word, Henry spins around on his heel and heads out through the classroom door, leaving me no choice but to follow.

Walking next to Henry through the crowded halls of Airington is a deeply strange experience. More people—teachers included—stop and greet him in the short walk from our social ethics classroom to our lockers than the total number of people I've spoken to since school started. That's not an exaggeration either. I can almost feel the tides of power ebbing and flowing around us, how everyone's attention shifts to Henry and stays on him as if he's glowing, and I think, briefly, that this must've been what it felt like to walk beside the emperor in the Forbidden City.

If only the emperor were me.

At last, we reach a quiet, deserted spot nestled between the lockers and the ayis' cleaning cabinets. We have a twenty-minute morning break before next class, so most students are rushing off to the school café at this time.

Henry stands with his back to the wall, scans the area twice to make sure no one's passing by, then says, "The app is ready."

I blink. "What?"

He sighs, takes his iPhone out of his pocket, taps onto something, and holds it up for me to see. A little blue logo shaped like a cartoon ghost blinks at me from the center of the screen, positioned next to Douyin and some kind of stock market app.

"Your app," Henry repeats. "Beijing Ghost. I've already trademarked the name, so if you don't like it, there's unfortunately not much we can do to change that."

"Wait—wait—so you're in?" I say, my mind scrambling to catch up. "You—we're really doing this?"

He gestures to his phone, eyebrows raised. "What does it look like?"

I grit my teeth. Would it really kill him to give a straightforward answer without sounding so condescending for once? A few choice words rise to my lips, but I force them back down. If he's gone ahead and made the app for me, then we're

officially business partners now, meaning it'd be quite un-
professional to tell him to shove his phone up his—

"I would've come to you sooner," Henry tells me, "but
there were a few logistics I still needed to figure out, and as a
general rule, I dislike talking about things before I have concrete results. So, if you look over here..."

He's talking faster than usual, I notice, his hand motions almost animated as he navigates the app's home page and points
out the key features. "The app essentially promises anonymity on both sides, for those in request of a service and those
carrying out the service—though of course, in this case, it'd
only be you. All users have to do is set up an account, fill out
a quick request form, and message you with any additional
questions or concerns they have. Then you can respond with
whatever price you're charging—I'd recommend starting at
around 5,000 RMB and raising the price depending on the
scale of the task—and if they agree, you enter into a binding
contract until the task is complete, and they've made their
payment."

"And how do they do that?" I ask.

A small, self-satisfied smile spreads over his lips. "I thought
about using cash at first—it's untraceable that way, and it'd
simplify the process—but then I came up with something
better." He clicks away from the app for a second and shows
me an official-looking email from the bank, addressed to
the owners of Beijing Ghost. "I asked a friend at the Bank of
China to help set up a private account just for this—under a
fake name, of course."

My head snaps up. "Isn't that..."

Isn't that illegal? The question dangles at the tip of my

tongue, but then, with a bubble of hysterical laughter, I remember that *everything* about this is at least a little bit illegal.

Alice Sun: Airington academic scholarship recipient. Honor roll student. Student council representative. And now criminal. Who would've thought?

"Isn't that what?" Henry prompts.

"Nothing. Never mind." I shake my head. Then I glance up at the app again, with its bright blue logo and sleek, professional interface, and can't help asking, "How did you get so good at this?"

"I had to design an app on my own to convince my father to let me help out at SYS. He wanted the company culture to be as meritocratic as possible." He combs back his messy waves with one hand, looking for a moment like the perfect picture of natural genius and nonchalance. "I was only thirteen at the time, so the app was obviously flawed, but it was proof enough that I could do...well, something."

I hide my surprise. I'd always assumed his father handed out work opportunities and privileges whenever he could, maybe even forced Henry into a high-ranking role at a young age. I'd assumed Henry never had to prove himself to anyone.

I make a vague sound with the back of my throat, and busy myself scrolling through the app. As much as I hate to admit it, Henry's right—it is easy to use. Not only that, but I can't find a single discernible fault.

"Well?" Henry leans forward. His dark eyes are alight, his chin angled up a few degrees, the sure, sharp lines of his body tense with something like anticipation. I realize he's waiting for me to give my opinion—no, for me to *compli-*

ment him, like some kid proudly holding up his artwork for a class show-and-tell.

My lips twitch. "I didn't know you had such a praise kink."

Surprise—maybe even embarrassment—flickers over his face. Then that calm, expressionless mask I'm so used to seeing immediately slides back into place, and I almost regret having spoken. "I do *not* have a—"

"Yeah, yeah, whatever you say." But when I turn and open my mouth to tease him further, I pause.

At this angle, under the fluorescent hallway lights, the fatigue shadowing his features is more noticeable than ever. He must've pulled at least two or three all-nighters these past few days just to finish working on the app.

And even though I know he's only doing it for profit, for his own interests, the words tumble from my lips anyway: "Thank you...for doing all of this. Really. It—it's even better than I imagined."

Maybe it's just a trick of the light, but I swear I see his ears turn pink.

"I'm glad," he says quietly, holding my gaze for what seems like a second too long.

I clear my throat and look away, feeling strangely self-conscious all of a sudden. "Right. Anyway, um. What do we do next?"

He responds by pulling another shiny new iPhone out from his pocket. "No one at our school knows this number," he explains, misreading my expression.

"You have two phones?"

"Three, actually," he says, his voice matter-of-fact. "One for work, one for personal contacts, and one for myself."

Whatever rush of gratitude I felt toward him just now immediately evaporates. My fingers curl into fists at my sides. I learned not long after I first came to Airington that comparing myself to people like Henry will only make me miserable, but I still can't help thinking about the battered phone in my own pocket, how Mama had to work overtime during the Spring Festival just to save enough money to buy it.

"All we need now is to get the word out about the app," Henry's saying, opening up a few different social media apps with impressive speed: WeChat for the local kids, Facebook Messenger for ABCs, WhatsApp for Malaysians, Kakao for Koreans.

"They're not going to believe you if you just say there's someone who can turn invisible," I point out. "Especially if you're messaging them from an anonymous number."

"No," he agrees. "Which is why I'm leaving that part out completely. All that matters to them is what the app can help them do, not how it's done."

Even though all of this is more or less my idea, now that it's really happening, I can't fight back the slow creep of doubt. What if everyone dismisses the app as a joke? What if they report it to the teacher? Or what if—

"Don't worry," Henry says without even glancing up, as if he can read my mind.

"I'm not worried," I grumble. I realize I've wrung my fingers into knots, and quickly force them to still at my sides. "How long do you think it'll take?"

He finishes typing out one last message on Kakao, then reaches for his other phone again. "Give it a minute."

I try to mimic his calm, his patience, start counting to sixty seconds in my head. I fight to keep my expression neutral, casual, to make it look like we're only going over some particularly difficult homework questions together. Anything to ward off suspicions from passing students when this thing works.

If this works.

It's true that news has a way of getting around in a school like ours, but could it really be that easy? That fast?

I only get to forty-five seconds when Henry's phone buzzes. The blue ghost logo lights up, glowing in quick pulses as if in sync with my rapidly pounding heart. A notification flashes over the screen: One New Message.

Henry could not look any more pleased with himself. He nods at me to open it and I do, trying to ignore the shaky feeling in my bones, the terrifying knowledge that there's no going back from this.

Immediately, a message from user C207 pops up:

is this legit?

I take a deep breath and reply:

Only one way to find out.

5

Coming here was a mistake.

This is all I can think as the taxi screeches to a halt outside Solana mall, narrowly missing a vendor selling shiny *Xi Yang-yang* helium balloons from the back of his bike. Lit up against the backdrop of a starless night sky, the sprawling shopping complex looks far bigger and grander than it did in the images I found on Baidu, the trees and wide storefronts all decorated with twinkling fairy lights. There's even an inky river flowing past a row of Western cafés on one end, the still surface reflecting the glow of water fountains.

Everything here seems clean. Fancy. *Expensive*, from the European architecture to the dressed-up girls in their twenties casually swinging designer bags over their thin white shoulders.

It's a completely different world from the tiny supermarkets that always stink of raw fish and the rundown shops near my parents' flat. A world suited for people like Rainie or Henry, not me. I can't help feeling like a dog who's wandered into wolf territory, every muscle in my body tensed, prepared for something to pounce.

"That'll be 73 RMB," the taxi driver tells me.

It takes me a second to understand what he's saying with his heavy regional accent, and when I do, I almost freak out. Solana isn't even that far from Airington; all the time we spent stuck in traffic must've driven the price up.

But then I remember that user C207 is covering my travel expenses for today, on top of the 20,000 RMB for if—*when*—I do my job well.

20,000 RMB.

The thought of that money filling up my brand-new bank account is enough to force my fears aside.

For now, at least.

I quickly pay the driver through WeChat, then scramble out of the taxi. The warm night air wraps around me like a cloak, and I'm grateful I decided to go with a simple sleeveless black dress for tonight—the only dress I have. Wearing my school uniform was obviously out of the question; I can't risk drawing any attention to myself before I turn invisible.

As I make my way toward the main entrance, sidestepping a young couple sharing lamb kebabs and a loud squad of international schoolkids (you can always just *tell*), I go over the to-do list in my head:

One, find user C207's father.

Two, follow him for the rest of the night without getting caught, or until—

Three, you gather substantial evidence that he is or is not cheating on his wife.

Four, send evidence to user C207.

Once I've reached the sliding glass doors, I pull out my phone and do another scan of the photos C207 messaged me yesterday, trying to commit the face in them to memory. This task would be a *lot* easier if their father didn't look like most wealthy men in their midfifties: beer belly straining against a crisp button-down shirt; short, graying hairs; ruddy complexion from too many free company drinks; and a roundish nose set over an even rounder chin.

Already, I've seen two or three businessmen passing by that bear a strong resemblance to the person I'm searching for. A terrible thought grips me: What if I end up stalking the wrong guy? It'd be so easy for me to blow it. And what then? The whole night would be wasted—a night that could've been spent finishing my ten-page history research assignment for tomorrow or revising for next week's chemistry unit test. I'd have to tell Henry and user C207 that I messed up, have to sit with the awful taste of failure I've spent my whole life trying very hard to avoid, and the whole plan would implode, and—

"Hey, you okay, kid?"

I jerk my head up. A beautiful, kind-faced woman who looks young enough to still be in college has stopped to peer over at me, her thick-lashed eyes wide with concern.

I realize I've been tapping my feet anxiously on the pavement like a scared rabbit, and I doubt my expression is too reassuring either. *Get your shit together, Alice*, I scold myself, forcing my feet to still. There's no way I can run a successful criminal enterprise if I have nerves of watery tofu.

"Oh yeah. I'm fine. Great," I say, mustering as much enthusiasm as I can. Maybe a little *too* much enthusiasm. The woman takes a small step back as if uncertain about my mental stability.

"Okay then, just checking..." There's a distinct Southern lilt to her voice—as in southern China, not Texas—making her words flow like water down a stream. After a few beats of deliberation, she turns around to leave, but before I can even breathe a sigh of relief, she pauses and asks, "Are you here with anyone? Your parents?"

God help me.

I know I have the kind of face that could easily be confused for a twelve- or thirteen-year-old's, but the very last thing I need right now is adult supervision. Time for me to put my lying skills to the test, I guess.

"I am, actually," I say. My voice sounds a few octaves too high. "Um, my parents are waiting for me over there"—I motion to a crowded line outside some Japanese BBQ restaurant in the near distance—"so I should really go..."

Without waiting for her to reply, I walk away at a speed that would probably impress our PE teacher, Ms. Garcia. I don't stop until I've turned into a dark narrow alley, tucked between two stores and hidden from view, then crane my neck to see if the woman's left.

She hasn't.

Not because she's searching for me, though, but because of the stout, gray-haired man heading her way, a wide grin stretching the faint wrinkles around his mouth.

Her father? I wonder.

Then he holds up a huge bouquet of roses that looks like a prop for a bad rom-com movie, and the woman squeals and runs to him, throwing her arms around his neck in a tight embrace.

So…definitely not her father then.

I'm about to leave and give the two of them some much-needed privacy, when the man spins the woman around, lifting his weak jaw up at an angle to offer a clearer view of his face, and I'm suddenly gripped by the feeling that I've seen him before, in a newspaper or—

The photos. Of course.

I pull out my phone again just to double-check, and sure enough, that same round plain-featured face is staring back at me.

But in the brief time it takes me to glance down and up again, the two have already broken apart, the woman now holding the flowers instead of the old man in her arms. She says something to him that I can't make out, and he laughs, a loud rumbling sound. Together, they set off down one of the brightly lit lanes by the river.

It's clear what I need to do next. I wait until there's a few more yards of distance between us, then follow them, like a ghost getting ready for its first haunting.

It turns out that stalking people is much harder than I thought.

The crowds in Solana seem to grow as the sky darkens, and more than once I find myself almost losing sight of my target, or forced to take a step back by a group of very evidently intoxicated young men.

"Hey, meinu," one of the men calls after me, making my skin prickle. *Meinu* means *beautiful girl*, which I guess is meant to be flattering, except people around here call pretty much anyone between the ages of twelve and thirty that. Even if that weren't the case, I'd rather fail a midterm than have some creepy guy comment on my looks.

I pick up my pace, trying to get as far away from the group as possible—and almost bump straight into the back of the old man and his girlfriend.

Heart pounding, I quickly duck around the closest corner before they can see me. They've come to a stop outside what looks to be a fancy Chinese restaurant—the traditional kind, with crimson lanterns swaying from the painted overhanging eaves and images of coiled dragons carved into the front doors.

A waitress dressed in shimmering black comes out to greet them.

"Cao xiansheng!" she says warmly. "Please follow me upstairs. We've already prepared your favorite dishes, and you'll be pleased to know the barramundi dish for today is…" The rest of her sentence is lost beneath an enthusiastic chorus of huanying guanglin and the clink of plates and champagne glasses as they move into the restaurant.

I try to follow. Now would be a great time to turn invisible, but of course my new curse—power, affliction, whatever— isn't cooperating when I actually need it. Based on the detailed records I've kept in my notebook, the invisibility thing tends to happen once every two days or so, and only when I'm awake. And since I haven't transformed in the past thirty hours, the probability of it happening sometime tonight should be high.

Should be.

But I know all too well that the universe doesn't always work the way it should.

Case in point: I've barely taken two steps forward when another waitress at the entrance holds up a hand to stop me. She's pretty in a mean-looking sort of way, her dark, eyeliner-rimmed eyes narrowing as they take in my appearance.

My gut clenches. Is it so obvious that I don't belong here?

"Do you have a reservation?" she asks in a clipped monotone voice, like she already knows the answer.

"Uh...yes, yes I do," I bluff, my mind scrambling for purchase. "My family's waiting for me upstairs—"

"Upstairs is the VIP lounge," she interrupts. Her eyes narrow further, and I can almost imagine the conversation she's going to have with her coworkers the second I'm out of earshot: *Did you see that weird little girl trying to get into the restaurant just now? You think she was trying to steal food or something?* "I'm going to need evidence of membership."

"Oh. Sure thing." I make what I hope is a convincing show of searching my pockets for a card I most certainly don't have. "Hang on—oh no. I must've left it somewhere... Let me just um—go get it..."

I'm rushing back out the door before she can think to call over a manager or security, cursing myself and my luck as I turn to hide behind the same corner as before. It's not like I should be expected to produce a VIP card out of thin air, but I have a feeling someone like Henry wouldn't run into the same problem. He could just stride in there with his quiet charm and confidence and perfect hair and they'd let him upstairs without a second thought.

I shake my head. No point making myself feel worse with imaginary scenarios—even though that seems to be what I do best. Tonight's mission has only just started, and I have to keep it together until my powers kick in.

However long that takes.

I end up standing outside the restaurant for what must be hours. Parents wheeling strollers and expats likely headed to the bars on Lucky Street walk past me, chatting and laughing in a messy blend of languages, oblivious to the panic crawling up my throat.

Come on, I urge my body, the universe, whichever one is listening. *Hurry up already.*

But another excruciating hour or so passes, with me feeling more idiotic by the second, before finally, *finally*, a familiar wave of cold washes over me, accompanied by an overwhelming surge of relief. I make myself count to three hundred, giving the cold time to sink in, then dart a glance at the tinted window behind me.

It's still disorientating and more than a little terrifying to not be able to see my own reflection, but right now I'm just glad the invisibility thing is working.

The restaurant is crowded when I slip inside—this time careful not to bump into anyone—and I have to blink a few times to adjust to the bright, lavish interior. Every surface has been polished until it practically glows, from the giant fish tanks out front to the traditional-style mahogany chairs arranged around the rotating tables.

Upstairs, however, the colors and noise level are more subdued, with dark panes of glass and wood pressing in on both sides of the narrow corridor. There's a luxurious lounge at the far end, the kind of spot where the richest of the rich are probably busy exchanging trade secrets or making arrangements to buy Greenland over tiny glasses of baijiu, but leading up to it are six private rooms. This must be where the old man and his girlfriend disappeared off to.

I tiptoe from door to door, silently thanking whatever God of Crime is out there that the walls aren't soundproof. Snippets of conversation float toward me, but it's not until I reach the fifth room that I hear what I'm looking for: a soft female voice, with a distinct Southern accent.

"...the hospital, but the doctors say it might be months before they can actually go ahead with the operation..."

"What?" A gruff male voice booms out, followed by a muffled *thud*, like someone slamming a fist on the table. "That's ridiculous!"

"I know." She sniffs. "And the only way to push forward the date is to pay an extra fee, but it's just—it's so expensive..."

"How expensive?"

A short pause. Then: "35,000 RMB."

"Baobei'r," the man says, rolling an *er* sound into the end of the pet name the way all old Beijingers do. "Why didn't you tell me sooner? That's hardly anything—"

"To *you*," the woman interrupts. There's the squeak of a heavy chair being moved, and I imagine her pushing away from him, a frown settling over her delicate features. "But for me—"

"Don't be silly. How many times do I have to tell you, baobei'r? What's mine is naturally yours..."

As the man continues spouting cheesy lines and words of comfort, I pull out my phone and hit Record. It's a good start, but a low-quality voice memo alone won't cut it. I still need photo evidence.

I'm trying to figure out how to get inside without opening the door myself when a waitress walks by, carrying an elaborate platter of fruit laid out on dry ice. All the lychees have been peeled and pinned into place with mini wooden toothpicks, and the fresh watermelons have been carved into the shape of blooming flowers.

With one elbow, the waitress pushes the door open, and I seize the opportunity to enter the room right after her.

It becomes clear to me at once why the private rooms are reserved for VIP members only. A glittering chandelier dangles from the high painted ceiling, casting flecks of light over the carpeted floor and full-length mirror on the wall like a much more expensive version of a disco ball. Beneath it, the old man and his girlfriend are seated around a table that looks big enough to fit twenty extra guests, the red tablecloth almost completely covered by an extravagant, mouthwatering spread of dishes. Most of them I've never even tasted before, only seen in ads or Chinese palace dramas: braised sea cucumber and abalone simmering in two little clay pots, white bird's nest soup glistening in a hollowed-out papaya like just-fallen snow.

I do my best to ignore the sudden sharp pang of hunger in my stomach. I was so nervous before coming here that I skipped lunch entirely—a mistake, I'm realizing now.

"Sorry to disturb you, Cao xiansheng," the waitress says, dipping her head and extending the fruit platter toward him like an offering to a king. "The manager asked me to bring you this complimentary fruit platter as a small token of his appreciation. We'll also be serving sweet red bean porridge at the end of your meal. Please enjoy."

The man waves a meaty hand in the air before she's even finished talking, evidently used to this kind of treatment by now.

After the waitress sets down the platter and turns to go, the woman instantly reaches for the lychees.

"Oh, these are my *favorite*," she sighs, chewing the small glossy fruit with such relish I feel like I should look away.

But of course, the man only leans in closer, smiling, then— to my absolute horror—starts *feeding* the lychees to her. I really should've charged more for this job. Resisting the urge to gag, I snap as many photos as I can on my phone, making sure to get a clear shot of both their faces even as something prickles at the edge of my conscience. It's not like I have any sympathy for cheaters who date women half their age, but my being here is still a blatant invasion of privacy. And the young woman—she was kind to me earlier. If these photos end up affecting her...

No. That's not for me to worry about. I *can't* worry. I'm just here to gather the evidence; user C207 can decide what to do with it.

I'm already planning the trip back to the dorms in my head, thinking of the homework I need to catch up on and the midnight snacks I can grab from the school kitchens if I'm still invisible by then, when my stomach growls.

Loudly.

I freeze. The woman freezes too, the half-eaten lychee falling from her open mouth, and I might've laughed at the cartoonish expression on her face if I couldn't feel my heart jumping to my throat.

"Did...did you hear that?" the woman whispers.

"I— Yes." The man's graying brows draw together. Then, in an unconvincingly casual tone, he says, "It must've been the air conditioner. Or the people in the next room."

"Maybe," the woman says, uncertain. "It just... It sounded so close to me. You don't think someone might be hiding...?"

The man shakes his head. Makes a *tsk*ing sound with his teeth, another attempt at nonchalance. "See, Bichun, this is why I told you to stop watching those creepy detective shows at night. It's bad for the nerves, and it's enough to send anyone's imagination into overdrive."

"I guess so..." Yet even as she says this, her eyes roam over a spot only a few feet away from where I'm standing. I tense every muscle in my body, afraid to so much as breathe. After a few beats of silence, the woman seems to relax a little, returning to her lychees—

But my stomach betrays me by rumbling again.

The woman jumps in her seat as if struck by lightning. "F-fuwuyuan!" she calls, her voice sharp with fear. "Fuwuyuan, quick, get in here!"

The waitress outside responds almost at once, the doors flying open as she hurries into the room, a heavy menu tucked under her arm.

"Is something the matter, madame? Was the fruit not to your liking or—"

"Forget the fruit!" The woman points a trembling finger in my general direction. "There was a...a noise..."

"What kind of noise?"

I don't wait around to hear the rest of their conversation. I tiptoe over to the opened door, grateful for the thick carpet masking my steps. Then I'm running—running down the winding stairs, past waiters carrying trays, and out into the open night.

It's not until I've rounded the restaurant corner that I let myself slow down. I'm panting hard. The back of my dress is soaked with sweat, and there's an awful stitch gnawing at my side, but none of that matters right now. Not when I've got my evidence.

Still gasping for air, I pull up the Beijing Ghost app on my phone and find all the photos and voice recordings I took in the restaurant.

Then I hit Send.

My dorm room is quiet when I walk in, the lights turned down low, veiling everything in shadow.

It's just past midnight, and usually around this time Chanel's jamming out to her K-pop playlist or doing some new aerobic workout or laughing hysterically on the phone with her other fuerdai friends about some joke with too much cultural nuance for me to understand. This silence is unexpected, unnatural; either Chanel's decided to become a monk, or something must have happened.

I drag my feet forward. The sharp spike of adrenaline I experienced at the restaurant has long given way to dizzying, mind-numbing fatigue, and all I really want to do is fall onto my bed and sleep. But instead, I turn the lights on to full brightness and search the cramped space for my roommate.

It takes a moment to spot her. She's curled up in the far corner of the room, her silk blankets pulled tight around her small frame, covering everything except her hands and face. Her eyes are swollen red.

She sets the phone in her hands down when she notices me standing there—but not before I see the photos flashing across the screen. The same photos I took only a few hours ago.

In my confusion, I think something nonsensical, like: she must've somehow taken my phone. But no, I can still feel the full weight of my phone in my own pocket. And it still wouldn't explain why she's been crying. What would the photos have to do with her...

Then understanding clicks into place.

Cao. It's a common enough Chinese surname—there are at least five or six Caos at our school—that I didn't think to make the connection earlier, yet now it seems obvious. The old man at the restaurant must be her father.

Guilt clamps down on my stomach. This whole time I was fantasizing about all the money going into my bank account, Chanel's life has been unraveling.

Still, she doesn't know that I know. The smart thing to do—the *safe* thing to do—would be to just leave it as that, act like nothing's wrong and spend the rest of my night catching up on homework. Let her grieve and rage however she wishes. I'm sure she has plenty of friends to comfort her anyway.

But as I stare at her sad, hunched-over form, all alone in the dark, an old memory ambushes me: a few months after we first moved in together, she'd found me lying facedown on the bed, uniform still on, my Chinese test shredded to pieces around me. A hideous 87.5% scrawled across one of the torn corners. We weren't close-close even then, but she'd plopped down beside me as if it were the most natural thing in the world and cheerily mocked every question on the test until I felt more like laughing than sobbing.

My heart wavers.

"Hey," I blurt out, taking a step closer even as I curse my own mouth. "Um… Are you all right?"

Chanel glances up at me from her cocoon of blankets. I half expect her to brush the question off, or maybe simply stay silent until I get the message and go away, but she replies quickly, with surprising violence, "Aside from the fact that my dad's a total asshole? I'm great."

I try to hide my shock. I can't imagine ever calling Baba something like that, not with all his lectures on filial piety and respecting my elders no matter what entrenched in my very bones.

"Sorry," Chanel says, maybe sensing my discomfort. She tugs the blankets higher over her face, so her words are muffled when she explains, "It's just been a shitty day."

I hesitate, then go to sit down on the floor beside her and ask, as if I were auditioning for Side Character Two in a high school drama, "Do you want to talk about it?"

She snorts, though it sounds a bit like a sob. "Aren't we already talking about it?"

"Right," I say, feeling dumb. Part of me is already regretting this conversation, but another part—the part that once hoped Chanel and I might become best friends—doesn't want to just leave it like this either. "I guess we are."

"I just. I don't get it." She sighs, blowing a stray, slightly wet strand of hair from her eyes. Picks up her phone, scrolls through another photo, then slams it down again with such force I almost jump. "I. Don't. *Get*. It."

I decide to stay silent.

"It just doesn't make sense. My mum never did—I mean,

this whole time, she's been busy preparing for his birthday. Can you believe that? She's booked his favorite restaurant, and his favorite band, and she even had a qipao tailored just for the occasion, and he's..." She tightens her grip on her phone, knuckles white. "What was he thinking? *Why?*" Then she turns to me, like she's actually hoping I might have an answer.

"It's not really about your mum though, right?" I say slowly. "I mean, if even Beyoncé was cheated on—"

Her eyes narrow. "Wait. How do you know that?"

"Know what?" I say, half wondering, in my sleep-deprived state, if she's talking about Beyoncé.

"I didn't say anything about my dad cheating just now. How do you know?"

Shit.

Panic seizes my throat. I choke out a vague *um*ing sound, my mind scrambling for some plausible explanation.

"Did Grace tell you?" she presses. "Because I specifically *asked* her not to say anything until I had evidence. Ma ya," she mutters, switching to Chinese. "That girl just can't keep her mouth shut—"

"No, no, it's not that. Really," I add when she casts me a look of disbelief. I realize that if there were an official report card for criminals, I'd be sitting on a low B or C right now; any straight-A criminal would go with the ready-made excuse, pin all the blame on Grace and simply move on with their lives. But seeing as Chanel's father has been deceiving her and her mother this whole time, it seems cruel to feed her another lie, no matter how small.

Besides, it might make things easier to have my roommate

in on the plan, to turn invisible in the mornings without raising any alarm that I've disappeared.

"So what?" Chanel says, watching me closely. "Who told you?"

"No one."

She frowns. "Then how…"

"Look, it's probably easier if I show you." I take out my phone and open up the app to my recent conversation with user C207—*our* recent conversation. Chanel's eyes lock on the photos of her father at the restaurant, then snap to the identical photos on her own phone. Her mouth falls open.

"*You*'re the person behind Beijing Ghost?" she demands. She inspects the photos again, holding the phone so close her small nose is almost touching the screen. Then she stares back at me. "Seriously? *You?*"

"You don't have to sound so skeptical," I say, not sure whether I should be offended by her reaction.

"Sorry. You just didn't strike me as the type to…you know."

I really don't, but there's no point in asking her to specify. So instead I ask, "Who did you think it was, then?"

"I'm not sure." She shrugs, the blankets sliding a few inches off her shoulders. "Henry, maybe? He's good with the tech stuff, and he's got his dad's entrepreneurial genes."

My jaw tightens. Henry, *again*. Even when he's not here, he's everywhere.

"Anyway," Chanel says, with a little shake of her head. "That's not the point. *How* did you do it? I thought—I don't know, maybe the app came with some kind of secret spy camera system—but the photo quality is perfect. And the angle." She jabs a manicured finger at the photo, clearly taken at eye level with her father and his girlfriend. "It's almost as if you were right there in the room with them..."

"Well, um." A nervous laugh escapes my throat. But better to get this over and done with, I suppose. "The thing is... I was. In the room with them."

Chanel laughs, too, but it's a sound of incredulity. "As if."

"I'm being serious."

"Yeah, you're *always* serious, Alice. But what you're saying— it doesn't make any sense. Like, at all. If you'd entered the room with my dad, he would've called security on you—"

"If he saw me," I interrupt. "But he didn't."

She stares at me, now looking a bit concerned for my sanity. "Again, I'm *hearing* you, I am. But I honestly don't understand how that would work, unless you could camouflage or turn invisible or something."

I know she's only joking, but I take the opportunity. "Actually, you're right."

"About...?"

"I can turn invisible. See"—I quickly zoom in on the photo for proof before she can protest—"that mirror in the background? If someone were standing there to take the photo, you should be able to see their reflection, right? Or at least a shadow. But here—"

"There's nothing," she murmurs, finishing the sentence for me. Then her brows crinkle. "You're sure you didn't just like, Photoshop this? Because I've seen Grace's Instagram posts, and photos can be *very* deceiving."

I wave aside whatever weird beef she has with this Grace girl, and look her straight in the eye. "Chanel, I swear I'm telling the truth. If I'm not..." I pause, trying to come up with the best way to convince her that I mean every word. "If I'm not…then let me get below average on every single test from now on. Let me end up rejected from all the Ivy Leagues I apply to. Let me—" I swallow. Even though this is all hypothetical, it's still painful to say out loud. "Let me do worse than Henry Li in absolutely everything."

Chanel's hand flies to her mouth, and I've never been so grateful for my competitive overachiever reputation in my life. "*No.* No way."

I nod grimly. "Yes. *That's* how serious I am."

I wait for realization to truly sink in this time. A long silence passes, and then—

"*Wocao!* I mean—wow. Holy shit. Holy *fuck*…" As Chanel makes her way through what seems like every single expletive in both the English and Chinese languages—some of which I don't even recognize—I'm struck by the ridiculousness of this situation. These kind of late-night, bare-all, *I-can't-believe-that-happened* conversations were exactly what twelve-year-old me would've wanted. Just never in these circumstances.

"When did it— *How* did it…" Chanel begins once she's managed to compose herself a little.

"I'm not completely sure," I admit. "There are still things I'm trying to figure out."

"*Wow,*" she says again on a drawn breath, eyes wide. She wraps the blankets tighter around herself and leans all the way back against the wall, as if unsure she can keep her body upright much longer.

"Yeah," I say awkwardly. "So, um—"

"Is this why you wouldn't go to the mall with me?"

"Huh?" I glance up at her, certain I've heard wrong.

"When we first moved in here. I asked you to go shopping with me a few times and you always turned me down. Is it because of this whole invisibility side gig you've got going on?"

"Oh no. Me turning invisible is a pretty recent thing," I tell her, still not understanding what this has to do with anything.

But then she offers me a brief, awkward sort of smile, sinks lower onto the floor, and it hits me that maybe she's drawn her own conclusion—the wrong conclusion—about why I never agreed to hang out with her. Maybe this whole time I was worried about the shopping and the expensive clothes, she's been under the impression that I simply don't like her very much. Which is wild. *Everyone* likes Chanel Cao; even the Year Thirteens who always march around the school as if they own the place sometimes invite her to go out clubbing with them.

Then again, now that I really think about it, it's hard to say if that's because of her or all those nightclubs her dad owns.

"Hey," I say. "About that. It's not that I didn't want to, you know. I really did—*do*. I just... Shopping isn't really my thing."

She lifts her head, her cheeks still damp with tears. Scans my face for a beat. "Are you being serious?"

I nod.

"Why didn't you just say so earlier?"

"I don't know. I just didn't think..." I trail off. *I didn't think it mattered*, I finish in my head. *I didn't think anyone would care.* But the very thought of saying those words aloud, of allowing myself to be vulnerable like that, makes me nauseated. Still, I force myself to add, "Now's not too late though, right? If you ever want to talk, or spend more time together... I'm here for you—" I gesture to my bed on the other side of the room. "Literally."

Somehow, my vague, fumbled explanation and bad joke seems good enough for Chanel, because she smiles. A real smile, this time, despite her puffy eyes and chapped lips.

Then she picks up her phone again and enters the Beijing Ghost home page.

"What are you doing?" I ask, cautious.

"What else?" she says with a small sniff, wiping the wet specks of mascara from her face. "Leaving you a good review."

6

I wake to the loud buzzing of bees.

No, not bees, I realize as I force my eyes open. It's my phone vibrating against my bedside table, the screen lighting up again and again in rapid succession as more notifications come flooding in. I fumble to pick it up, my stomach already knotting with anxiety.

The last time I received this many alerts at once was when I forgot to call Mama three days in a row during exam season, and she thought I'd been kidnapped or hospitalized or something. I'd felt so guilty afterward that I promised to message her at least once a day, just to let her know I was safe. And even with everything going on—even on a night like last night—I've honored that promise.

But if it's not Mama frantically checking that I'm still alive…

My confusion lifts, then returns with double the intensity when I spot the little Beijing Ghost icon beside what must be over fifty new notifications. Did someone manage to hack the app?

Wide awake now, I untangle the cheap, thin sheets from my legs and jump down from bed, yanking my phone free from its charger. Then I scroll through the messages, and a silent laugh of disbelief rises to my lips.

I'd thought Chanel was only joking about the review last night, but it turns out she really went ahead with it. Not only that, but it must've been pretty convincing—convincing enough to cause a 770 percent spike in user activity overnight.

My pulse quickens as I read over the new requests. There's an odd fluttering sensation in the pit of my stomach, caught somewhere between nerves and excitement and impatience, like that feeling I sometimes get right before heading into an exam.

I filter through the smaller requests, the ones that wouldn't make me much money and probably aren't worth my time, and a few troll messages asking about weird sex stuff. Then I come to the most recent work order, and pause.

The message is surprisingly detailed and long enough to be an essay, and even comes with its own nondisclosure agreement attached, but that's not what makes an alarm bell go off in my head. It's the request itself; the user wants me to remove a series of nudes from Jake Nguyen's phone before he can send them out.

Everything I overheard from Rainie's conversation—or supposed audition—in the bathroom comes rushing back to me. It all seems like too much of a coincidence. Besides, almost everyone knows Rainie and Jake have been on and off since last year, and their most recent split was ugly. Apparently Rainie burned 100,000 RMB worth of the gift bags Jake gave her in a fit of rage, and Jake responded by hitting every bar and club in Thailand over the summer break.

But the nudes—that's definitely a new development. It wouldn't be the biggest scandal to hit our school, of course, not since Stephanie Kong's potential Olympics career was cut short by a leaked sex tape, but it's no small matter either.

After some deliberation, I type in the private chat:

This counts as child pornography, you know that right? Why don't you go to the school, or the police?

My suspicions are confirmed when the user replies, almost immediately:

it's complicated. i can't risk anyone finding out abt this...would do more harm than good, tbh.

but you'll help me, right??

I haven't had a chance to form a response yet when new messages pour in:

please?

this is rly urgent.

like he told me he'd send the pics to his friends when/if he felt like it i tried to talk to him but he's blocked me on all social media alr. even facebook.

i don't know what else to do...

I can practically feel Rainie's panic radiating through the other side of the screen, and with each new message I read, I can also feel my own anger simmering. Rising. First there was Chanel's cheating father, and now this. If nothing else, these couple of days have served as a great reminder of why I'm glad to be single.

More messages pop up:

sorry, i didn't mean to spam u...i get u must be busy & there's probably lots of ppl messaging u rn...

i'd be happy to pay u early if that speeds things up

would 50,000 RMB be enough?

I'll admit—it does feel wrong to capitalize on her desperation like this, to charge money for the kind of help I should be offering for free, even if 50,000 RMB might mean nothing to her and her family.

But I would also be lying if I said my heart didn't skip a beat at the number.

50,000 RMB. That's more than what Mama makes in a whole year.

I glance at the time on my phone. It's still half past five in the morning, giving me enough time to sign the NDA, revise for my Chinese tingxie quiz, and—ideally—come up with a game plan before first period.

I shoot back:

Ok. I'll try my best.

Then I yank my uniform over my head, grab my school bag, and slide out the door, keeping my steps as light as possible so as to not wake Chanel up. After everything she went through last night, it's the least I can do.

Henry and I are the first people to enter the English classroom.

Well, technically, that's a lie—our teacher, Mr. Chen, is already seated behind his desk. He's busy shuffling around piles of marked papers when I walk in, a Styrofoam coffee cup dangling from his mouth, his oil-black, shoulder-length hair combed back in a low ponytail. Out of all the teachers at Airington, Mr. Chen is probably the most talked about, and by far the most respected; he's written for the *New York Times*, had lunch with the Obamas, published a poetry collection on the Asian diaspora experience which was later nominated for a Nobel Prize, and got his law degree from Harvard before he'd even turned twenty, then gave up a six-figure job at a prestigious New York law firm on a whim to teach all around the globe.

He is, in short, everything I want to be.

"Ah. Alice." Mr. Chen smiles widely when he sees me. He smiles a lot, Mr. Chen, despite the fact that there's very little to smile about at eight o'clock on a Thursday morning.

Then again, if *I* were a successful, award-winning Harvard law grad-slash-poet, I'd probably be grinning like an idiot even at my own funeral.

"Morning, Mr. Chen," I say, smiling back and forcing as much enthusiasm into my voice as I can. This is a strategic move, on my part. When it comes time for the teachers to help us write letters of recommendation, I want to be remembered as someone "upbeat" and "positive," with "excellent people skills"—never mind if that's the complete opposite of my actual personality.

Of course, now that I might be leaving, all my efforts could be for nothing...

No. I crush the thought before it can fully form. I have Beijing Ghost now. A source of income. People who want to pay me *50,000 RMB* for a single job.

Everything can still work out the way I want it to.

"...consider that English program?" Mr. Chen is saying, a meaningful look in his eyes.

It takes me a second to figure out what he's talking about. He'd recommended this prestigious two-month writing course to me and only me at the end of last year, and I'd let myself get excited for exactly five seconds before erasing the whole thing from my mind. The program cost about as much as my parents' flat, and even if I *were* rich and had the time to spare, I'd probably invest in a coding boot camp like the one Henry went to in Year Nine. Something with a high ROI.

But obviously I can't tell *Mr. Chen* that.

"Oh, yes. I'm still thinking about it," I lie. My smile is starting to feel even stiffer than usual.

To my relief, Mr. Chen doesn't push the matter. "Well,

no rush. And in the meantime… I have something for you." He holds up a paper with my tiny writing scribbled all over it. It's last week's English test: an essay and two long-answer questions on symbolism in *Macbeth*. "Good job."

My heart stutters a beat, the way it always does when I'm about to receive academic feedback of any kind. I grab the paper and quickly fold it in two so that Henry, who's walking toward us, can't see my score.

"And you too, King Henry," Mr. Chen says with a wink, handing him his test over my shoulder. I don't remember who came up with the ridiculous nickname first, but all the humanities teachers seem to get a real kick out of using it. I've always found it a bit too on the nose. After all, everyone knows Henry is the equivalent of royalty at our school.

I have a nickname, too, though only my classmates sometimes call me by it: Study Machine. I don't mind, to be honest—it highlights my main strength and suggests at control. Purpose. Ruthless efficiency.

All good things.

As Henry thanks the teacher and strikes up a conversation about some extra readings he did last night, I step off to the side and sneak a glance at my score.

99%.

Relief floods through me. If this were any other subject, I'd already be beating myself up for that deducted 1%, but as a rule, Mr. Chen never gives out full marks.

Still, I can't celebrate just yet…

I turn to Henry when he's finished talking. "What did you get?" I want to know.

He raises his eyebrows. He looks more well rested than he

did the last time I saw him; his skin smooth as glass, dark hair falling in neat waves over his forehead, not a single wrinkle to be seen on his uniform. I wonder, briefly, if he ever gets tired of being so perfect all the time. "What did *you* get?"

"You tell me first."

This earns me an eye roll, but after a pause, he says, "Ninety-eight percent."

"Ah." I can't help it—my face breaks into a wide smile.

Henry rolls his eyes again, and heads to his seat. He unpacks his bag slowly, methodically: a shiny MacBook Air, a clear Muji pencil case, and a thick binder with colorful annotated tabs running down the sides. He arranges them all in straight lines and ninety-degree angles, like he's about to take one of those esthetic Studygram photos. Then, without lifting his head, he says, "Let me guess, you got ninety-nine percent, then?"

I say nothing, just smile some more.

Henry glances up at me. "You realize it's rather sad that your sole source of joy comes from beating me by one percent in an English unit test?"

The smile slides off my face. I scowl at him. "Don't flatter yourself. It's not my *sole* source of joy."

"Right." He sounds unconvinced.

"*It's not.*"

"I wasn't disagreeing with you."

"I—ugh. Whatever." Despite the fact that there are literally a million other things I'd rather do—including walking barefoot over Lego bricks—I take the seat beside him. "There's something kind of important I need to discuss with you…"

Henry's expression doesn't change when I sit down, but

I can still sense his surprise. It's an unspoken yet universally acknowledged rule that the seat you take at the very start of the year is the seat you stick with.

Which is why, when my usual desk mate and Airington's top art student, Vanessa Liu, comes through the door a few seconds later, she freezes in her tracks. This might sound like an exaggeration, but it isn't; she goes *completely still* from head to toe, even as more students trickle in behind her. Then she marches over to me with the sort of betrayed, wounded look one would usually reserve for when they catch their boyfriend cheating on them with their best friend, or something worse.

"You're sitting *here*?" she demands, her thin voice stretching into a whine. When I don't respond, just give her a small, apologetic smile, she pouts and continues, "You're leaving me at our table with *Lucy Goh*?"

"What's wrong with Lucy?" I say, even though part of me suspects I already know the answer.

Lucy Goh is one of the rarities at our school; thoroughly lower middle-class, with white-collar parents working at small local companies. She's kind to everyone around her—she once baked the whole class personalized cookies for our end-of-year party, and she's always the first to run over when someone falls in PE class—but she's not an art prodigy, like Vanessa, or a musician, like Rainie, or particularly good at any of her subjects. And that's the problem. Here at Airington, there are many different tickets to respect—talent, beauty, wealth, charm, family connections...

But kindness is not one of them.

"Like, yeah, she's nice and everything," Vanessa is saying, fluffing her bangs with one charcoal-smeared hand, "but when it comes to group work..." She pauses, then leans forward like she's about to share a juicy secret, though her voice is still loud enough for the whole class to hear her next words: "She's kind of useless, you know what I mean?"

Her sharp cat-like eyes crinkle at the corners, and she's looking at me like she expects me to laugh or agree.

I don't.

I *can't*. Not when my stomach seizes up as if I'm the one she's bitching about.

And maybe it's because I'm aware of Henry sitting close beside me, watching and no doubt judging this whole exchange, or because I'm still riding the power high of my test results, or because there's a chance everything might *not* work out and I'll be gone from Airington in a semester, but I do something wildly out of character: I say exactly what I'm thinking. "Really? Because I'm pretty sure she does more work than you do."

Vanessa's eyes widen.

I shrink back in my seat by instinct, suddenly scared she's going to punch me or something. Too late, I remember that in addition to all her prestigious art awards, Vanessa also won the national kickboxing championships last year.

But all she does is let out a loud high-pitched laugh.

"Damn. Wasn't prepared for a roast, Alice," she says, her light, teasing tone not quite matching the flash of anger in her eyes. Before I can backtrack, however, she marches to our usual table—*her* table now, I guess. I have a feeling I won't be sitting next to her anytime soon.

"Wow," Henry says once Vanessa's out of earshot.

"Wow *what*?" I demand, cheeks flushed, regret already twisting into my gut. There's a reason I never get confrontational with anyone at school, and it's not because I'm a coward—well, not *only* because of that. With all the connections my classmates have, I can't burn a single bridge without burning a hundred more bridges by association. For all I know, I might've just ruined any chance I had of one day working at Baidu or Google.

"Nothing," Henry says, but he's looking at me like he's never really seen me before. "It's just—you can be quite surprising sometimes."

I frown. "What's that supposed to mean?"

"Never mind. Nothing," he repeats. Looks away. "Anyway, what were you saying earlier?"

"Oh, right. About the next task—"

"Wait." He opens up to a blank Pages document on his laptop, and motions for me to write what I want to say on there.

I type: srsly? we're passing notes like we're in year six now?

To which he immediately responds: Yes. Unless you want everyone eavesdropping on us right now to know you're Beijing Ghost.

I look up just in time to catch four people staring our way with great interest. Point taken.

So I spend the rest of class filling Henry in on Rainie's request and planning how to proceed via laptop, occasionally looking up at the board to pretend I'm taking class notes. It's not like I'm missing much anyway; Mr. Chen's handing back papers and going over the answers to our latest test, and most of the "model answers" he uses are either Henry's or mine. *See*, I'm almost tempted to tell Henry as my classmates copy down my answers word for word. *Here's another source of joy.*

But when I play the sentence over in my head, I'm not sure if it makes me sound less pathetic or more.

The period flies by with surprising speed. And when the bell rings, sending everyone else scrambling out of their seats, Henry and I are the last to leave.

In theory, it shouldn't be difficult to delete a few photos from Jake Nguyen's phone, especially when I have the element of surprise on my side.

In theory.

But after observing Jake over the next few days and tailing him whenever I turn invisible, it becomes clear that the guy basically carries his phone *everywhere* with him—in class, on the basketball court, even on his way to the bathroom—as if it's his firstborn child or something. He's like a parody of the tech-obsessed, easily distracted Gen Z kid; always scrolling through memes on Twitter or Moments on WeChat or photos of his friends' new customized Nikes on Instagram. On numerous occasions, I'm tempted to just slap the phone right out of his hands and be done with it.

Soon, five whole days have passed and all I've gotten out of my invisible spying sessions is his iPhone passcode (which is literally just *1234*) and the knowledge that Jake Nguyen secretly watches *Sailor Moon* in his spare time. To be honest, I'm not quite sure what to make of the latter.

What I do know, however, is that the longer this drags on, the greater the chances of Jake sending the photos out. And according to Rainie's increasingly desperate messages, he's threatening to do it very soon.

Then, early on Wednesday morning, as I'm getting ready for school, Henry calls me.

My hands freeze over my skirt zipper. I don't know what's weirder—the fact that he's *calling* me, as if we're still in the early 2000s, or the fact that it's *him*.

"Hello?" I say, tentative, lifting the phone to my ear with my free hand. Part of me is convinced his number has been stolen.

Then his voice comes through the line, crisp and smooth as ever. "Alice. You busy?"

"No—well, I mean, I'm just getting dressed," I say without thinking.

"Oh." There's an awkward pause. "Right."

I quickly yank my zipper all the way up and sit down on the edge of my bed, my cheeks heating. "Wait, never mind. Forget I said that." Across the room from me, Chanel is snoring softly. I press the phone closer to my ear. "So, um. What's up? Why are you calling?"

"It's about the latest task."

For some reason, the first feeling that pools into my stomach is…disappointment. But *of course* it's about the latest task. Why else would he be calling? "Go on."

"Given how slow business has been, I've taken it upon myself to observe Jake's movements around Mencius Hall these past few days—truly one of the lowest points in my life so far, I might add—and it seems there might be a small window of opportunity for you to delete those photos of his…"

I swallow my surprise. Out of courtesy, I've been keeping Henry updated on my progress—or, well, the lack thereof—ever since our first English class together, but I never expected him to go out of his way and gather information on his own.

Part of me is grateful, obviously. Another part of me hates the fact that he's spotted an opportunity before I did. It makes it feel like he's winning, which is ridiculous.

This isn't meant to be a competition.

Still, I can't help the hot stab of irritation in my chest—nor the strange chill that follows it, like a winter draft blowing over me, except all the windows are closed...

Oh.

Henry continues talking, completely oblivious to what's happening. What's about to happen. "See, the only time Jake leaves his phone in his dorm is when he's showering. So I was thinking, if I could wait in the halls near his room and pretend to accidentally spill something on him—something you'd have to wash off, like orange juice—you'd have around eight or nine minutes to—"

"That sounds great," I cut in, suppressing a shiver as I push myself off the bed. My hands feel like ice. No, *everything* feels wrong, somehow, the walls of the dorm room swelling up around me like an open sore, and my heart speeding up with it. Just because I've experienced this shit before doesn't make it any less terrifying. Any less unnatural. "You think you'd be able to do that in like, ten minutes? I'm heading over."

"Er...right now?"

The cold has spread all the way down to my toes. I need to move. And quickly.

"Yeah," I manage.

"Right, well, there's a slight issue I was about to get to—you know Jake's roommate, Peter? He's still in the dorm, and from the sounds of it..." He pauses. A door creaks, and somewhere in the background, I swear I hear *beatboxing*, of all things. "…he's currently busy recording a new mixtape. Or perhaps it's another one of his political rants. If I'm honest, it can be quite hard to tell the difference—"

"What do we do then?" I cut in, urgency leaking into my every word. "I mean—*crap*, I forgot about the roommate situation—"

"I can probably help with that," someone says from behind me.

I almost drop my phone.

When I whirl around, Chanel is standing there in her silk pajamas, still a little bleary-eyed from sleep but smiling.

"Chanel, I…" I say, too stunned to form a complete sentence.

"This is for your Beijing Ghost thing, right?" she clarifies. "Sorry, I couldn't help overhearing just now."

Henry's voice cuts through the phone line. "Wait. *Chanel?*"

"Yes, hi, Henry," Chanel says into the phone, her grin widening. "How do you feel about us working together again?"

"Since when did you two work together?" I demand, the same time Henry says, a trace of incredulity in his tone, "You told her about Beijing Ghost?"

"Yeah, yeah, Henry and I've known each other since we were kids," Chanel explains quickly, like it's not really worth mentioning. "SYS collaborated with my father"—for a second, the corners of her lips turn down—"on a few promotional campaigns for his night clubs."

"Oh." I shouldn't be surprised. Sometimes it feels like all the Airington students and their families belong to a single intricate, complex web of power, one I can see but can never enter. Not without getting trapped inside it like some pesky fly.

"And Alice told me about your app last week," Chanel goes on, speaking to Henry now. "But it's kind of a long story, and we're apparently very short on time." She turns back to me. "So. Can I help out or not? God knows I need the distraction."

I'm aware that this kind of decision should warrant careful evaluation, a comprehensive risk assessment and *at least* two long lists detailing all the pros and cons of getting a third person involved. But I'm also acutely aware of the cold spreading fast over my body.

"Okay," I say. "You're in."

7

"This feels so *weird*," Chanel mutters for at least the tenth time as we creep down Mencius Hall. She keeps glancing back in my direction, as if checking to see if I'm still there. "I mean, I really can't *see* you. Like, at all."

"Well, what did you expect?" I whisper. My eyes scan the mostly empty corridor. It's early enough in the morning that most students haven't woken up yet—I guess they don't share my need to be productive before 6:00 a.m.—and the ones who have are already off to breakfast. The good news is there won't be too many witnesses around in case things go wrong.

The bad news is Chanel and Henry will look a lot more suspicious standing around here.

"To be honest, part of me thought... I don't even know what I thought," Chanel continues under her breath. "But things like this don't just happen to—"

"*Shh*," I hiss. A boy I've seen around campus a few times

walks past us, but not before he shoots Chanel an odd look. He must think she's talking to herself.

"Sorry," Chanel tells me once he's gone, barely moving her lips this time.

"It's fine." I try and fail to slow my rapidly pounding heart; my nerves have been going into overdrive ever since we left our dorm. "Let's just get this over with."

To my immense relief, Henry is already standing in position outside Jake's dorm just as we agreed earlier, a full cup of coffee in one hand and a history textbook in the other. As Chanel and I slow to a stop behind one of the many large decorative pot plants lining the corridor, Henry knocks on Jake's door, then takes a few steps backward.

A long moment passes. Nothing happens.

The knots in my stomach tighten. What if Jake's already left his room? Or what if he sensed something was wrong, that Henry's been acting weird and spying on him from afar? No. That couldn't be possible. Right?

But then the door swings open, the low, rhythmic thump of a bass emptying into the corridor, and Jake shuffles out in plastic slippers. He's wearing only a loose white tank and boxers, his spiky black hair sticking up everywhere. He stifles a yawn. Blinks around in confusion.

"Who was that just now?" he grumbles.

This is Henry's cue.

Henry walks forward, textbook held up in front of him as if distracted, as if he hasn't been waiting outside this whole time, and bumps straight into Jake. Almost in slow motion, the coffee cup tumbles out of Henry's hand, and the dark liquid splashes everywhere.

"What the *fuck*." Jake stumbles backward, hands flying to his soaked shirt.

"So sorry. I didn't see you," Henry says at once, making a good show of looking guilty. A few drops of coffee splattered onto him too, and as I watch, he slowly wipes his cheek clean with a faint grimace. "I could get you a new shirt if—"

Jake shakes his head, though he still looks pretty pissed. "Nah, whatever, man. I just need to go wash this shit off."

With that, he disappears back into his room, snaps something that sounds like, "Peter, my man, could you please stop rapping for *one goddamn second*?" and reemerges with a towel draped over his shoulder and an expression that screams murder.

As he storms off to the bathroom, Chanel makes her move.

When I'd asked Chanel on our way here how, exactly, she planned to get Peter out of his room, she'd simply winked and replied in a matter-of-fact tone, "My feminine charms, of course."

I'd thought she was joking.

But as I follow her into Jake and Peter's room, she makes a straight beeline for him, hips swaying to the beat of the bass, and calls, her voice almost a coo, "*Peter!* I've been looking for you."

The bass stops. Peter jerks his head up from what looks like a miniature recording studio in his corner of the room, complete with a keyboard and microphone and everything. "Uh…Chanel?" He blinks at her. Puts a self-conscious hand over his Star Wars pajamas, as if he can somehow block them from view.

"Sorry, I'm not interrupting anything, am I?" Chanel asks,

her eyes wide. She steps closer to Peter, until there are only a few inches of space left between them. "I just really needed to find you."

Peter lets out a nervous laugh. "Okay... Uh, why though?"

"Oh my god. Why do you think?" Chanel says with a coy smile, like they're sharing an inside joke. She swats his shoulder, but leaves her hand there, her fingers curling slightly over the fabric.

"You...want to borrow something?" Peter attempts, his eyes darting back and forth between Chanel's hand and her face.

And even though he's barely said anything of substance, Chanel breaks into giggles as if he's just told the funniest joke in the world. "*No*, you idiot," she says affectionately. "My dad's thinking of hiring some new DJs for his nightclub, and he wants me to help him pick. But then it just hit me that like, we have a freaking *expert* right in our year level."

"Oh," Peter says. Then Chanel's words seem to actually register; his face flushes. "*Oh*. I mean—I wouldn't call myself an expert, but—"

"Come on, you don't have to be modest with me." Chanel leans in closer, long lashes lowered, and I don't know whether to laugh or cringe or applaud her commitment. "You're talented as hell, and you know it. Everyone knows it."

Peter just turns redder.

Suddenly, Chanel pulls away. Places a hand on her hip and studies him. "So you'll do it with me?"

"Do...what?"

She arches a delicate brow. "Come up with a list of good

DJs, of course. I've already got a few names on my laptop, if you want to come check it out now."

For a brief moment, Peter hesitates, like he suspects this might all be a prank. But it turns out Chanel's *feminine charms* are pretty persuasive, because he rises from his chair, still trying to conceal his pajamas from view, and says, "Uh, sure. I guess. Let me just—let me get changed first."

"Great! I'll wait outside."

Chanel beams at him and struts out the door, and I quickly avert my gaze as Peter starts tugging off his shirt. I listen to the squeak of the wardrobe door, the soft clatter of plastic hangers as he searches for something to wear, to his muttered curse— *"Aish!"*—when he bangs his leg against the corner of his bed.

Then he's gone, and I'm left standing all alone in his room.

I've never really been inside a boy's dorm room before— apart from Henry's, of course—and the more I stare around, the more I realize Henry's taste in interior decoration must be an exception.

There are three giant computer monitors and headphones set up over the desk, rainbow lights flashing from the gaps between the keys. Protein bar wrappers littered everywhere. Two posters of some NBA star and that popular Chinese idol so many guys seem to love—Dilraba Dilmurat—plastered over the gray walls. Socks and underwear strewn across the floor in crumpled balls.

When I inhale, I catch a strong whiff of peanut butter, and something that might be cologne.

Wrinkling my nose, I search through the mess for Jake's phone. I spot it only minutes later, half tucked beneath his pillow. A small sigh of relief escapes my lips. For some reason, I'd thought this part would be a lot harder.

But then I enter the numbers *1234*, and the phone buzzes. The words *wrong passcode* flash over the screen.

I frown. Try again.

Wrong passcode.

My mouth runs dry. I'd watched Jake type in those exact numbers just this Monday, which means he must've changed his passcode sometime yesterday. A few more wrong attempts and I'll be locked out of his phone for good.

But his new passcode could be *anything*.

I try to ignore the slow creep of despair. I can't mess this up. I can't. There's no saying whether I'll ever have the chance to access Jake's phone again, or if it'd even matter two or three days from now, when Jake's already sent those cursed photos out.

Besides, Henry and Chanel have already done their part. Now they're counting on me to do mine, and more than anything else—more, even, than the idea of failure—I hate letting people down.

Okay, think, I urge myself. *What numbers might be relevant to him?*

I pull out my own phone, wait for what feels like an eternity for my VPN to connect, and do a quick search through Jake's Facebook. Then I enter the date of his birthday.

Wrong passcode.

Shit. I chew on the inside of my cheek so hard I taste blood. Desperate, I Google a list of the most common iPhone passcodes, and try the second option after *1234: 0000.*

Still nothing—and only one attempt left.

No, it's fine. It's fine. I force my breathing to steady. *Don't you dare panic. Just—just imagine you're Jake Nguyen. You're a straight-C student who spends his weekends clubbing and says "lol" out loud and doesn't drink anything besides protein shakes and alcohol. You think you're super hot because you've got an undercut and use a shit ton of hair wax. You're the kind of asshole who would keep the nudes of your ex-girlfriend and threaten her with them. You...*

I scan the room for more information, and suppress a groan. *You apparently also have an opened box of extralarge condoms sitting right on your nightstand.*

Now, if you were to change your passcode, what would it be?

An idea comes to mind. A ridiculous, absolutely laughable idea.

I almost hope for Jake's sake I'm wrong as I type in the numbers *6969*, but the phone doesn't buzz this time.

And just like that, I'm in.

I shake my head, a laugh and a sigh jostling in my throat. Rainie really should've broken up with him sooner.

I'd feared it would take too long for me to find the actual photos, that Jake might've created some secret file for them or hidden them using a cryptic code he alone could decipher, but when I click into his photo album, my eyes immediately find a folder named with only the peach butt emoji.

Classy.

Rainie's nudes show up at once, along with photos of two other girls I've never seen before. I delete them all, then make sure to clear them out from the "Recently Deleted" folder too.

I'm about to put the phone away when I hear footsteps. Then, Jake's voice, slightly muffled through the door—

"You're still here?"

I realize he must be talking to Henry. That Henry's been outside this whole time…doing what? Standing guard? Waiting for me?

Or does he not trust me to get the job done on my own?

"Of course," Henry says steadily. "I wanted to see if you were okay."

"If I'm okay?" Jake echoes, a note of suspicion creeping into his voice. "Dude. It was *coffee*, not poison or some shit."

When Henry doesn't reply to that, Jake huffs out a sigh. "Okay, man, I didn't want it to come to this but… You've been hanging around here a lot, you know? Like, I know your room's nearby and all, but I mean *right here*, specifically, and way more than normal. So…either you're trying to steal something from my dorm or you're like, secretly in love with me."

I expect Henry to freeze up, maybe deny it or make some bad excuse and leave as soon as possible, but he replies with perfect calm, "Yes."

There's a significant pause.

"Y-yes?" Jake stammers, clearly as taken aback as I am. "Um…to what, exactly?"

"Yes to the latter, of course."

It takes every ounce of willpower in my body not to snort out loud. I wait for Jake to call him out on his bullshit right away, but I've clearly underestimated Jake's confidence in his own charms, because a second later he stammers out:

"O-oh, well… I mean, don't get me wrong, my man, you're great and all. Really. And the whole being gay thing, that's—like, I'm totally cool with it. You know, love is love is love and all that…" He clears his throat. "But I just—I don't really feel the same way about you."

"Ah."

"Yeah... But, like, no hard feelings, right? We good?"

"Certainly." Henry pauses. "And I do apologize if I've made you uncomfortable by hanging around here so often. In fact, I'll be leaving *right this minute...*"

I know this is my cue to get the hell out of here, but something makes me pause. Scroll through Jake's photo album again. I'm not even sure what I'm looking for until I come across a video taken of Jake a few months back.

Blood pounds in my ears. Adrenaline and fear and something like excitement shoot through my veins in a dizzying rush.

Could I? *Should* I?

And I guess it all comes down to this: I don't know whether it'd be morally right to take matters into my own hands, but I do know that Jake is an asshole. I also know that Rainie's been worrying herself sick for what must be months now, and that this kind of situation isn't uncommon at all, yet somehow it's always the girls who get blamed for it, who are slut shamed and silenced and forced to shoulder the consequences. And I know that Rainie and I aren't friends, that we've barely even spoken to each other apart from our one awkward conversation in the bathroom, but I still can't help feeling angry on her behalf.

I still can't resist the urge to teach Jake a lesson.

My fingers fly over the keyboard, almost as if acting on their own accord. For once, I'm grateful rather than embarrassed to have sent my teachers so many homework questions and follow-ups in the past; I've got every single one of their emails memorized.

By the time Jake pushes open the door, grumbling something about coffee and having too many people fall in love with him, I've done what I need to. I glide past him, swift and silent as a battleship in the night, finally ready to return home after winning an unlikely war.

We're in English class when Mr. Chen opens up the email. I made sure he would. The email subject says nothing but "Class 12C, Jake Nguyen: Urgent—please show in class." Everyone can see it, too; Mr. Chen loves showing us video analyses of our texts on YouTube, so his laptop is always connected to the projector.

Across the room, Jake's face goes blank with confusion at the sight of his own name on the screen.

I suppress a smile, feeling almost giddy with anticipation. *Finally*, I want to sing. Only an hour has passed since I fled from Jake's dorm room and finished packing for school, but it seems like an entire lifetime ago, with every moment in between spent waiting for the scheduled email to come through.

"Now what's this?" Mr. Chen muses out loud, his eyebrows raised.

Jake blinks. "I didn't…"

But the rest of his sentence is drowned out when Mr. Chen clicks onto the attached video. Immediately, a BLACKPINK song blasts through the speakers at full volume, so loud that half the class jump in their seats.

Then the Jake in the video comes into view on the screen. His gelled hair is shorter than it is now, his skin still burnt a dark gold from the summer break, and he's clearly intoxicated, his cheeks so red they practically glow. His eyes are half-shut as he sings along to the song, flailing his arms about and stamping his feet in an uneven rhythm as if trying to do the choreography as well. Judging from the family portraits and giant porcelain vases in the background, it looks like he's at someone's house, but the place has been redecorated to resemble a nightclub. Flashing colored lights dot Jake's low V-neck top and sweat-coated forehead, and more teenagers hoot and clap and cackle like wild witches in the background.

Someone in the video screams over the music, their words slurring together so they're just barely comprehensible, "Who d'you reckon's the hottest girl in the year level?"

Jake yells back some name I can't quite catch, and shoves his flushed face into the camera. Then, raising his voice, he adds, "She's so—she's *so-oo* fucking hot." His lips stretch into a sloppy smile. "Like, dude. Have you seen her ass? She could sit on my face and I'd—"

Mr. Chen quickly shuts his laptop, but the damage is already done.

"Jake," Mr. Chen says after a long pause. He stands up, the screech of his chair cutting through the silence—and even then, I don't think I've ever heard the class this quiet before. "A word outside, please?"

Jake's face looks almost as red as it did in the video. Stuffing his hands in his pockets, his head bowed at an angle, he shuffles after the teacher into the corridor.

The door has barely closed behind them when the class erupts into chaos. Loud whispers and notes of laughter swirl around the room, friends leaning far over their desks and jumping out of their seats with wide eyes to discuss what they just saw:

"Oh my *god*."

"I can't believe…"

"What the hell was he thinking? Did someone hack his phone?"

"The secondhand embarrassment is real. Like, I'm literally cringing so hard right now—"

"Did you *see* Mr. Chen's face? He looked like he was ready to resign—"

"I always knew Jake Nguyen was a fuckboy. You can just tell by the hair—"

"No wonder Rainie dumped his sorry ass. Seriously."

"*Ugh*, I can't believe I used to have a crush on him in Year Seven. Someone kill me now…"

As my classmates continue talking over each other, Henry peers at me silently from the seat next to mine, and I read the question in his dark eyes: *Was this your doing?*

I say nothing, just shrug and pretend to focus on my *Macbeth* notes, underlining the words *revenge* and *desire* and *guilt*.

But I know, somehow, that he can read the answer in my eyes too.

"I heard Jake Nguyen has detention every day for the rest of the month," Henry tells me on our way to class the next day, "for deliberately distributing inappropriate content and"—he makes air quotations with his fingers—"behaving in a way that doesn't represent Airington's school values."

"Good," I say, unable to help feeling a sharp surge of triumph. Hopefully the punishment will teach Jake to be a little more careful about his actions—and if not, then at least the other girls at our school might think twice before dating him.

As we round a corner in the crowded hall, I turn to Henry. "Oh yeah. Speaking of Jake—I probably should've said this earlier but…" I pause, the words I've prepared since yesterday burning in my throat. Why is it so hard to be nice to him? What is it about the words *thank you* that makes me feel so disgustingly vulnerable?

"But?"

Just say it, I command myself. Looking away and resisting the overwhelming urge to cringe, I tell him, "I just wanted to thank you for that little performance you pulled the other day. Guess you're a pretty decent actor or whatever."

Great. Even when I'm trying to be nice, it sounds like I'm mocking him.

But Henry's lips tug up at the corners as if I've just paid him the biggest compliment in the world, and says, "Well, of course I'm a great actor. It's one of my many strengths."

"Is humility one of them, too?" I say dryly.

"Naturally."

I roll my eyes so far back in my head I almost see stars. But as we exit the building and walk past a group of tiny Year Sevens who stare after us as if we've just stepped out of a magazine cover—one of them saying in an awed, breathless kind of voice, *"Damn, I didn't know Henry Li and Alice Sun were friends"*—my faint annoyance is pushed aside by pleasure. It's nice being noticed. Really nice.

"You know," I muse out loud, "if it weren't for the fact that we hated each other's guts, we'd probably make an impressive power duo."

I expect Henry to raise his eyebrows at me as usual or make a cutting remark, but his footsteps suddenly slow beside me.

"Wait. We hate each other?"

He says this as if it's actually news to him. As if we haven't spent the past four years exchanging little snide remarks and glares across opposite ends of every room. As if I didn't drag myself to last semester's optional chemistry revision sessions with a thirty-nine-degree fever just so he wouldn't beat me on the final exam.

I whirl around to face him, squinting into the sunlight, and for the briefest moment I catch something almost like hurt flicker across his features—

No. I must be imagining it. There are few things in this world that have the power to hurt Henry Li—things like a sudden drop in SYS's stocks, or his name coming last on the Forbes 30 Under 30 list.

Certainly not me.

"What did you *think* this was?" I demand, motioning to the space between us.

"Well, I'm not entirely sure." He stares at me a beat. Slides his hands into his back pockets. "A fun competition?"

"Fun," I repeat in disbelief.

But then again, *of course* he sees our four-year rivalry as a fun competition. For someone like Henry, who will always have his father's business, his family's wealth as a safety net, everything is just a game. There are no true consequences. No real threats. He could fail a thousand times in life and still sleep easy, knowing there will be food waiting for him at home, medical insurance for his parents, more than enough money in the bank.

Henry and I might share similar goals and grades, but at the end of the day, we will never be the same.

"Do you seriously hate me?" Henry says, a strange, unreadable expression on his face. And maybe it's just the angle from where I'm standing, but his eyes look suddenly lighter in the sun, more gold than their usual coffee black. Softer, somehow. "Well?"

I cross my arms over my chest, weighing out my response.

Yes, is the obvious answer. *I do hate you. I hate everything about you. I hate you so much that whenever I'm around you, I can barely think straight. I can barely even breathe.*

But when I open my mouth, none of that comes out. What I say instead is, "Don't you... Don't you hate me too?"

Immediately, I regret it. What a ridiculous question to ask. He's obviously going to laugh at me and say *yes*, the way that I should have just now, and whatever sense of comradery we've built over these past couple of weeks will collapse, which will then affect our efficiency in completing Beijing Ghost tasks. But it's not just that. For some reason, the thought of him telling me he hates me—right here, out loud, in plain English—feels like a punch to the chest. Which is *even more ridiculous*, because—

"No."

I blink. "Huh?"

"No, Alice." The faintest movement in his throat. I still have no idea what his expression means, why his voice sounds so strained. "I don't hate you."

"Oh." My mind goes blank. "Well, that is... That's something. For sure."

That was not a legitimate sentence, Alice, I scold myself.

"A very good thing to know," I try again. "Glad we spoke of it."

Neither was that.

Thankfully, I'm saved from what's shaping up to be one of the most awkward exchanges of my life by a new phone notification. I turn around and open up my Beijing Ghost messages. To my surprise, it's from Rainie again:

i don't know how u did it but...thank u.

you're my hero.

I stare and stare at the message, read it three times over, and feel my heart lighten. Because this—this gives me a spark of hope. To know that I can live in a world where Rainie Lam would voluntarily call me a hero, even if she doesn't know Beijing Ghost is me. To think that even the richest and most influential of Airington's elite would thank me, *need* me, however briefly, and that my powers—my strange, inexplicable, unreliable powers—have actually been able to help somebody...

I hold the phone to my chest and inhale deeply. Never before has the summer air tasted so sweet.

I move through the requests quickly after that.

As I do, my life changes shape, fits into the mold of a new, bizarre routine: I spend my mornings going through new Beijing Ghost messages and choosing the most feasible tasks, lunchtimes developing a plan of action with Henry and sometimes Chanel, and classes only half paying attention to the teacher as I wait anxiously to turn invisible.

And on the days when I *do* turn invisible, and make that same mad dash out the classroom door, I always make sure to come back with a stolen, forged note from the nurse's office, explaining a fictional chronic health condition I have that unfortunately makes me puke my guts out from time to time. It's enough to get the teachers off my back about my sudden, spontaneous absences—that, and the fact that I haven't fallen behind on any schoolwork.

Because when all my Beijing Ghost tasks are finally done for the day, I trudge back to my dorm, exhausted, and study, cramming lecture notes and slides and graphs into my brain until five or six in the morning, just in time to watch the watery sunrise through the window. Only then do I allow myself to be human and nap for about an hour. Two hours, max.

By the time November rolls around, I can't remember the last time I woke up without bloodshot eyes and a terrible, pounding headache, like someone has taken to squeezing my skull for fun. The trick to working through the pain, I've discovered, is by forcing myself to conjure up worst-case scenarios, to picture a future where I don't make enough money and have to leave Airington. It's like the reverse of guided meditation:

You're walking into the classroom of your new local school. You're sweating visibly, a heavy bag of books you haven't read gripped to your chest. All the students and teachers stare at you. The bell rings, and you take your first pop quiz: twenty-five pages of tiny Chinese characters you can hardly understand, much less answer. You feel sick. The test results are posted for everyone to see the next day. You push through the crowd, heart pounding, and find your name at the very bottom of the list...

Compared to that, staying up all night feels almost like a luxury.

But despite everything, I'd be lying if I said some part of me didn't enjoy the constant stream of tasks, the new notifications lighting up my phone. No, maybe *enjoy* is the wrong word. It's not about happiness; it's about power. It's the thrill of being needed, of knowing things other people don't.

In the space of two months, I've learned more about my classmates than I have in my five years here—like how Yiwen, daughter of a billionaire, has been stealing entire plates of cupcakes from the café before school every day; how Sujin, another billionaire's daughter, runs her own karaoke bar and spends all her money funding global warming research; how Stephen from Year Ten and Julian from Year Eleven have actually been making out behind the koi ponds when everyone thinks they're busy taking photos for the yearbook; or how Andrew She and Peter Oh's parents are running for the same global director position at Longfeng Oil, and in fear of their latest campaign ideas being stolen, have advised their children to stay far away from each other.

Secrets, I'm realizing, are their own kind of currency.

But even better is earning *real* currency, the satisfaction of seeing the numbers in my new bank account rise:

70,000 RMB.

100,000 RMB.

120,000 RMB.

More money than I've ever seen in my life. But even then, I know I could still earn more. I have to earn more. I still need another 130,000 RMB if I want to stay at Airington until I graduate.

Ten more tasks, I tell myself, and I'll be able to make that much. Twenty more tasks and I'll be able to pay for not just Airington, but an entire year of college.

It's addicting. Intoxicating.

Who cares if I'm so busy I can barely breathe?

"Maybe you really are a ghost," Chanel jokes to me one morning, when she sees me in the exact same position at my desk as the night before: head bent over my Chinese textbook, shoulders almost hunched to my ears. "The kind of invincible ghost that like, doesn't need to eat or sleep or pee or anything, just runs on willpower alone. Seriously though," she adds, peering at the tiny annotations and Post-it notes covering my textbook page. "How the hell are you keeping up with all your subjects?"

I don't reply to her at the time, but the answer comes almost two weeks later, like some sort of sick joke.

And the answer is: *I'm not.*

When I hurry into history class on Friday, I freeze.

All the desks and chairs have been rearranged. Spaced out around the classroom in neat, single files, instead of the usual messy clusters that are meant to inspire "group work."

Most of my classmates are already sitting down, zipped-up bags tucked away under their seats, faces set in solemn lines as they methodically place their pens out in front of them. Someone sighs. Someone else mimes slitting their throat.

There's a palpable tension in the air.

"What's going on?" I say aloud.

Mr. Murphy, who's handing out a thick stack of papers, pauses and gives me a small, odd smile, like he thinks I've just made a bad joke. "The thing you've been waiting for all week, of course."

I blink at him. "The thing…?"

The smile slips from his face. He frowns. "Surely you haven't forgotten about today's test, Alice? I mentioned it in class a week ago."

At the word *test*, panic seizes my chest with such intensity I almost stagger back a step. A stone forms in my throat.

"*What?* But I didn't—I—" I swallow, hard. People are starting to stare at me now, Henry amongst them. My face heats.

My fingers fumble for the planner in my bag, for proof that there is no test, there can't be, that this must be a mistake. I have a perfect, color coded system, developed over my five years of school here. Foolproof. Red for important things and events, blue for homework and assignments, green for extra-curricular activities.

But when I flip open the pages to last week's entry, there's red *everywhere*. Almost all of it is Beijing Ghost stuff, but squeezed right in between the lines *find out if Vanessa Liu's been bitching about Chung-Cha behind her back (waste of time tbh— Vanessa bitches about everyone)* and *find Daniel Saito's locker combination*, written so small I have to squint to decipher my own handwriting, are the words: *Chinese Rev history test: next Friday.*

The stone sinks to my stomach.

No.

"Alice?" Mr. Murphy looks at me, making very little effort to hide his surprise. His disappointment. I want to cry. "The test is starting soon..."

"Y-yes, of course," I choke out, forcing myself down into the closest empty seat. I duck my head and search for my pencil case with shaking fingers, but not before I catch the expressions on my classmates' faces: variations of pity, amusement, smugness, and most pronounced of all, *shock.*

A few summers back, some director at LinkedIn was invited to our school to talk about the importance of "personal branding" in the twenty-first century, and I've devoted the past five years to developing and strengthening mine. I'm *Alice Sun*, the type A, straight-A student, the sole scholarship recipient, the perfectly programmed Study Machine, the girl who will help you get full marks on your group project. I do everything that is expected of me and more. I never under-perform in important unit tests, much less forget when they're taking place—until today, that is.

My gut roils.

So much for personal branding.

Just when I think I couldn't possibly feel any worse, Mr. Murphy comes around to my desk, hands me a blank test paper and says, very quietly, "Even if you forgot about the test, Alice, you're a smart girl. I'm sure you'll still do well."

He's wrong.

Because even though I'm smart, I'm not *that* smart. Not the kind of prodigy-level smart you would expect to find at Harvard, the kind that would allow me to skip all my classes and still rank first in every test, that would make everything come easily. I don't say this in a self-pitying way, either; I've long acknowledged and accepted my limitations, and done my best to compensate for them with sheer willpower and hard work.

But without hard work, I doubt I can scrape so much as a B+ on this test. Even if I could, I've never been able to perform well when I'm panicked. And I'm panicking hard right now. My heart feels like it's about to explode in my chest, my fingers shaking so badly I almost drop my pen.

No. Focus, I urge myself. I look up at the ticking clock. Seven minutes have passed already, and my test paper is still blank.

Normally, by this point, I'd have written enough to cover two entire pages.

I attempt to answer the first question ("To what extent did the Warlord Era prove a turning point in the development of the revolution in China?"), but all that's running through my head is *fuck fuck I'm so fucked* in a maddening, highly unhelpful loop.

When I check the time again, another minute has already passed. And all around me, people are writing, answering each question perfectly, scoring every mark, and I—

I can't do this.

Oh god, I can't do this.

I take a deep, shuddering breath that fails to fill my lungs. Another. It sounds like I'm hyperventilating. Fuck. Am I hyperventilating?

"Alice?" Mr. Murphy crouches down beside me. He's whispering, but it's pointless. Almost comical. With the whole room silent, everyone can hear him. "You look a little ill. Do you need to go to the nurse's office again...?"

More eyes turn to me. Pin me down in place.

All while I'm trying to remember how to breathe like a normal person.

I don't trust myself to speak—I'm not sure I'm even allowed to, under test conditions—so I just shake my head. Force myself to write a few sentences, slowly, shakily, over the printed lines.

It's complete bullshit, of course. I have no dates memorized, no key events that I can recall. I'd turned invisible for half our class on the Warlord Era, and must've missed the important points.

After a few seconds of excruciating silence, in which Mr. Murphy seems to confirm that I'm not going to faint or throw up at his feet, he stands up and returns to the front of the room.

Meanwhile, the clock ticks on like a bomb.

★ ★ ★

"Please put your pens down."

I glance up from my test paper, where my writing crawls over the page like spiders, nearly illegible in my frenzy. Evie Wu and I are the only people left in the class; the test was short enough that everyone else turned it in early. Henry left the classroom before half an hour had even passed, his stride confident, his face calm.

Evie's face, on the other hand, must look a lot like mine: bright red and shiny with sweat, as if she's just finished running a marathon. When she hands her test to Mr. Murphy, I notice that the entire back page is empty, save for one or two hastily scribbled words.

"Thank you very much, Evie," Mr. Murphy says. Then pauses. "I hope you didn't find this test too difficult. I'd hate to have to give your mother another call..."

Again, he's whispering, and again, it serves absolutely no purpose when I'm sitting less than five feet away, close enough to catch every word.

Evie's eyes dart to me, clearly mortified, and I feel a swell of sympathy. Evie is the only student at Airington who's had to repeat a year, but it's not her fault. Even though she has a Canadian passport, she was never actually taught any English growing up. Once, I caught a glance of Evie's history textbook, and saw Chinese translations and annotations written in the margins for almost every word, little question marks drawn over certain phrases, entire blocks of text highlighted to mark out parts she didn't understand. I could almost feel the frustration pulsing out of those carefully marked lines.

The worst part is that Evie's a *genius*, and not just in math and physics, but languages too. She's in the most advanced Chinese class, and Wei Laoshi always gushes over her poems and essays and suggests not-so-delicately how he'd be happy if we could write with a tiny fraction of her skill, even goes so far as to compare her to Lu Xun—one of the most famous writers in modern China.

So, really, it's only the English that's the issue.

Maybe that's why Mr. Murphy is whispering so loudly now. Why he's speaking at half his usual speed, enunciating every syllable. He used to speak to me like that, too, when I first came to Airington, despite my insistence that English was my first language. Only after I aced five tests in a row did he seem to believe me.

Evie mumbles something back that I can't quite hear, rises from her chair and quickly gathers up her things.

Once she's left, Mr. Murphy turns to me.

"Can I have your test, Alice?"

I realize I've been gripping the paper to my chest like a lifeline, my knuckles almost white. I drop it. The pages flutter out like wings.

"Y-yes. Of course," I say, pushing it across the desk. I know the wise thing to do would be to just leave it at that, scrape up the little dignity and self-esteem I have and walk away, but instead I blurt out: "I'm sorry. I'm so, *so* sorry—it's really bad, I know it is, but I swear I don't usually—I'd *never*—"

"Don't stress about it," Mr. Murphy interrupts, with a little chuckle. "Besides, I've taught you for almost five years now, Alice. Your definition of 'bad' is rather different from that of your peers."

But rather than reassure me, the kindness in his voice—so

sincere, and so unearned—only makes something inside me fissure. To my absolute horror, a pressure begins to build in my chest, climb up to my throat. My eyes blur.

Mr. Murphy looks alarmed. "Hey—"

It's as if someone's turned on a switch.

When I start crying, I can't seem to stop. Short, violent breaths rock my entire body, a disgusting amount of tears and snot flowing down my face even as I try, desperate, to wipe them away. I cry so hard my chest physically *hurts*. My head feels light. I sound unhinged, like an inconsolable child, a tortured animal.

I sound like I'm about to die.

"Hey," Mr. Murphy says again, lifting a hand as if to pat my shoulder, then thinks better of it. Fear creases his bushy brows, and I wonder, dimly, if he's scared I'll sue him for psychological damage or something. Two years ago, a student in Year Thirteen did just that when he failed a major chemistry test. His parents were both lawyers; the student won in the end. "It's okay."

I manage to suppress my sobs long enough to stammer out: "S-s-sorry, I wasn't"—I hiccup—"I wasn't even planning to cry...or I'd"—I hiccup again—"I'd have l-let you know in advance..."

Mr. Murphy's lips twitch slightly at that, like he thinks I'm trying to be funny. I'm not. I've just never cried at school before, not even when I broke my arm during an intense dodge-ball game in PE, or that time when Leonardo Cruz called the prom dress Mama made for me *cheap-looking* in front of everyone. I never wanted any of my classmates or teachers to see me like that—distressed. Discomposed. Weak.

But I guess today is a day of firsts for everything.

"You know, in all my years of teaching," Mr. Murphy says, when my sobs have quietened a little, "I can't remember the last time anyone reacted so…violently to a bad test experience." He's not smiling anymore. "Is there something going on, Alice? Issues at home? Relationship drama? Friendship troubles?" His expression grows more uncomfortable with every question. "Because you know, there are…*resources* at Airington for that."

When I look at him, confused, he clarifies, "We have excellent school counselors who'd be more than happy to—"

"N—" The unspoken word lodges in my throat. I shake my head instead, violently, to get my point across. I don't need someone to recommend meditation apps and listen to all my problems. I need to get my shit together. Pull my grades back up. Make more money.

I need to get out of here.

"I—I think I'm fine now," I say on a shaky breath. "And I have to get to class. So I'll—" My voice threatens to crack again, and I gesture to the door.

Mr. Murphy purses his lips. Studies me for a beat.

"All right," he says finally, with an awkward smile. "Well… just. Just take it easy, okay?"

"Okay," I lie, already turning around to go.

Mr. Murphy means well, I know, but his words play over in my head like a taunt. What he doesn't understand—what most people here don't understand—is that I don't have the luxury of taking it easy.

If I'm not swimming as hard as I can, feet thrashing at the waves, I'm drowning.

★ ★ ★

Henry is waiting for me outside the classroom.

This, in itself, is not unusual. I can't pinpoint when exactly it started, but Henry and I have gotten into the habit of walking to our classes together. It's a simple matter of practicality. Necessity. We share the same classes for almost every subject, after all—a fact I used to deeply resent—and we always put those extra four or five minutes to good use, strategizing and fine-tuning and outlining the next Beijing Ghost tasks under our breaths as we walk. Sometimes I'll even pull out my planner, or a clipboard.

But something's different today.

I notice it in the way Henry looks at me when I walk out, the way he flinches as I draw near. It's such an odd sight I'm almost convinced I've imagined it. I don't think I've ever seen Henry Li flinch before.

Yet even odder is the expression that settles over his features like a shadow:

Concern.

Concern for *me*, because… I was hyperventilating during our test just now? Because it's clear I've been crying? Because he overheard my conversation with Mr. Murphy?

There are so many possibilities. All of them make me want to run far away in the opposite direction.

But before I can turn around, he steps toward me.

"You forgot about the test," he says. Not *are you okay?* or *how did it go?* or *do you want to talk about it?* Maybe he isn't that concerned after all.

I run my tongue over the sharp edges of my teeth. "Yeah, I know. And I swear, if you're going to rub it in—"

"No," he says. Quickly. "That was not my intention."

And even though it's the last thing I'd expect myself to do, especially when I still feel like my world is about to end, I can't help it: I snort.

He frowns. "Is something funny?"

"No, no, nothing," I say, shaking my head—then stop abruptly, when the motion makes pain spike through my skull. At this rate, I can't even tell if the migraine is from sleep deprivation or from bawling my eyes out.

Henry says nothing, but his frown deepens.

"Okay, fine, you really want to know? It's just—you just sound so *posh* all the time, oh my god." I straighten my posture to match his and mimic him with an exaggerated British accent. *"That was not my intention."*

"I do *not* sound like that," he says, affronted.

"You're right. You sound even posher. Why are you still here, anyway?" I ask, looking over his shoulder to scan the emptying hall. "Shouldn't we be getting to class or—"

"English is canceled for the day. Mr. Chen was invited to deliver a lecture at Peking University." He hesitates. "The email came a few minutes ago, when you were..."

When I was having a mental breakdown.

"Ah," I say, suddenly far too aware of the damp patches on my blazer from when I used it to wipe my face. The puffiness in my lips and cheeks. The dry, uncomfortable ache in my eyes. I turn my head, feigning interest in the glass display to my left. Glossy certificates catch the artificial light of the hall, the golden, italicized text gleaming like magic: *Rachel Kim: First Place in IGCSE History. Patricia Chao: Best All-Rounder Award. Isabella Lee: Perfect Score in IB Geography.*

All legends. All names that continue to adorn our halls, remind us of their greatness, long after the students themselves have graduated.

The sound of crinkling paper pulls me from my thoughts. I glance back to see Henry reaching for something in his bag. "Do you want—"

"Oh, it's fine, I can just get some from the bathroom," I say, assuming he's about to offer me a tissue.

But then he's holding up one of those White Rabbit milk candies I saw him eating in his dorm, the creamy white wrapper smooth, almost the same shade as his outstretched palm. Confusion flickers over his features when he hears the end of my sentence.

We both pause. Catch our mistake.

God, why does everything have to be so awkward when I'm around him?

"Uh. Never mind." I hold out my hand. "Guess I could do with some candy." As he passes it over, his fingers brush against mine. Just once, briefly, there and then gone. So warm and light they could be confused for the flutter of birds' wings.

It feels nice. *Too* nice.

I retract my hand as if I've been burnt.

"Thanks," I mumble, busying myself with peeling the wrapper and bringing the candy to my lips. Immediately, the thin, papery outer layer melts on my tongue, and the rich, mildly sweet taste fills my mouth.

It tastes like my childhood. Like the long, luxurious summers in Beijing before I left for America, before my nainai passed away. Mama rarely let me have sweets, saying it was a waste of money and bad for my teeth, but every morning during the holidays, Nainai would hobble out to the local grocery store and buy little packets of White Rabbit milk candy, hiding them inside her handkerchief. Whenever Mama wasn't looking, she would sneak one to me with a wink.

But my memories of her more or less end there.

She only called on my birthdays after we moved across the sea, said she didn't want to inconvenience us as we tried to settle in, that she knew we were busy. Then, sometime after I turned nine, she died alone at home. A stroke. Preventable, if only she had the money to pay for a proper checkup and medical treatment, to ask for help when she wasn't feeling well.

Baba and Mama didn't even tell me she was gone until the day of the Qingming Festival.

My throat burns at the thought, at the injustice of it all, but this time, at least, I manage to force the tears back before they can form.

I don't know why I'm so emotional today.

I sneak a quick glance at Henry to see if he's noticed, but he seems suddenly fascinated by the awards display too.

"It's been ages since I last had one of these," I say, more to break the awkward silence than anything. "They were my favorite childhood treat."

He turns to face me, his expression impassive. "Mine too." He says this almost reluctantly, with great caution, like he's disclosing some kind of confidential business information. "My mother used to give me one whenever I had a bad day at school."

"Really?" Surprise leaks into my voice, and not just because I can't imagine him ever having a bad day at school.

Not even a subpar day. "I thought you'd have grown up eating all that fancy, expensive stuff."

His eyebrows arch. "Fancy, expensive stuff?"

"You know what I mean," I say, annoyed. I recall the lavish feast spread out before Chanel's father and the young woman, the delicacies arranged in their clay bowls and tiny crystal plates. The food of emperors, of kings. "Like bird's nest soup or sea cucumber or something." As soon as the words come out of my mouth, I realize how ignorant I must sound. How painfully obvious it must be to Henry that we were raised in two separate worlds, that I've only witnessed but never experienced the casual luxuries he must take for granted in his life.

I wonder if he feels sorry for me, and anticipatory anger rattles in my stomach like a snake as I imagine him tiptoeing around the subject, trying to play down the obvious discrepancies between our childhoods: *They weren't* that *expensive*, or *We only had those once a week.*

But in reality, he just shrugs one shoulder and says, "I never really liked sea cucumber, actually. They used to creep me out when I was a kid."

"Yeah, well, they do look a bit like slugs," I mutter, and he laughs.

I stare at him, taken aback by how his entire demeanour seems to change: the sharp, regal lines of his face softening, white teeth flashing, his shoulders slipping forward from their usual stiff posture. He's so closed off all the time that I didn't even think Henry was *capable* of laughing. For a moment I wonder what we might look like from an outsider's perspective: just two teenagers joking around and sharing candy and chatting together after class. Friends, maybe. The thought startles me.

Then Henry catches me staring, registers the visible shock on my face, and sobers up at once, like he's been caught doing something he shouldn't. The curve of his ears turn pink slightly.

"Well, anyway." He slides his hands into his blazer pockets. "I should probably go. Study. Our midterms are soon."

"Oh. Okay."

But he makes no immediate move to leave. "Will you be all right? After..." He trails off, once again leaving it to me to fill out the rest of his sentence. "Either way, it's not as if a bad grade would bring your average down so much, right? So long as you do well in the midterms, you could still be ranked second in the class."

I bristle, the remnants of that brief, tender moment we shared earlier vanishing like smoke. *We're not friends*, I remind myself. We're competitors. Enemies. Only one of us can win in the end.

"I don't *want* to be ranked second." I surge forward until I'm standing right in front of him, hating that I have to crane my neck just so we're at eye level. "If I'm not first, I'm nothing."

He merely looks amused. "Is there really such a substantial difference? I doubt your report card—"

"It's not just about how my report card looks," I interrupt. "It's about losing my winning streak with the Academic Award next year. It's about what people will think of me."

"It doesn't matter what people think—"

"Bullshit," I say hotly. "That's bullshit, and you know it.

Perception is *everything*. Money would just be colored paper if we didn't all think it was important."

"Cotton, actually."

"What?"

"Contrary to popular belief, money is mostly made out of cotton," he says, as if this is life-changing information. "Just thought you'd want to know. But do go on."

The idea of murdering him flits through my mind.

"My point is," I say through gritted teeth, "when a large enough number of people collectively care enough about something—no matter how superficial or arbitrary or inherently worthless it is—it starts to carry value. It's like when people say it doesn't matter where you get your education, but watch how fast they change their attitude, their tone when you tell them you go to Airington." I suck in a breath, curl my trembling hands into fists. "Even just now. Mr. Murphy was already looking at me differently because I—" I swallow. "Because I fucked up on that one test."

Surprise flashes across Henry's face. I don't think anyone at Airington has ever heard me swear out loud before. It's kind of liberating, really. Cathartic. It even makes me feel a little better—

Until one of the classroom doors down the hall swings open, and Julie Walsh steps out.

Her narrowed eyes instantly land on me, and she comes marching straight over, thin heels clacking, sleek blond hair bobbing with every step, her lips pressed into a tight line. As she draws closer, the strong, sickly sweet scent of her perfume hits my nose. I try not to choke.

"Such foul language," she hisses, shaking her head. "Honestly, after everything we've taught you here at Airington, is *this* really how you wish to conduct yourself?"

A mixture of embarrassment and annoyance snake under my skin. I'm tempted to tell her about the number of Chinese and Korean swear words students have used right in front of her face in the past week alone, but because I still have somewhat of a will to live—and because I'd never throw the other kids under the bus like that—I decide against it.

"Sorry, Ju—" I catch myself just in time. "Dr. Walsh."

"Hmph. You certainly should be." She sniffs. "Don't let me catch you swearing again, Vanessa Liu, or there *will* be consequences."

I look up at her, stunned. Like Mr. Murphy, she's been teaching me for *five years*—surely she must know who I am? My name, at least? Besides, Vanessa and I don't even look remotely alike; her face is sharp and long whereas mine is wide, her nose petite while mine is round, and her skin is at least five shades paler thanks to all her Korean skincare products. Anyone with eyes should be able to tell the difference between us.

I wait for Julie to realize her mistake, to correct herself.

She doesn't.

Just stares me down with those cold blue eyes like she expects me to apologize again.

But instead, all I say is, "It's Alice."

Her face goes blank with confusion. "What?"

"I said, my name is Alice. Not Vanessa."

"Huh. Is it now?" she finally says, unconvinced, looking for a second as if she actually believes I might've mixed up my own name. When I nod, she gives me a tight-lipped smile that isn't much friendlier than a glare. "Well, pardon me, *Alice*. But my earlier point still stands, of course."

"Of course," I echo.

Satisfied, she spins around on her noisy heels and leaves. As soon as she's out of earshot, Henry mutters, "Charming, isn't she?"

On this, at least, we can agree.

Next week, an ominous poster appears over the Year Twelve lockers, with the following words printed out in large, block letters:

15 DAYS LEFT

It takes everyone a while to figure out what the poster's referring to.

"Maybe it means fifteen days left until my will to live runs out," Vanessa Liu suggests as she crams a mountain of textbooks into her overhead locker, slamming it shut with a roundhouse kick that makes the walls tremble.

Someone behind me snorts. "Sounds about right."

"Oh! Oh—I know!" Rainie says, her eyes widening, lips parting in a perfect O. Ever since the whole Jake incident, she's been a lot more enthusiastic about everything. "Maybe it's for the Experiencing China trip!"

"But, like, that usually happens in late November," Chanel points out.

"Then what about—"

"Isn't it obvious?" I say, louder than I mean to. Almost the entire year level goes quiet and turns to me, expectant. My face burns at the sudden attention. Still, I hold my ground and explain, "There are only fifteen days left until our first midterm exam. The teachers probably put the countdown up to remind us."

Immediately, faces fall. Smiles fade.

"Well, trust the Study Machine to know," someone says. It isn't the first time I've heard this sort of joke, but there's an awkward pause after the familiar words, and I know the people from my history class are still remembering what happened in our last test.

My face grows hotter with embarrassment. Shame.

Who knows how long it'll take me to build up my reputation again?

As people finish cramming books and laptops into lockers and start heading outside for lunch, most of their conversations turning to revision and how far behind they are and how they haven't even really read *Macbeth* yet for English, just the SparkNotes summaries, my phone buzzes.

Another Beijing Ghost notification.

I've already lost track of the number of requests I've gotten, but my heart still stutters in my chest as I find a dark, empty corner in the hall, turn with my back against the wall so that no one can see my screen, and read over the latest message:

Okay to call?

Surprise flutters inside me. This is definitely new.

It can be done, though. Henry's been fine-tuning the app for weeks in his spare time, claiming it's a great way to put the skills he's learned at SYS into practice, and now there's a call option that distorts the voices on both ends to ensure anonymity. I've only used it once before, in a brief test run with Henry and Chanel. Though I wasn't a *huge* fan of how the feature made me sound like Darth Vader, everything else worked pretty well.

So I message back: Sure.

And almost instantly, the call comes in. I do a quick scan of the locker area before I pick up. The place is empty. Good.

"Hello?" I say, wedging the phone between my ear and shoulder.

"Wei?" The voice distortion feature works so well I can't even tell if it's a boy or girl speaking. But I can hear the slight hitch in their breathing, the nervousness in their tone when, in slow, carefully enunciated Mandarin, the person asks, "Do you speak Chinese?"

"Oh—um, yeah, no problem," I say, switching to Mandarin too.

A sigh of relief. "Great. And...whatever I say next—you won't tell...?"

"Of course not," I reassure them. It's what most users ask when they first start using the app: *You promise this will stay private? You promise no one else will ever know?* "Everything is strictly confidential."

"Okay." Another sigh, but this one is heavier, drawn out, as if they're bracing themselves for what's next. "Okay. What I want is..."

They trail off. Go silent for so long I pull the phone away from me, check to see if I've accidentally disconnected the call. I haven't.

Then, in one desperate, breathless rush, they say: "I want answers."

"Answers?" I repeat. "I'm afraid you'll need to be more specific than that."

"Exam answers. For the history midterm. Ideally a week before the actual exams so I can, you know…so I'd have time to memorize them."

"Right." I fight to keep my voice neutral, free of recognition, even though I can already guess who the user is. Can picture her vividly, with her head bowed over last week's history test, frustration flushing her cheeks. "I see."

One of the first things that shows up on Beijing Ghost's homepage is that we have a no-judgment policy. Because, let's be honest, if you're hiring some anonymous person to carry out the kind of tasks you can't get caught doing yourself, the last thing you want is moral scrutiny.

But this feels different from the previous jobs. If Beijing Ghost has a strict no-judgment policy, then Airington International Boarding School has a *very* strict no-cheating policy. A few years ago, a kid in Year Ten was found cheating on his final exams by copying his textbook out on toilet paper in the bathroom beside the exam hall. He was kicked out within weeks, and to everyone's indignation, we haven't been allowed toilet breaks in exams ever since.

But the worst part isn't even that. The kid's parents were so ashamed that they flew all the way over here from their company in Belgium, and bowed repeatedly to the principal, his teachers, and classmates, apologizing with every bend of their spine.

I'd die before I put my own parents through such a thing.

Maybe Evie Wu can sense my hesitation through the phone, because she hurries to explain, "I know it's bad. Trust me, I don't want to be doing this either. But... I don't have any other choice. If I fail this exam again, my mother..." A shaky breath. "No. No, I *have* to pass. I must. And I can't without the answers..." Her voice drops to a whisper. "I can't do it on my own."

"Okay," I say.

"Okay, you'll do it?"

The hope in her voice—the strain of guilt in it, too—kills me a little. Makes my resolve weaken. But still, I correct, "Okay, I'll *think* about it."

My neck is starting to ache from holding the phone in place for so long—or maybe it's from stress. I shift position, press the phone to my other ear, just in time to hear her say, "...can pay you more. Double your usual rates, if that's the issue."

It's not the *issue*, but I make a note of it anyway. "Look, I want to help you, I do. I just need to consider—well, everything. The logistics. The risk." The fact that if I procure the answers, *I'll* be cheating too. "How about I get back to you in a day or two?"

"Yeah." She sounds disappointed. "Yeah, okay. Wait— before you go. Can I ask you something? You don't have to answer if you don't want to," she adds quickly.

I pause, alert. "What is it?"

"So I heard about this app from a friend. A few people, actually. I've also read all the reviews. And a lot of them are curious—me, included... How do you manage to do it? All of these tasks without being seen? You're not—" She breaks off for a second, laughs, the sound quiet and nervous. It makes me feel intimidating in a way I never imagined I could be before. "You're not actually a ghost, are you?"

She says this like a joke, but there's a trace of genuine fear in her voice. I wonder, briefly, what would scare her more: me being a ghost, or me being a human girl with the inexplicable power to turn invisible. I wonder what would sound more believable.

"Why not?" I say in the end. "Anything is possible."

The rest of the school day passes in a blur.

I drift from class to class, bump into people in the halls, do the in-class history exercises robotically, hand them in early. And even though I haven't made my mind up yet about the request, I linger once everyone's gone.

Mr. Murphy starts at the sight of me. Blinks rapidly, like he's scared I might start crying again. "Alice." He folds his hands over his desk. "What's up?"

"I was just wondering," I begin, going over the lines I've rehearsed for the past hour in my head, "since I know I didn't do that well for the last test—"

"I haven't marked those papers yet."

"Still," I insist. "I have a pretty good idea of how I did, and—I'm not going to lie, I feel...horrible about it, which is why it's more important than ever that I perform well in our midterms." I make myself look right at him, and pray that my expression is earnest, rather than terrified. "And so I—I was wondering if you've already written the midterms...? And if you've got a revision guide ready, like you did last year? I mean, I obviously don't want to rush you or anything but—"

"Oh no, don't worry," Mr. Murphy says with a light chuckle, evidently relieved I'm back in control of my emotions again. "I just finished writing your midterms yesterday—would've gotten it done earlier, honestly, if it weren't for my kids." He makes a *you-know-the-struggle* kind of face, and I nod just to speed things along, even though I obviously don't. "The revision guide should be ready soon too. I'll send the class an email once I've got it printed out for next class—how 'bout that?"

"That'd be *perfect*," I say, offering him my best straight-A student smile.

He smiles back, not suspecting a thing. I'm still Alice Sun, after all. Even if I messed up on my last test, there's no way I'd ever dare cheat. "You know what's so great about you, Alice?" Mr. Murphy says as he stuffs today's worksheets into an already overflowing, see-through folder. Even though Airington keeps making grand statements about being a completely "paper-free school," he's one of those teachers who's always preferred physical copies. "You're so driven. So determined. No matter what happens, you just have a plan and you do it—and you do it well too."

Normally, this kind of praise would make me giddy with joy, but my chest only tightens.

"You'll go far with that mindset of yours," Mr. Murphy continues, gazing out into the empty classroom as if he can see some glorious vision of my future shining right there before us. "I'm certain of it."

It's too much. I feel so guilty that I barely manage to stutter out a thanks, just grab my books and go.

★ ★ ★

When I get back to the dorms, Chanel is in a bad mood.

I know this because she's lying on our bedroom floor in her BTS pajamas and feasting on three giant bags of spicy strips at 11:00 p.m., breaking the intermittent fasting thing she's been practicing religiously since the start of the school year.

"Want a latiao?" she asks when she notices me, holding up one of the bags. Her fingers are red with chili oil.

"Um, no thank you." I walk closer, careful not to step on her hair. "Is…everything okay here?"

"Yeah, of course," she says. But she's an even worse liar than I am, and terrible at holding things in. After only a few beats of silence, she throws up her hands like I've got her at gunpoint. "Okay, okay, fine. But you're going to think it's ridiculous."

"I won't," I promise quickly.

"You're going to think *I'm* ridiculous."

I blink at her, confused.

She heaves a loud sigh, props herself up on one elbow, and says, "I failed my chem test."

"Oh."

I don't know why I assumed it'd be something a lot more dramatic, less…normal. Maybe I've come to think of people like Chanel as living on a whole separate plane of existence, elevated from mundane struggles and concerns like getting a bad grade.

"See," she says, groaning and falling back on the floor with a significant *thud*. "You're judging me. I can feel it."

"I'm not," I say, trying to collect my thoughts. "And it's not like… I mean, grades don't matter that much anyway…"

I wince. The words ring awfully false and hypocritical to my own ears. "Sorry. That was so obnoxious."

Chanel snorts. "It was, a little."

"So—okay, I do get why you'd be upset about it. It sucks. But also, if it helps… I genuinely don't consider our academic records to be like, the ultimate indicator of human value or whatever."

She looks up at me. "You really think that?"

I nod.

"Then why do you kill yourself studying all the time?"

"Well, it's different for me…" I immediately cringe again, and hurry to explain, "Not in like a special snowflake sort of way but… I don't know. I guess grades are the only thing I have power over. The only thing I have."

The second I say this aloud, I realize how sad it sounds.

"That's not true," Chanel tells me, and I expect her to sprout some vague, corny line about how I still have so much untapped potential and my whole life ahead of me, but instead she simply says, "You have me. And you have Henry."

I stare at her. *"Henry?"*

"Mm-hmm."

"As in *Henry Li*? The one at our school?"

"The one and only."

"Henry literally wouldn't bat an eye if I dropped dead at his feet," I say, half laughing now. "Or, no, he'd probably tell my corpse to not dirty his shoes."

"You might think that," Chanel says, stuffing three spicy strips into her mouth at once and speaking between chews. "But trust me, he cares a lot more than he lets on." She arches an eyebrow at me. "He cares about *you* a lot more than he lets on."

Heat rises up the back of my neck, followed by a sharp, inexplicable thrill of pleasure. "Don't be ridiculous," I say loudly, more to myself than to Chanel.

"I swear on my favorite LV bag I'm telling the truth," she insists, raising one hand dramatically in the air. Then she pushes herself up into sitting position, her eyes suddenly serious. "I've known that kid and his family for—what? Seven years now? And, yeah, he's always worked like he has a fire lit under his ass. Hell, he used to listen in on his dad's business meetings and draw up all these solutions for SYS when he was a freaking *ten-year-old*. But I've never seen him this... devoted to a project before. Like, ever."

"He's only like that because we're business partners," I point out. "And he gets to make a profit out of it."

"Sure." She rolls her eyes. "Because we all know that's the only thing missing from Henry Li's life—money."

I decide to ignore what she's implying. "You don't have to lack something to want it. And everyone wants money."

"Not *everyone*," Chanel protests. When she sees the look I'm giving her, she adds, "Like monks, for example. My uncle's a monk, you know. Lives in a temple in Xiangshan and eats only lettuce and everything. He doesn't want money at all."

"That's nice. Good for him."

She snorts.

"Really." I move over to sit down beside her. Before she can turn the topic to Henry again, I say, "But back to your chem results..."

"You sound like my mum," she grumbles.

"I'm not going to lecture you, I promise." I raise my hand, too, mimicking the oath she made just now. She shakes her head and laughs. "I was actually just thinking—and this isn't directed at you personally or anything—but...if you had the opportunity, would you ever cheat on the next test? If it was a matter of pass or fail?"

She considers this for a moment. "I don't think so," she says finally. "But only because I'm not that desperate."

"What do you mean?"

"Well, you know how it is." She shrugs. "A lot of the kids here were born when the one-child policy was still around. They literally have their entire family—all their aunts and great-aunts and their grandpa's cow—just *counting on them* to succeed, not to mention how many of them have parents who immigrated just so they could get a foreign passport, a better education, a better life, whatever. And with that kind of pressure weighing down on you all the time... It can push you to do extreme things. It makes failure a nonoption. Unthinkable. You know what I'm saying?"

I do know. I know all too well what she means.

But my next decision still doesn't come easily.

In the dead of night, long after Chanel's fallen asleep, I make lists.

Lots of them; pros and cons, risks and costs.

I map out where and how I'd be able to find the exam answers, the probability of me getting caught in the process, the chances of me getting kicked out, thrown into jail (which *sounds* super melodramatic, I know, but according to a quick Google search, two students were actually sent to jail for cheating a year ago).

I think about why I'm doing this. I think about why I want—no, *need*, always need—the money. More money. I think about how ironic it is, that in order to become the person I'd like to be, I might have to do the last thing others would expect of me. I think about guilt and karma and survival and how being good doesn't ever promise you anything in this world—only power does that.

Power I finally have.

And as the night drags on, I can't help but think of Mama.

I think of the thin, ugly cut slicing through her worn hands, where once there was an open gash, flowing blood, a dark red river running past her fingertips.

I remember the sound of the robber breaking into our store—the only Asian grocery in our tiny rural Californian town, how proud Baba was to be the owner of the very first one, to "share a slice of our culture" with the locals there.

I remember Mama's sharp cry of alarm—then *pain*, the metallic clatter of the knife hitting the floor. The robber's grunts as my father raced to the cash register, tackling him from behind.

The shrill blare of the sirens afterward.

I'd been helping stack the back shelves when it happened, two cartons of salted duck eggs balanced precariously in my hands. And I'd just *stood there*, frozen, my body shutting down in shock. Only once the scene had already unfolded and the police had arrived was I finally jerked back into motion, the cartons falling to my feet, the soft crunch of egg shells all I could hear over my ragged heartbeat.

The police were nice enough about the whole incident, but dismissive, the way parents might console a crying child. *Look, we get you're upset,* one of the older policemen had told me, patting my shoulder a few times. I fought the urge to slap his meaty hand right off. *But there's no evidence this was a hate crime. I mean, this kind of stuff can happen to anyone, you know? Try not to think too much into it.*

And maybe he was right. Maybe it really was just a matter of bad luck, bad timing. Maybe the person standing behind the cash register could've been a tall blond man with a nice smile, whose words came out smooth and unaccented when he called out for help, and the same thing would've happened.

Maybe.

But here's the thing about living in a place full of people who don't look like you—whenever shit like this happens, you can't help but wonder if you've been singled out for a reason.

After the incident, I felt certain Mama would run out of the hospital and book the first plane ride back to China. But I'd forgotten this was a woman who'd grown up in the after-math of the Cultural Revolution, who'd poured ice water over herself every night for a month just to stay awake studying for her gaokao. She was not so easily fazed. In fact, she seemed more determined than ever to remain in America *(What we do wrong, huh? Your Baba and I work hard, pay tax, obey law— then this man stab me and I run like criminal? How come?).*

In the end, it wasn't fear that sent us packing for Beijing, but money. Or, well, the lack of it. Our little grocery store never brought in much cash to begin with, and whatever my parents managed to save up, they spent it all on me—on tuition, piano lessons, swim classes, weekend Chinese school.

Then came the recession, and business seemed to sputter to a stop entirely.

My parents fought it at first, because that's just what they did; they tried, they fought. When things didn't work, they fought harder. They started selling things to stay afloat: Mama's favorite jade bracelet, Baba's only winter coat, a porcelain vase, the dining table. Mama found a job as a janitor at the nearest hospital, the closest thing she could get to her old nursing career in China, and Baba made a few extra coins every day by collecting and recycling used plastic bottles.

But even then, it wasn't enough. Nowhere close.

The breaking point came on Chinese New Year. We celebrated it alone in our dark, rented home, sitting around the plastic tablecloth that now served as the table, passing around a plate of those frozen, store-bought dumplings we'd heated in the microwave.

Mama had taken one bite of the dumpling and gone very still.

"What is it?" Baba asked in Mandarin, peering over at her with concern. "Does it taste that bad?"

She said nothing.

"Because we still have a few cups of instant noodles left," Baba continued. "I could boil the water now—we might even have an egg—"

Then Mama's face crumpled. Her voice cracked. "I—I want *real* dumplings."

"What?"

"I want to go back," Mama whispered, her dark eyes misting over. It terrified me, seeing her like that. She hadn't even shed a tear when she was stabbed. "I want to go *home*."

Understanding passed over Baba's face like a shadow. He reached across the tablecloth and put one hand over hers, covering up the half-healed scar. "I know," he said quietly. "I know."

We flew back to Beijing a few weeks after that, our first and last shot at the American Dream over, the chapter unceremoniously closed. But I never stopped thinking about the sacrifices my parents made, the pleading look on Mama's face when she said it, almost like a child—*I want to go home*—and how the only reason they left home in the first place was because of me.

Even now.

I relive every moment of those final bitter months until my brain threatens to melt in my skull and my eyelids begin to weigh a thousand tons.

And right before I drift off to sleep on my desk, what I think is this:

My parents didn't work this hard for me to only get this far.

10

"You're stress pacing again," Chanel observes from her dressing table.

I'm not just stress pacing—I'm the textbook definition of anxiety right now. My heart is beating so hard I can feel it in my throat, and my mouth tastes like ash. Ever since I messaged Evie Wu on Beijing Ghost this morning, telling her I'd be willing to help her cheat, my nervous system has been on the verge of breaking down. And I hate it, truly. I hate everything about this.

But I need to honor my choices.

"You also look like you're going to throw up," Chanel adds helpfully.

"I won't," I tell her, just as my stomach lurches. I fight back the rising swell of nausea. "I mean—oh god, I hope not."

"Hey," she says. She tears open a new face mask packet, dabbing the excess foam on the pale insides of her wrists. "Not to be super gross, but like, if you *were* to throw up...do you

think your vomit would be invisible as well? Because technically it'd be outside your body, but if it was also *produced* by—"

"Chanel?" I interrupt.

"Hmm?"

"Please stop talking."

She manages to stay quiet for a full minute, pressing the
mask onto her skin, before she says, "Will you at least tell me
what kind of task you're doing today that's so—"

"Nope," I say, and she responds with an exaggerated pout.
"And careful, your mask is going to wrinkle."

She stops pouting at once, settling instead for a stiff poker
face as she hurries to smooth out the edges of her mask again.
If I wasn't trying so hard to keep my lunch down, I might've
laughed.

"Anyway," I say, completing another lap around our tiny
dorm room. My feet refuse to stay still. "I'm not withholding
information this time because I don't trust you. But the less
people know, the less likely things will go horribly wrong—
and the less liable you'll be."

"But *Henry* knows."

I grimace. "Yeah, well. That's because I need him for something. Speaking of which…" I glance up at the clock, and my
heart seizes. 5:50 p.m. It's time.

Oh my god. This is really happening.

When I speak again, my voice comes out as a squeak. "I—I
should go find him now. Get this over with."

I leave everything except my phone in the dorm and rush
outside, barely catching Chanel's quick "good luck!" as the
door swings shut behind me.

Henry and I agreed to meet by the main entrance of the

humanities building at 6:00 p.m. At exactly 5:59 p.m., we both arrive at the same time, and I have to give it to him—Henry might be unbearably pretentious, but at least he's punctual.

He also happens to look especially put together today; his dark blazer freshly ironed, his tie straight, not a single hair out of place. I almost laugh. He looks like he's about to deliver a speech to the school, rather than help me pull off a crime.

"Alice," he says when he sees me, ever so polite.

"Henry." I return his greeting with a mock salute, mimicking his formal tone.

Faint irritation flits over his face. Good. If Henry is in the mood to bicker with me, then at least I'll have something to keep me distracted from my nerves—

"Are you nervous?" he asks.

Or not.

"Why would you think I'm nervous?" I snap, reaching over his shoulder to yank open the door.

"Well, you appear to be shaking."

I follow his gaze, and hastily hide my trembling hands in my pockets, pushing past him into the building. "It's cold," I mutter.

"It's twenty-two degrees right now."

My jaw clenches. "What are you, the weatherman?"

"Really? The weatherman?" His voice is light, amused. "Not your best insult, Alice."

I try to stab him to death with my eyes. Unfortunately, it doesn't work.

I keep walking.

The corridor is almost completely empty, as it should be. No student wants to stay behind after class, especially when our dorms are only a courtyard away, or when they can take a Didi to the Village or Solana. But for the teachers, it's a different story. Most of them bike to school, and like to hang back in the classrooms until after dark, when the streets outside aren't as crowded and the probability of being run over by a car is significantly lower. Mr. Murphy is one of them.

Sure enough, the lights in the history classroom are still on. Through the small window in the door, I can make out his figure hunched over the teacher's desk, stacks of papers laid out before him. It looks like he'll be busy marking them for a while.

Perfect.

Now I just need to turn invisible.

"Sometime soon would be good," Henry murmurs from close behind me, as if reading my mind.

I scowl but don't reply right away, gesturing for him to follow me into one of the narrow adjoining corridors—far enough so that Mr. Murphy can't hear us. The place smells like fresh printer ink and whiteboard markers. It smells like integrity, like academic success.

Another wave of nausea rolls over me.

"I've already *told* you," I say as I resume my pacing. "I can't control when exactly the invisible thing happens. It just *does*."

Henry doesn't move, though his eyes follow me as I walk, back and forth, back and forth. Someone once told me my stress was contagious, that it spilled right out of me. But maybe Henry is immune to it, untouchable, like he is with most things.

"In that case," Henry says, "how can you be certain it'll even happen tonight?"

"I mean, I'm not." I sigh. "But it's happened much more

often in the evenings these past few weeks, and I can make a…a reasonable prediction based on the existing patterns. Like menstrual cycles."

For a brief moment, Henry looks stunned. "I beg your pardon?"

"Menstrual cycles," I repeat, very clearly, glad to see him squirm for once. "You know, like you can keep track of what time of the month it happens and know roughly when to expect it, but sometimes it still manages to catch you off guard. It's like that."

"Ah." He nods, schooling his expression back into one of calm. "Right."

And just like that, my momentary rush of satisfaction leaves, and the anxiety returns with double the intensity. I quicken my steps, wring my hands together. It's a wonder Henry isn't dizzy looking at me.

This is, without a doubt, the worst part of every mission: not the fear of getting caught, or even the guilt gnawing on my conscience, but the *uncertainty*. Never knowing when I'll go invisible or when I'll go back to normal.

Only a couple weeks ago, I'd spent an entire day standing around the school hall, waiting for my powers to kick in so I could finish what should've been a simple Beijing Ghost task. They never did. Henry had been surprisingly understanding about it, even though he'd chosen to wait with me too, but I can still taste the sharp, sour note of failure, still feel the heavy frustration of relying on something completely out of my control.

"Just relax," Henry tells me, after I've paced the length of the corridor at least twenty times. If I were counting my steps, like Chanel does, I'm sure I'd have reached my daily goal by now. "Even if this task doesn't go as we initially planned... What's the worst that could happen?"

I make a little noise of disbelief. "Please, *please* tell me you're joking."

"I assure you I'm quite serious."

"Oh my god," I say. Shake my head. "The worst thing—I mean, there are literally *so many* worst-case scenarios I don't even know where to—"

"Like what?"

"Um." I pretend to think hard for an answer. "Like, *getting expelled*?"

"I highly doubt they would expel us. We're the best students they have," Henry says. States it, just like that, as if it's an indisputable fact.

My heart snags on the *we*, the casual compliment in those words, but I push on.

"No? They could also involve the police, throw us into jail—"

"A few of my dad's friends are lawyers," he says breezily. "Amongst the best in the country. Even if the evidence was stacked up against us, we'd still win the case."

I twist around so fast my shoes squeak against the polished floor. "See, this is why I can't stand people like you," I seethe, jabbing a finger in his direction. "You think that just because you're all smart and wealthy and attractive you can just do whatever the hell you want—"

"Wait." Something shifts in the black depths of his eyes. "You think I'm attractive?"

"Oh, come on, don't act like that's such a huge revelation,"

I snap. "I'm pretty sure even the guys in our year level think so. I mean, really, when we had those diving lessons last year, everyone in the stands was straight-up *gawking* at you as if they'd never seen a shirtless guy before, and later, when you did that photoshoot for the school magazine, and they made you wear that ridiculous suit—I couldn't even—you just..." I trail off, suddenly all too aware of the heat in my cheeks, the anger curled in my chest that no longer feels like anger, but something else.

Something worse.

"Just—whatever." I clear my throat. "Anyway. What was I saying?"

Henry cocks his head to the side, a slow smile spreading across his lips. "You were telling me how much you hate me."

I bite my tongue, quickly avert my gaze. Try to will the strange feeling in my stomach away. Eventually, when I decide it's safe to look at him again without my skin bursting into flames, he says, "Do you feel better now?"

"Huh?"

"You tend to stop being so scared when you're angry," he explains.

Confusion bubbles inside me. "How—how do you know that?"

"I notice," he says simply.

Another statement. Another phrase thrown into the air for me to decipher. But I can't wrap my head around it. What does he mean, *he notices*? And how could he be aware of something about me that I wasn't even aware of myself? It just doesn't make sense. It doesn't make sense, because *no one* notices—

A sudden chill snakes down my spine, crawls along my legs, my wrists. A thousand pinpricks of ice. I go cold all over—painfully, unnaturally cold—and I understand what *this* means, at least.

It means it's time to get to work.

"Henry! What are you still doing here?"

Mr. Murphy looks up from his desk as Henry and I walk in, his eyes sweeping right over me.

"I was hoping you'd still be in, Mr. Murphy," Henry says with one of his rare, grossly persuasive smiles. Bright eyes. Shining teeth. Faint dimples in his cheeks. Even I'm almost tempted to believe what comes out of his mouth next. "Do you have a few minutes to spare? I was hoping to look at some of the primary sources from the Opium Wars—you know, since you said we'll be learning about that next—but the librarian wouldn't let me go near them without your approval…"

It's perfect—the slight reluctance in his voice, like he's afraid to inconvenience the teacher; the eagerness without appearing *over*eager; the sincerity in the way he holds Mr. Murphy's gaze. And, of course, there's the one factor others wouldn't be able to replicate, no matter how great at lying they are: his reputation. He's King Henry, every teacher's favorite student, the one who always talks to them about extra course material, advanced readings, debates new theories with them just for fun.

I never thought I'd see the day where I was *grateful* for Henry being such a teacher's pet, but here we are.

Mr. Murphy sets down the paper in his hands. His tone

is friendly, slightly teasing, when he asks, "Primary sources, hmm? And this couldn't wait until tomorrow?"

Henry ducks his head, making quite the convincing show of looking sheepish. "Well, I was reading about the First Opium War this afternoon and it's all just so interesting—terrible, obviously, but interesting—and when I remembered the library had some of the original texts... I suppose I got carried away." He shoots Mr. Murphy another smile, softer this time, embarrassed, and my heart does a weird little somersault in my chest. "Sorry, you're right. It's not that important—"

"No, no, I didn't mean that," Mr. Murphy says quickly. He stands up, his chair rolling back a few feet and hitting the wall with a dull *thud*. "It's great that you're so passionate about your subjects, Henry. And I'm more than happy to go with you—right now, in fact." As he says this, he tucks his laptop under his arm, and makes a motion for Henry to lead the way.

But Henry hesitates, his eyes falling on the laptop. For the first time, I sense a fissure in his mask of calm. "You don't—you don't have to bring that with you. It'll be really quick."

I swallow the lump of fear in my throat and step closer, studying Mr. Murphy's reaction carefully, searching for any signs of suspicion, of confusion. But he just sighs and shakes his head.

"I know, but I think it's for the best. I've heard a few funny reports lately..."

My stomach lurches.

"What reports?" Henry asks, tensing too.

"Oh, well, nothing to be *overly* concerned about, I'm sure," Mr. Murphy says with a wave of his free hand. "Just stories of things disappearing here and there from lockers, phones and laptops being hacked. Stuff like that." He nods toward the door. "You good to go?"

Henry straightens, but not before his gaze darts in my general direction. "Yes. Yes, of course." He doesn't ask Mr. Murphy about his laptop again, or persuade him to leave it behind, and I don't blame him; if Mr. Murphy's already on guard and vaguely aware of what's been going on, it wouldn't take much for him to suspect something was off.

But once Henry and Mr. Murphy have left the classroom, leaving me alone, invisible, the laptop I need gone, I can't help feeling absolutely idiotic. My heart sinks all the way down, my head pounding. What am I supposed to do now? Follow them to the library, try to steal Mr. Murphy's laptop when he's not looking? Try again another day? But even with Henry's reputation—even if Henry claimed to have found a never-before-seen primary source from the Daoguang Emperor himself—I doubt the teacher would be so trusting if Henry were to come find him two nights in a row.

No, there has to be some other way. Maybe I can access Mr. Murphy's laptop from his phone or my phone, or maybe he has a copy of the exams sent to his email, or maybe—

Maybe he has a physical copy lying around somewhere.

Around *here*.

With a sudden, dizzying surge of hope, I remember the thick folder Mr. Murphy always carries with him, how he likes to print things out, says he finds it hard to read things on a screen.

I rush to his desk. It's a complete mess, highlighters and half-marked papers scattered everywhere, one last bite of jianbing going cold on a dirty plate. But right there, buried beneath it, is the see-through folder I last saw Mr. Murphy with.

Slowly, inch by inch, I pull the folder free as if it's a Jenga block, careful not to move anything else on the teacher's desk. The folder's been crammed full with worksheets, copies of the syllabus, past test rubrics, excerpts from the textbook readings...

There doesn't seem to be any kind of organization system, not even a single colored tab. All I can do is flip page after page as the folder grows unbearably heavy in my clammy hands, my heart racing, terribly conscious of the ticking clock and how many minutes have passed since Mr. Murphy and Henry left.

My senses seem to have sharpened, too, like a rabbit's when it fears it's being hunted; every rustle of movement in the corridors outside startles me, every creak of the door or tap of the branches against the windows makes me freeze. I can smell the leftover food from the staff's office upstairs—seafood, and something sour—and feel the sweat forming on my skin in cool, perfect beads.

And still I force myself to keep rifling through the giant folder, keep searching, scanning the blur of text for the words *Year 12 Midterm* or *History Exam* until—

Finally.

Finally. There it is.

Adrenaline floods my veins as I take out the exam and answer booklet with shaking fingers, holding them up under the fluorescent classroom lights. For a second I'm so stunned by what I'm about to do I almost drop them, but I steady myself. Grab my phone and snap a photo of the first page, then the second, the third.

I'm close to finishing when I hear it—

Voices.

"...difficult to believe the emperor really was so ignorant. If you read between the lines of that letter, it seemed more like one last, desperate attempt to avoid trouble," Henry's saying, his slow footsteps falling behind Mr. Murphy's quick, noisy ones. He's speaking louder than usual—no doubt to warn me they're about to come in.

No. Not yet.

I'm on the very last page now, but my shadow keeps blocking the words—

Then realization hits me like a boulder, almost knocking the breath out of me: *my shadow.* If I have a shadow, then I must've turned visible again, and if I'm visible when Mr. Murphy walks in here... If Mr. Murphy sees me...

Shit.

Panic invades every cell in my body. I twist the paper around in the light and snap a photo, then stuff it back into the folder and shove everything under the dirty plate again in one rapid, frenzied movement. I don't know if it's in the exact same position as before, but there's no time to check.

The doorknob creaks. Turns.

Mr. Murphy opens the door just as I throw myself onto the ground, squeezing into the gap under his desk. The space is tiny; I have to tuck my knees under my chin like a fetus, wrap my arms tight around myself like a vise.

My heart is pounding so hard I think I might die.

"Thanks again for everything, Mr. Murphy," Henry says.

He sounds less than ten feet away. "I know how busy you must be..."

"You're too polite," comes Mr. Murphy's response from nearby. He's walking, drawing closer and closer, and—

Oh god.

His worn, leather shoes suddenly appear in my line of vision, only a few inches from my leg.

I retract further, press up against the hard surface of the desk, fold into myself until I can barely breathe, but still he's too close. He only needs to look down to know I'm here. He only needs to listen carefully to hear my furious heartbeats, my uneven gasps for air.

I'm trapped.

The thought sends a new jolt of hysteria through me. I'm trapped and I can't see any way of getting out. Not undetected. Not without consequences. The inevitable begins to play in my mind like a horror film: Mr. Murphy accidentally dropping a pencil or paper and seeing me crouched here, hiding at his very feet; the shock flashing through his eyes, even more pronounced than when I broke down over my test in class, and the realization that'll follow shortly afterward, that I must be here for a reason. Then he'll look at his desk, notice how the folder is maybe two inches to the right from where he'd left it, how the corner of the exam booklet is bent, and put two and two together, and then—

"Is there something else you need, Henry?" Mr. Murphy asks. He lowers himself into his seat, and I watch in silent horror as the chair rolls forward...

There's no room for me to retreat. The front wheels ram into my right foot, crushing my toes. A white-hot bolt of pain shoots through me, and I have to bite down on my tongue to keep from crying out.

Please let this stop, I pray, not even sure who I'm praying to. *Please, please let him get an urgent call, or have to get up to use the bathroom, or let the fire alarm go off sometime soon…*

But neither the chair nor Mr. Murphy moves.

"Well, actually…" Henry's voice floats over from the other side of the room, and I can tell from the pause that he's trying to stall. He must know I'm still here. We talked about this before, albeit briefly; I would text him once I was safe outside, and if not, he would create a distraction to buy me time. I just hadn't counted on him to remember.

For a second, I allow myself to hope.

Then I hear his footsteps moving in the opposite direction, and my heart falls. Confusion clouds my mind. What the hell is he—

A crash breaks through my thoughts: the unmistakable sound of flesh slamming into cement, like someone's body hitting the floor.

Then a gasp—

"Henry? *Henry!*"

The chair rolls back and in a flash of brown, Mr. Murphy's shoes disappear from view. I hear him run toward where Henry must have fallen and I don't think. I just move. Ignoring the pins and needles in my legs, I scramble out from under the desk, almost banging my head against the corner, and sprint for the back door.

In the dark of the corridor, I sink into the shadows, panting, catching snippets of Henry's conversation with Mr. Murphy as I creep farther away from the classroom.

"…haven't had much to eat. Don't worry, this has happened before…"

"…to the school nurse? They might still be in—"

"No, no, that won't be necessary. Really, it's fine. I didn't mean to startle you…"

The night air is cool when I step out. Sweet with the fragrance of begonias blooming in the school gardens. I close my eyes and inhale, hardly daring to believe what I just managed to get away with. What Henry just did. When he talked about creating a distraction, I never would've imagined he meant *fake fainting.*

It's all so bizarre that a bubble of laughter bursts from my lips, and suddenly my whole body is shaking with hysteria, the much-needed release of tension. I don't know long I stand there, waiting, light-headed and almost giddy with relief, but soon I hear voices. Henry and Mr. Murphy's. Some of their words are muffled by the front door, but I can make out Henry's continued insistence: *"I'm fine, I'm fine. I can go see the nurse myself."*

Mr. Murphy must believe him—or maybe he simply knows better than to challenge Henry's stubbornness—because there's the squeak of shoes, of heavy footsteps moving away, while another set draws closer.

The door creaks open.

"Well, that was a thoroughly humiliating ordeal."

I twist around.

Henry is standing behind me, his expression calm, hands in pockets, the collar of his shirt rumpled. A reddish-yellow bruise has started to bloom over the curve of his left cheekbone, a violation of his otherwise perfect skin.

Without thinking, I grab his face in one hand and tilt it up to the moonlight, inspecting the injury. It looks swollen. Painful.

"Holy crap, Henry," I say, no longer laughing. "You didn't have to go that far—I mean, I'm grateful, obviously—so grateful—but... Does it—does it hurt?"

He doesn't answer me, but his eyes widen slightly. Flicker to the point of contact between us, where my hand is still cupping his cheek.

I let my hand drop and step back, mortified.

"Um, sorry. Really don't know why I just did that..." I shake my head, hard, as if I can somehow shake the awkward moment away too. *What is wrong with me?* "Do you need a bandage though? Or ice? Or one of those cloth things they tie around..." I trail off when I see the corners of his lips twitch with ill-suppressed amusement. "Is this somehow *funny* to you? Because you could've been seriously—"

"I appreciate the concern," he says. "But I'm honestly fine. I promise. I've done this before."

I stare at him. "*What?* Why?"

He hesitates, and I can almost see the gears in his mind working, trying to decide how much information he can afford to disclose. Finally, he says, "It was a long time ago... when I was seven or eight. My father had signed me up for violin lessons and I really, *really* did not want to go..."

It takes me a minute to understand what he's saying, to grasp the sheer absurdity of it. This is truly the last thing I'd expect from Henry Li. "Wait. So you'd fake faint just to get out of violin lessons?"

"I only did it once." He grimaces. "All right, *twice*. But in my defense, it was very effective; the violin teacher was so concerned for my well-being she personally asked my father to keep me home."

I choke out an incredulous laugh. "And you couldn't have just—I don't know, faked a cough or a cold like a normal kid?"

His expression doesn't change, but his eyes harden. "That wouldn't have been enough. So long as I was physically conscious, my father would've insisted that I continue with my studies, push through until I was perfect." He turns his head away from me, the moonlight washing over his stiff profile, lining the slight furrow in his brows, and I realize, with an odd pang, that the conversation is over.

I also realize that for all the glamorous magazine profiles and interviews and SYS-related news I've devoured in my attempts to better understand my competition, I don't know Henry that well at all... Yet now, more than ever, I kind of wish I did.

A few beats of heavy silence pass. Then Henry asks, "Do you have everything you need?" His voice is formal again, perfectly professional. I hate it.

"Oh—yeah." I pat the front of my blazer, where my phone is. "I do."

But as we make our way slowly back to the dorms, the exam answers saved and safe in my pocket, the promise of a sizeable payment awaiting me, I can't shake the feeling that I've left something invaluable behind.

11

As exams loom closer, I keep waiting for Mr. Murphy to find me.

Alice, I imagine him saying at the end of class, his expression unusually stern. Maybe he'll have his folder ready by his side, a secret recording device I failed to notice, all the incriminating evidence he needs. *Would you care to explain this?*

Each time I enter his classroom or pass by him in the halls, I feel violently sick. My palms go all clammy and I have to swallow back the nausea, barely mustering the energy to return his smiles and occasional nods of greeting.

The paranoia is so bad that I start having nightmares about it: strange, disturbing nightmares where Mr. Murphy faints before me and I rush over to help him only to be tackled to the ground, police sirens screeching around me until I wake up with a start; or I'm about to enter the examination hall when I realize I've forgotten to put clothes on, and Jake Nguyen leaps onto the teacher's desk, declaring that being naked is a sign of guilt, all while Henry catches my eye from across the hall and whispers: *Have you no shame?*

Needless to say, my sleep quality hasn't been great.

"I feel like Lady Macbeth," I mutter to Chanel the morning before our first exams. "You know, like after a bunch of people die and she starts hallucinating about all the blood on her hands because it's a super not-subtle manifestation of her guilt—"

"Alice, *Alice*," Chanel interrupts, putting a hand on my shoulder. "First, it's really bold of you to assume I have any idea what you're talking about, because I haven't read *Macbeth* yet—"

"But—but the English exam's *tomorrow*—"

"Exactly," she says. "That gives me a whole twenty-four hours to get the gist of it."

"I think you're severely underestimating the complexity of Shakespeare's work."

She ignores me. "Second of all, I still don't know what your little mission with Henry was since *someone* won't tell me, but I'm sure it's going to be fine. You haven't been caught a single time so far, have you?"

"No," I admit. "But still. I just… I have a bad feeling."

"You always have a bad feeling," she says with a wave of her hand. "Your body like, functions on bad feelings. In fact, I'd be very concerned if you *weren't* high-key stressed about something right now."

"I guess," I say, not entirely convinced.

But then exams come and pass in a blur of late nights and last-minute revision and adrenaline, and nothing out of the ordinary happens. Mr. Murphy thanks us all for our hard work with a round of Kahoot on ancient Chinese history (it gets a little intense; pencils are thrown, angry fingers are pointed, and Henry and I end up tying for the lead) and promises he'll mark our exams within the next week. The teachers start handing us forms and brochures for our upcoming Experiencing China trip to Suzhou, and soon it's all that anyone can talk about. The leaves on the school's wutong trees turn gold, then a withered brown, falling and scattering over the courtyard like shredded notes, and such a pervasive cold creeps in by mid-November that even the Year Thirteen guys stop playing basketball outside during lunchtimes, hogging the limited space in the school café instead.

And through it all, the Beijing Ghost tasks keep coming.

More pregnancy scares and sex scandals and embarrassing photos taken drunk at an exclusive party in Wangjing. More instances of unrequited love and friendship worries and panic attacks and crumbling families. More messages detailing stories of exes and vigorous competitions and bribery and secret insecurities. This is the unexpected side effect of the app: the tasks feel like more than business opportunities now.

They feel like confessions.

Of course, I've always known that my classmates at Airington lead completely different lives from mine. But I've never looked beneath the shiny, polished surface of their million-dollar condos and private drivers and wild shopping sprees. Never considered that the people I've bumped into countless times in the corridors, made vague small talk with about upcoming tests, are people I might've actually been friends with. Exchanged secrets with. Reached out and comforted.

Instead, I've spent my five years here completely oblivious to everything outside my own studies.

Henry, on the other hand, doesn't seem surprised by *anything*.

"Hmm," is all he says when I show him the latest request at the end of our social ethics class.

"Hmm?" I repeat, incredulous. "Did you even read it?"

His eyes shift from the phone to my face, a gel pen twirling around and around between his long slender fingers. "Yes, of course. In its entirety."

"And you—you knew about this?"

"No," he says calmly, voice low enough for just the two of us to hear. Everyone else is busy pretending to jot down Julie Walsh's board notes on Discrimination in Developing Countries, their hands already reaching for their bags and laptop cases, ready to run out of here the second the bell rings. "But I find it rather plausible. Her artistic statement for her final project last year doesn't align at all with her coursework this semester. Either she underwent a drastic change in world views over the summer, or those views weren't hers to begin with."

I shake my head in disbelief. Even by the usual Beijing Ghost standards, the anonymous message currently loaded up on my phone is...well, shocking.

Apparently, Airington's favorite art prodigy, Vanessa Liu, has been buying all her art ideas and designs from some older university student. The source wants me to follow her to Shimao Tianjie, or simply *The Place*, tomorrow—one of those high-end, inner-city places I never visit—where she's meant to be meeting up with the student for another little exchange.

"But I've seen her draw," I insist, keeping my voice down too. "She's—I mean, she's *talented*. I don't understand why..."

"Talent isn't the same as genius," Henry replies, with all the secure, unaffected ease of someone who's spent his life in the latter category and knows it.

A familiar thorn of envy—of *want*—digs into my side.

I set the phone down. "Well. I guess I'll find out tomorrow night."

Henry glances up, and for the first time since I brought up this subject, he looks interested. When he speaks again, he seems to choose his words with care. "Would you...perhaps like some company?"

"From who?" I say, confused. The whole point of Beijing Ghost is that I'm meant to operate alone: undetected, unseen.

He raises his brows. Waits.

"What, *you*?" I say it like a joke, but his expression remains completely serious.

"Why not?" He holds up the pen he's been spinning. "Exams are over. We've both got some extra time on our hands. And I go to The Place all the time. I could be of some help."

"But. But if someone sees you—"

"We can go there early," he says readily, shrugging. "I'll show you around a bit, then head back on my own when you find her."

"But you—I just—"

The pen stills in his grip. He cocks his head a few degrees, his gaze steady on me, sharp and assessing and intensely black beneath the classroom lights. "What?"

And I don't know what. Only that the idea of meeting

him alone outside school at night makes my stomach dip as though I've just tumbled from a great height. I mean, sure, we've been walking to class together and I've even been inside his dorm room, but this...with only the two of us...this is—

"I won't be able to focus with you there," I blurt out, then realize exactly how that sounds.

His lips twitch. It's the same half-suppressed smile he wears when he's making his grand closing statement in a debate tournament, or when he knows the answer to a particularly hard question in class, or when he's making an impressive business pitch. It's the smile he wears when he's about to get what he wants. "Are you saying you find my presence distracting, Alice?"

"N-no. That's not at all what I..." I clear my throat just as the bell rings, drowning out the rest of my half-formed protests. When the loud buzzing finally stops, Henry speaks up before I can.

"I'll see you tomorrow night then." For some reason, he sounds weirdly excited.

The Place looks like something straight out of a movie. The high-budget kind.

It's an absolute behemoth of a road, with multilevel luxury brand stores and futuristic, glow-in-the-dark signs and rooftop restaurants crowded together along the sides, and a massive outdoor screen stretching from one end of the road all the way to the other, blocking out the hazy evening sky above it.

A clip of a dragon swimming through pools of gold is playing on the overhead screen when Henry and I step out from his driver's car. The light is so bright it casts a golden sheen over everything, from the smooth pavement tiles to the rich midnight fabric of Henry's button-down coat and the knife-edged angles of his face.

He's dressed even better than usual today; his hair is all soft and freshly combed and falling just above his eyes, and he has on a crisp white shirt underneath, the collar strategically undone, the sleeves peeking out every time he moves his arms around. Maybe he's heading off to a big event after this. A tech convention or something.

Then again, *everyone* here looks awfully stylish. Half the girls we pass on our way down the road could very well be models, with their velvet thigh-high boots and designer belts and bouncy, curled hair.

I run a self-conscious hand over my own plain shirt and leggings, then shake the thought away.

I'm not here to walk a runway; I'm here to complete a task and get my money.

Besides, if all goes according to plan, I'll be invisible soon anyway.

"So. Where do you want to go?" Henry asks, his steps falling in line with mine. Our shoulders are just close enough to touch, which, I realize, isn't something I should be noticing.

I shoot him a strange look. "Wherever Vanessa is. Where *else* would we go?"

"We could grab dinner first… Maybe walk around a bit—"

"And possibly miss out on our target?" My voice rises an octave with incredulity. Henry's always been annoyingly cavalier about all the Beijing Ghost tasks, but even for him, this seems a frivolous suggestion. "Or risk bumping into her before we gather our evidence? All for a—a meal? I don't think so. Plus, I ate a granola bar before coming here. I'm good."

He makes a small, exasperated noise with the back of his throat. Stops walking so abruptly I almost trip. "Alice."

"What?"

But whatever he's about to say is lost to the swell of orchestral music in the background. The screen above us flickers, and the brilliant wash of gold light is replaced by vivid hues of red and pink. Projected roses bloom over the giant screen's corners, magnified to the size of the outdoor dining table we've stopped beside, and images start flashing over the center.

Couple selfies. Shots of a pretty girl in her late twenties clearly taken by someone who knows her on an intimate level: pictures of her posing at a beach, smiling from the opposite end of a dinner table, hugging a cat and teddy bear in the comfort of her kitchen.

Then snippets of text pop up on the screen as well, written in pretty, enlarged italics.

*You're beautiful...
I've loved you ever since
we met in high school...*

Gasps and cheers arise from the many onlookers around us as they realize the same thing I do—

It's a proposal.

"This seems very unnecessary," I mutter as I scan the rapidly gathering crowd. People are running—actually *running*—to some distant spot outside a Guess store, where I can vaguely make out the shape of a man bending down on one knee. As cheesy as the proposal is, if Vanessa happens to already be here, she seems like the type who'd join the crowd. Maybe I could spot her from here, and follow her...

"I think it's rather romantic," Henry says lightly, while more roses threaten to take over the entire illuminated screen.

I whip my head back to stare at him. "If this is your idea of romance, I'm somewhat concerned for your future girlfriend."

Girlfriend.

The word hangs in the cool evening air between us, and if I had the energy and resources and brainpower to invent a time machine just so I could go back and retract that one sentence, I would without hesitation.

Henry and I have spoken about plenty of things over the past few months. Exams. Criminal activity. Bribery. The Boxer Rebellion. How we both achieved the same perfect English test score in Year Ten but I received more praise.

But we've never touched upon the topic of relationships. Of romance.

It's not as if I haven't *thought* about it in his presence, haven't occasionally wondered about things I shouldn't, dwelled a little too long on the shape of his lips, but to speak it aloud and acknowledge it feels like a kind of surrender.

It doesn't help that Zhang Jie's hit ballad "This Is Love" is now blasting at top volume from the speakers.

Or that Henry's gazing intently down at me.

"Anyway," I say, raising my voice over the music, praying he can't distinguish the reddish glow of the screen from the heated redness of my cheeks. "I'm happy for the couple and all, but we should really, uh, focus on finding Vanessa..."

To both my disappointment and relief, Henry doesn't say anything else as he follows me down toward the crowd. The girl must've accepted the proposal, because people are clapping wildly and wolf whistling, and off to the side of all the commotion is—

"Shit," I hiss under my breath, grabbing Henry by the sleeve and dragging him behind a nearby pillar with me.

"What—" he starts to say, but I clamp my hand over his mouth, forcing him farther back against the stone, out of view, my own body pressed up to his. Close enough to feel the heat of his skin. The warm tickle of his breath on my cheek.

My heart thuds louder in my ears.

Vanessa was there. *Is* there.

Carefully, one hand still pinning Henry in place, I sneak a quick glance out at the crowd again. Vanessa doesn't seem to have spotted me. She's standing next to a tall wiry guy maybe a few years older than she is; someone I've never seen before. The university student.

It must be him.

The two of them linger a few beats longer before turning in to the French-style bakery café on their left, their figures soon obscured by the colorful display windows.

I release a small sigh.

All I have to do now is turn invisible and follow them inside. I'll need close-up evidence; photos of the exchange taking place, pictures of the university student's face, and the artwork involved.

"Er... Alice?"

Henry's voice comes out muffled through my palm, and only then do I realize how close we still are. How easy it would be, in our current position, to stand on tiptoe and tilt my head just so and—

I lurch back. "Sorry," I apologize hastily, bringing my hand back down. "I was scared she'd see us."

"No worries." His tone is equally dismissive, nonchalant, but the tips of his ears are a deep pink.

Or maybe, in his case, it really is just the effect of the glowing screen.

"I should turn invisible now," I say out loud, more to fill the silence than anything.

"Indeed."

An awkward beat passes. Then another.

Nothing happens.

I keep waiting for the familiar chill to descend over my body, wash over me like a bucket of ice water, for the hair on my arms to rise, but all I feel is...warm. Whole. Flushed from my proximity to Henry, from the way he's looking at me, his lips red in the places I pressed my fingers to; from the ballad still playing in the background, the soft piano notes tangling together, the vocalist singing throatily about love and loss and want and how it feels to be truly seen.

And I'm just standing here, as blatantly visible as ever, my shadow falling firm over the pavement at my feet.

"Perhaps you can try again later," Henry suggests after about fifteen minutes of this. "Take a break and whatnot."

"I can't." I shake my head fast. "There's not enough time—for all we know, she's probably already taken the art—"

"Then let her."

I gape up at him, uncomprehending. "But that means—then I'll *fail the task*—I can't just *fail*—"

"Well, it seems like this isn't something you can control at present."

He's right. He's right, and it's horrible. My powers have never been the most reliable, I know that, but to have them abandon me at a time like this, when Vanessa is *right there* in that café and I've traveled all the way here, feels like the worst possible betrayal.

"Come on." Henry waves a hand. "Even if you do turn invisible in time, we might as well walk around while we wait."

But I don't turn invisible that night. What I end up doing instead is following Henry down the length of the crowded road, watching the screen glow and change scenes every few seconds, from a vast stretch of ocean to an ancient Chinese palace to a phoenix unfurling its fiery wings. He buys this inflated disk-like toy thing from one of the vendor carts parked outside a busy Zara shop, and even though I'm half-convinced he only wants to see me fumble with it and laugh at me, I try throwing it up in the air. It flies much farther than I thought, carried along by a mild breeze. We take turns with the disk afterward, until it inevitably becomes a ridiculous, intense competition to see how far we can throw, and soon I'm yelling at him to mark out the exact spot the disk hit the ground because I *swore* I won that last round.

And I almost forget about Vanessa and the art scandal and turning invisible at all.

I'm too busy watching the screen's green-blue light move over Henry's skin like water, the challenge set in the sharp line of his jaw as he makes his way back to me.

Is this how it feels? I wonder as I throw the disk up high again and watch it soar, weightless, over the heads of happy families and giddy teenagers, friends drunk on a wild night out. To be someone like Chanel, like Rainie, like Henry? To come to a place like this on any old weekday and just...have fun? Just *live*, without worrying about opportunity costs and paying out school fees?

I'm still thinking about this on the quiet car ride home, my fingers poised over my phone, a half-finished message typed out on the screen.

Unfortunately, I was unable to fulfill your request for Beijing Ghost...

I read it over, tasting the bitter failure in those words, and sigh. Delete everything. Tonight's assignment should've given me 25,000 RMB, but all I have now is an unwritten apology and one fewer client and a pressing need to make up for all the lost money whenever and however I can. I squeeze my eyes shut briefly, go over the calculations inside my head until my chest tightens, stuffed full with panic and flashing numbers. Even with the 160,000 RMB in my bank account now, I'm still over 80,000 RMB short. And the next deadline for our school fees is due in less than three weeks.

80,000 RMB.

The tightness in my chest suddenly feels a lot like exhaustion. Like despair.

I'm yanked from my spiraling thoughts when my phone buzzes. Not a Beijing Ghost alert, but a WeChat message. From Xiaoyi.

Yan Yan! Have you eaten yet?

I've attached a link on best foods to help counter excessive han energy in women… I think you should find useful—you can share with friends too. Most important is to drink ginger and brown sugar water while on period (I sense yours is starting soon)

And how is your little situation going? Is all under control?

I'm so mortified by what she's written above that it takes me a moment to register which "little situation" she's referring to.

My chest tightens. It's been a while since my invisibility powers felt so completely *beyond* my control. I might as well be honest about it.

Not really, I type out.

She replies right away, as if she'd sensed this answer was coming as well. Ah.

Then that means you have not seen the light yet.

Don't worry, Yan Yan. You will get better soon.

I stare at the message for a long, long time and decide that I have absolutely no idea what she means. I can only assume she's alluding to some Chinese proverb.

Still, it's nice to have an adult tell me everything will be okay. Even if I'm not so sure that's true.

12

The next week, a teacher asks me to stay behind after class, but it's not Mr. Murphy, as I feared—it's Mr. Chen.

His expression is stern as I approach his desk, a faint wrinkle appearing in his forehead, the way it does when he's going over a particularly difficult passage in our texts. Fear pulses through me.

"I wanted to talk to you about your English essay, Alice," he says.

"My essay?" I repeat, like an idiot.

"Yes. From your midterms."

"Why? Was it—was it bad?" The words tumble out of my lips before I can stop them, like water gushing from a broken dam. I hate that this is always my first instinct: self-doubt, anxiety, the nagging feeling that I did something wrong.

But Mr. Chen puts my worries to rest with a firm shake of his head. "On the contrary—yours was one of the most well-written essays I've read in years. And I don't say that lightly."

"Oh," is all I can think to say as the compliment sinks in. *One of the most well-written essays I've read.* And that's coming from Mr. Chen, the same teacher who was invited to speak at Peking University only weeks earlier, who received his education at *Harvard.* I've never had drugs before—never plan to in my life—but I imagine this is what the high must feel like. "Wow."

"Wow indeed," he says, but he doesn't smile. "That's not the main reason I asked you to stay behind, though." He taps a finger absentmindedly on his desk like a pen, as if deciding how best to phrase his next question. "Do you remember your main contention for the essay?"

I try not to look too taken aback. "Um, roughly."

"So you remember how you positioned yourself in…*support* of Macbeth and his actions?"

Now I see where this is going.

"It was only for the exam," I say quickly. "To make an interesting argument. I obviously don't believe you should go around killing people to gain power—or for any reason, really, unless the person you're killing is about to wipe out the human species or something, but that's a whole different topic. And I wasn't saying that he was *right* either. Just—sympathetic."

"Just sympathetic." Somehow, when Mr. Chen repeats something, he sounds all wise and philosophical.

"I mean his ambition," I say, feeling the need to clarify further, especially as his contemplative silence drags on a beat too long. "The fact that he goes after what he wants."

"Well then, Alice." Mr. Chen clasps his hands in front of him, peers at me across his desk. I feel vaguely as if he's about

to give me a test of some kind. "Since we're on the topic—
tell me. What is it that *you* want?"

"What do I want?" I echo.

He nods, expectant.

But the open-endedness of the question catches me off
guard, knocks the air out my lungs as a million answers surge
up to meet it—

I want to be respected. I want to be rich. I want to become
an acclaimed civil rights attorney or a business director at a
Fortune 500 company or a Pulitzer Prize–winning journalist; I want to be a professor at Harvard or Oxford or Yale, to
walk those gleaming lecture halls with my head held high and
know that I belong; I want to inherit a giant multimillion-
dollar company, like Henry, or be bold and gifted and inno-
vative enough to pave my own path in some niche field, like
Peter, or to have endless opportunities to stand before thousands of people and be seen, like Rainie; I want my name to
be spoken at Airington long after I've left, for all my teachers to be proud that they once taught me, to say to future
students, "you heard of that Alice Sun? I always knew she
would make it"; I want glory, recognition, attention, praise;
I want to buy my parents a brand-new apartment with floor-
to-ceiling windows and a balcony that overlooks a glittering
green lake, to earn enough money to treat them to roast duck
and fresh fish every day; I want to be great at what I do, no
matter what I do; I want, I want, *I want*—

Yet just as quickly as it balloons, the wild longing in my
chest deflates.

With a sharp jolt I feel all the way down to my bones, as
if I've fallen from a great height, I remember who I am, and

who I am not. I can't afford to think so far ahead into the future, to be so frivolous with my plans. I should only be focusing on making enough money to cover my school fees and bills for this year, then next year, then the year after that...

Maybe I was lying just now about why I find Macbeth so sympathetic. Maybe it's because I understand what it's like to want things that do not belong to you.

But of course, I don't tell Mr. Chen any of this.

"I want to get good grades. Graduate. Get a job in whichever field my strengths lie."

His brows furrow, like he doesn't quite believe me. "Not what you're passionate about?" he asks delicately.

I lift my chin. "I'm passionate about being good at things."

There's a defensive edge in my voice, and Mr. Chen must hear it. He drops the subject.

"Well, all right then. I suppose I should let you go to lunch..."

"Thanks, Mr. Chen."

But as I turn to leave, he adds, very quietly, "You're still a kid, you know."

I falter. "What?"

His eyes are kind, almost sad when he looks at me. "Even if it doesn't feel that way now, you're still only a kid." He shakes his head. "You're too young to be this...hardened by the world. You should be free to dream. To hope."

My conversation with Mr. Chen plays over and over again in my head as I make my way over to the cafeteria. Most people have eaten and left already, and only the Chinese cuisine bar is still open, so I grab a tray of rice and braised pork ribs that have already gone cold and nibble at my food half-heartedly, the chopsticks held loose in my hands.

You're still a kid, you know.

Coming from any other adult, the words would've seemed condescending, easy to laugh at and brush off, but I could tell Mr. Chen really *meant* them. Which is almost worse, somehow. It makes me feel too vulnerable.

Exposed.

It's like that time I wrote a poem about my family in Year Eight, thinking it was only for an English assignment, but the teacher insisted on reading it aloud to the whole school at assembly, her voice reaching an emotional crescendo as she described the old callouses on Mama's hands, her own hands rising and falling in exaggerated movements. People approached me about it afterward, kind and gushing and sympathetic, and part of me basked in the positive attention, while the other part—a bigger part—wanted nothing more than to flee.

I guess that's the thing: I've spent my whole life longing to be seen, but I've also come to realize that when people look too closely, they inevitably notice the ugly parts too, like how the tiny cracks on a polished vase only become visible under scrutiny. Like Mama's callouses, hidden from the world until the teacher had to go and read my poem into the microphone, into the silence of the giant, filled auditorium.

You're still a kid, you know.

The back of my neck prickles. Something sharp and hard lodges in my throat, like a shard of bone, even though the pork ribs on my tray are still untouched. I give up trying to eat.

This isn't how it's supposed to go.

Mr. Chen had said my Macbeth essay was one of the most well-written essays he'd read in *years*, which is the kind of praise I usually live for, lap up like a starved dog, but he hadn't looked impressed at all.

Only concerned.

"Alice! Hey, girl!"

I jerk my head up and spot Rainie making a beeline for me from the other end of the cafeteria table, a wide grin on her face. Her glossy hair has been tied up in a high ponytail, and it bounces elegantly over her shoulders as she sits down beside me. Another thing I wasn't expecting to happen today.

"So. What class is next?" she asks cheerily.

"You have art for fifth period," I inform her, thinking this must be why she came here. Since I've long fallen into the habit of memorizing Henry's timetable every school year, I know pretty much everyone's class schedules by heart. But she just shakes her head and laughs.

"Oh my god, *Alice*," she says, in that fond, exasperated tone people tend to use around close relatives. "Girl. I know what *my* class is. I'm asking about yours."

I blink at her. "Um… I have a spare period. Why?"

"Because. I'm trying to be your friend." She makes this sound like it's the most natural and obvious thing in the world, when I could easily name at least two thousand other reasons for someone of her social standing to seek out someone like me. But as she continues smiling, not budging from her seat, I realize that more people *have* been approaching me lately, sometimes waving in the corridors or striking up conversations out of the blue.

I guess hanging around Henry and Chanel so much in

public is the real-life equivalent of getting the verified check mark on social media: it sends a clear signal to the world that you're someone worth paying attention to.

Or maybe it's also because of Beijing Ghost. Even if no one here knows I'm the one behind the app, I've still spent these past months learning about all their secrets, their greatest fears and desires and insecurities, from Rainie's photos to Evie's test scores. Maybe that's the kind of thing you *feel*, instinctively, that draws people together like an invisible string, even if they're not aware of the full truth.

In theory, this should make me proud. This is what I've always wanted, after all: to be noticed, to be approached. But just like Mr. Chen's remark, it somehow feels wrong.

If Rainie notices my mini existential crisis, the way I'm gripping my chopsticks too tight, she doesn't show it. Instead, she leans back and starts scrolling through what has to be at least a hundred new notifications on her phone, pausing and rolling her thick-lashed eyes when she gets to the latest one.

"Still can't believe they're raising the prices again," she says with a snort. "The sheer nerve."

My heart seizes. "Wait. What?"

"The school fees," she says casually. "Didn't you know? They sent out an email about it a few months back."

"I—I don't..." All the school's emails go straight to Mama and Baba, but between their long work hours and old phones and the crappy connection in their little flat, sometimes things slip through the cracks. Important things. My heart starts pounding faster.

"Here. This is just a reminder for the upcoming deadline. The original email's down below." She scoots closer, holding her screen up for me to see. I can't read anything at first—can only stare at the tiny black numbers, the harsh white light, my stomach writhing. Then the figure comes into painful focus. 360,000 RMB.

No.

That's a 30,000 RMB jump from what it used to be, and that's only for one school year. It's too much. It's more than what I have, what I could possibly earn before the fee deadline in seven days, even if I were to complete another Beijing Ghost task—

I'm only dimly aware of what Rainie is saying. "...first heard about it. Apparently a bunch of the other international schools have raised their prices too, beginning from next semester—*such* a rip-off. My dad's company had like, a mini fit when he sent them the receipt."

"Right," I manage. The cafeteria suddenly feels too small, or maybe it's just my lungs that have shrunk. *360,000 RMB.* It's the kind of number that should be overwhelming, apocalyptic, *illegal*, that should send everyone at this school into mass panic, but Rainie looks mildly annoyed, at best.

Then again, of course she is. Most of my classmates have their parents' companies covering their school fees, their private drivers, their giant condos. Everything. That would explain why I never heard about the raised prices until now, too; this is nothing more than a minor inconvenience to them, hardly worth dwelling on for longer than a few seconds.

Case in point: Rainie's already launched into another conversation topic—this time about the midterm exams, and how they should be graded on a curve, and wasn't that English essay question so vague, and—

"Oh yeah, did you hear about Evie?" she asks.

If I wasn't already on edge, I most certainly am now. My spine goes rigid, half my thoughts still stuck on the school fees, trying desperately to calculate how much more money I need to make in the next week. "What—what about Evie?"

"Apparently, she smashed her history midterms—for her standards anyway. Got like, eighty percent or something. Pretty impressive, huh?"

I search Rainie's body language for any hidden, darker meaning behind her words, but she just tightens her ponytail, flips it over her shoulder, and sighs.

"I'm happy for her, honestly," she continues. "She's gone through at least ten different tutors in the past year, and none of them helped. Guess she finally found the right one."

"Mm," is all I reply, terrified that my voice will break and give me away if I try to speak. What could I possibly say? *Yes, I, too, am so glad she found the right tutor. Her final score was definitely because of that, and not because she received the literal answers to memorize days in advance. For sure.*

Then my phone buzzes, the vibration almost violent against the thin fabric of my skirt, and all thoughts of Mr. Chen and Evie and the raised school fees are driven away as I read the new message on Beijing Ghost.

"Repeat what you just said."

Henry is staring at me from the other end of his dorm room, his expression the closest thing to shock I've ever witnessed on him. He runs an agitated hand through his hair, shakes his head. Sits down on the edge of his bed, which is perfectly made, as usual. Sometimes I wonder if he even sleeps on it.

"Which part?" I ask.

He doesn't reply, but his eyes dart to the door. He's been doing this a lot—ever since I ran in here and shut the door firmly behind me, afraid that people in the hall might overhear our conversation and call the police on us. He'd flinched as if I were trapping us inside a prison, looking almost…*nervous*. Tense. His back too straight, his fingers restless. If I didn't know better, I'd think he was more upset about the closed door than what I just said.

"Which part?" I say again, when it becomes clear he hasn't heard me.

"All of it."

"Are you serious?"

"It's a fair lot to take in, don't you think?"

I roll my eyes, but he's right. It is a lot to handle; I wouldn't have come here straight after school otherwise.

So I repeat it all. Everything from the latest Beijing Ghost message.

I tell him about Andrew She and Peter Oh, how their parents' rivalry at the same company has been escalating in recent weeks, how one of them is meant to be promoted soon, but the company hasn't reached a decision yet on who is the best pick. All Andrew knows is that whoever gets promoted will be the marketing director for every branch in Eurasia and receive a seven-figure salary each year, and it's everything his father has been working for since his early twenties, but his father isn't so confident about his chances at winning.

In fact, his father is *so* uncertain about his chances that he's willing to use other methods. Simpler, crueler methods that are sure to produce results.

Like kidnapping the other guy's son.

The Experiencing China trip will be the perfect opportunity, Andrew She had written. He hadn't mentioned his own name, only Peter's, but I'd known about them and their parents' feud long enough to guess just from the context. *We'll all be staying at the Autumn Dragon Hotel for four nights in a row, and you know how these trips go—the teachers will have trouble supervising us all at night. The whole process should be smooth. Easy for someone like you. My father will send some of his men over, keep them hidden in a room on a separate floor. All you have to do is ensure Peter makes his way to them, and take his phone. It's essential, however, that you create no disturbance whatsoever, so that by the time anyone even notices he's gone, it'll be too late.*

Then, as if he could sense my horror through the phone, he'd added, *Don't worry. We won't cause him physical harm in any way, and when the time comes, we'll release him on our own. What we need is merely for Mr. Oh's son to go missing during a vital time in his campaign, long enough to distract him, upset him, severely affect his everyday performance. Then the promotions will be announced, and Mr. Oh will have lost but miraculously won his son back, and everyone will be happy.*

"Did he actually say that?" Henry asks, incredulity lifting his brows. "That *everyone will be happy*?"

I nod.

"Good god," he says on a drawn breath. He's silent for a while, processing, though his eyes still flicker to the door every few seconds. "Was there anything else?"

"No. Nothing," I lie quickly. What I don't tell him is that

by some awful coincidence, or maybe some twisted sign from the universe, Mama had messaged me right after Andrew did. She'd received Airington's reminder email about the change in prices too, having missed the first one.

Have you made your decision yet? she'd asked, then attached three brochures for cheap, low-tier local schools near our compound, as well as one for a school in Maine. *If not, it's time to start thinking about next step. Airington's fee deadline is in one week. After that, you'll automatically be un-enrolled from school.*

In other words: I need to somehow make over 100,000 RMB in the next seven days, or accept that I'm screwed and start cleaning out my school lockers. But where am I supposed to get that sort of money? Where else, if not from Andrew?

As I fight off another wave of panic, Henry's voice breaks through my thoughts.

"You know, I always figured Andrew She was a bit of a snake."

I frown at him. "Really? But the guy's so…so *nice* and scared of everything all the time. He looked close to wetting himself when Mr. Chen called on him in class the other day."

Henry just nods as if I'm helping him prove a point. "Makes sense. It's usually the cowards who resort to such crude, extreme tactics."

Or the desperate, I add in my head, but don't say.

"Well, coward or not, he's definitely not messing around." I walk over to his bed and show him the last message Andrew sent me. "He's offering us one million RMB for this task alone." When I first saw it, the number didn't even seem real. It still doesn't. *"One million."*

"Wait." Henry turns his full attention to me, and I can't

help but shift under the weight of it. "You're not really considering this, are you? The plan is absurd. And we both know Andrew isn't very bright."

But he's rich, which is what matters.

"I mean, I'm not saying I'd be *thrilled* to get involved in a toxic decade-long intercompany rivalry and kidnap a minor—"

"That's a really great way to start a sentence," Henry says drily.

I glare at him and continue, "But if you think about it, this one large crime pays the same amount as ten or eleven medium-sized crimes, so we're actually just...just maximizing profit and minimizing sin."

He makes a sound caught halfway between a laugh and a scoff. "So what's next, then? Actual murder?"

"Obviously not—I'd never—"

"Really? Never?"

"*No,*" I snap. "How could you even *think* that? Andrew said himself that Peter wouldn't be harmed. That's completely different from—from taking someone's life."

"I don't know, Alice," he says, his dark gaze unreadable, pinning me in place. "A few months ago, I wouldn't have thought it possible for you to consider kidnapping your classmate either."

Anger surges up inside me, hot and sharp and sudden, cutting my words into blades. "Oh my god, Henry, don't be such a *hypocrite*. You didn't say anything when I told you about the exam mission—"

"Well, it was clear you'd already made up your mind—"

"Then it's all my fault. Is that it?"

"No." His voice is infuriatingly calm. It makes my skin itch. "No, that's obviously not what I'm saying—"

"Or do you regret it?"

"Regret what?"

"This." I point to him, to me. "Because I made it pretty clear from the beginning that this wasn't going to be a fun charity project—"

"If my memory serves me correctly, I signed up for an *app*, not a criminal organization—"

"Then quit."

The words come out harsher than I intended, and my mouth goes dry as they shoot forth to meet their target. It's too late to retract them.

A muscle strains in Henry's jaw; a rare sign of emotion. "Do you not know me at all?" he says after a long pause. "I never quit anything."

You quit violin, I almost counter, but the memory of him confiding in me about his lessons, his lovely features illuminated by moonlight, the mottled bruise stretching over his cheek like a shadow, suddenly threatens to overwhelm me. Softens the acid on my tongue.

Even now, I can still make out the faint outline of the bruise on his face.

"I never quit anything either," is what I say instead. "Which is why I think—I need to see this task through. I'm so close to…"

To earning enough money for me and my family. To feeling safe for once in my life. To never having to worry about those awful school brochures again. One million RMB. Do you have any idea what that means to me?

But the question sounds ridiculous, even in my head. How could he? He's Henry Li.

"I'm just so close."

"Close to *what*?" He sounds genuinely confused.

"You wouldn't get it," I mutter. I look away before he can question me again, and the vestiges of my anger turn heavy in my stomach, draining all the fight out of me. "I know you think I'm a bad person," I say quietly, and without meaning to, I leave an opening at the end of the sentence, room for him to step in and say, *that's not true.*

But he takes a beat too long to respond. "...I don't—"

"Whatever." I straighten, stride over to the window. The sky hangs gray and heavy with unshed rain, and from afar, the pale, bare branches of the wutong trees planted around the playground look like bones. "It's fine if you think that. Really. I"—for a fraction of a second, my voice cracks, and I force it to harden—"I was never trying to be a hero anyway."

"You could be, though," Henry says quietly.

"Don't be naive."

"Why no—"

"*Because,*" I snap. "Because this isn't a Marvel movie. It's not about good versus evil—it's just about survival. And even if it were," I add, dragging a finger down the cold pane of glass, "I'd rather be the villain who lives to the end than the hero who winds up dead."

I turn back around, just in time to catch the look on Henry's face. It's not disgust, as I expected, or even shock. His lips are set in a tight, unyielding line, but his eyes are soft. Strangely tender.

As if I've given away something about myself without re-alizing it.

"Look, I don't need your approval, Henry," I say, deter-mined to ignore that expression, the way it makes my chest ache like a pressed bruise. "I just need to know if you're fully prepared to do this mission with me."

Seconds tick by.

Minutes.

A century of him sitting there, not saying anything, kill-ing me with his silence. But just when I'm about to give up and walk out the door and pretend all of this never happened, he nods, *yes*.

"Good," I say, and it's not until the word leaves my lips that I realize the extent of my relief. It startles me. Unsettles me. Maybe I care about this partnership more than I want to admit.

I quickly push the thought aside.

"All right then. Let's start brainstorming how we're going to do this whole kidnapping thing now, hmm?" I retrieve a pen from my pocket, and point at the calendar hung up over his desk, a colored sticky note marking every important event. Written in his handwriting, so neat it looks as if it's been typed up and printed, are the words *Experiencing China trip*. Only three days away. "We don't have much time to waste."

13

There's a strange hum of energy in the air as we board the train at Beijing Railway Station.

It's not just because of the enormous crowd moving with us, pushing past and into the narrow compartments: young, sunburnt workers heaving pots and plastic duffel bags over their shoulders, eager to return to their hometown over the weekend; mothers clutching their purses tight to their chests, yelling and gesturing wildly for their children to follow; gray-haired businessmen negotiating deals on the phone at the top of their voices as they fumble around for a charger.

It's excitement, anticipation, wholly unique to Airington students alone. Everyone knows that Experiencing China trips are where Things Happen. After all, the combination of long train and bus rides, luxurious hotels in a foreign place, and nonschool-related activities completed in close proximity of one another seems almost *intended* to create drama. Friendship circles are broken and rearranged. Long-time couples split and exes hook up again. Secrets are revealed, scandals are made. Like when Vanessa Liu lost her virginity behind a Buddhist shrine on our Year Nine trip to Guilin, or when Jake Nguyen managed to sneak his way into the hotel bar during our Year Ten trip and got so drunk he launched into an hour-long monologue about how he felt inferior to his brother, while Rainie—who was still his girlfriend at the time—stroked his hair and fed him sips of water.

But the same scandals that shocked me this time last year now seem so small, so trivial. So *normal*.

Compared to what I'm meant to pull off in the days ahead, they feel almost like a joke.

"This should be our compartment," Chanel tells me when we reach the middle of the carriage, shoving her giant suitcase through the opened doors with surprising ease. "I travel alone a lot," she explains, catching the look on my face, and without another word, helps me roll my suitcase inside as well.

"Oh—thank you."

I wonder if it's obvious to Chanel that I don't travel a lot at all. In fact, apart from my plane ride in and out of America, and the previous Experiencing China trips—and only because the school fees cover them—I haven't gone anywhere outside of Beijing.

So it's with fascination that I take in our tiny train compartment: the kettle set out on a folded table, the identical bunk beds sticking out from the walls, the space in between them so narrow only one person could possibly stand there at a time.

"Not a great place for the claustrophobic," Chanel remarks as she squeezes her way through behind me, plopping down on one of the lower beds. "Or for anyone, really."

It's still bigger than my parents' bedroom. A faint pang twists through my stomach at the thought, but I just smile and nod. I was prepared for this to happen, after all; within the Airington school gates, it's still fairly easy to pretend that everyone's the same. But out here, well…

"Qiqi! Guolai, kuai guolai—zai zhe'er!"

The loud, rapid Mandarin exclamations cut through my thoughts, and I turn toward the noise.

A short, middle-aged woman is wheeling two suitcases into our compartment, one of which is covered in a bright pink Barbie design that makes Chanel's eyes twitch.

Seconds later, a little girl no older than six comes skipping into the compartment, a doll clutched to her chest, her high pigtails bouncing with her every step. This, I assume is the Qiqi the woman was yelling for.

"Oh!" The little girl stops short at the sight of me and Chanel. Then she breaks into a wide grin, pointing at us with her free hand. "Jiejie! Da jiejie!"

The woman glances in our direction for the first time and pauses too. I wait for the flash of surprise that usually arises when strangers see our uniforms, but then I remember we're in casual clothes: Chanel, wearing a lacy blouse that rises just above her pale, flat midriff, and me, in a faded sweater and jeans Mama bought at Yaxiu Market a few years ago.

Instead of surprise, a crinkle appears between the woman's drawn-on brows, like she's not sure if Chanel and I are traveling together or not.

"Jiejie hao," Chanel greets politely, and only then do the woman's features smooth out, her lips lifting into a smile at the subtle flattery; being called *jiejie*, older sister, instead of *ayi*, for older women.

I quickly copy Chanel's greeting, but the woman is already preoccupied, her gaze fixed on Chanel as if they might've met somewhere before. Then, in that same brisk, accented Mandarin, she says: "I'm not sure if anyone's ever told you this, but you look a lot like that famous model—what's her name again…"

"Coco Cao?" Chanel offers.

"Yes!" The woman claps her hands together and beams. "Yes, exactly!"

"Oh, right, well…" Chanel tucks a strand of hair behind her ear, and with a practiced air of nonchalance, says, "That's my mother."

The woman's eyes widen. "Really?"

"Really."

"Qiqi!" the woman suddenly calls her child, who's busy tucking her doll into bed, her little face puckered in concentration. "Qiqi, guess what? This is a *real model*. Isn't she pretty?"

"Model's daughter," Chanel corrects, but she looks a little pleased at all the attention, the evident awe awash over the woman's face.

And I'm happy for her too. Of course I am. But as the train lurches into motion and the woman sits down beside Chanel as if they're old friends and starts gushing about her mother's latest appearance on *Happy Camp*, I get that feeling extras must have on large movie sets: like my presence might count for something, but it doesn't *really* make that much of a difference.

Watching them out of the corner of my eye, I make a silent vow to myself that one day, strangers like that will notice me as well. I will not stay in the corners, feeling sad and silly and small, my pride eating away at itself.

No, I will do something great, and they will all know my name.

But until then, I decide to put my time to better use than listening to Chanel's incredibly detailed skincare advice. Retreating to the very end of my bunk bed, I take out the printed, annotated map of the Autumn Dragon Hotel from my bag and force myself to study it.

I've already spent the previous two days memorizing every possible route to the twentieth floor—where Andrew She's men will be waiting—and marking out the busiest spots, the corridors and corners where there'll likely be the least number of security cameras. And still, I retrace the routes over and over again with my fingertips, try to visualize how the night will go in my head, prepare for the worst-case scenarios—where to stop, where to flee, where to hide.

The world around me starts to fade, as it always does when I enter this zone of intense concentration; in fact, if I forget about the whole illegal aspect of the mission, it's almost like studying for an exam.

At some point, the air conditioner kicks on at full blast, and I shiver in the sudden, unforgiving cold, hugging the blankets tight around my body with numb fingers. But the cold only grows, the temperature dropping by what feels like ten degrees per second, and as my teeth start chattering violently, I remember, dimly, that it's late autumn. There's no reason for the train's air conditioning system to be on at all...

I recognize the exact moment I turn invisible.

I recognize it, because the little girl, Qiqi, happens to be looking in my direction, and her eyes go rounder than her doll's. She brings a small hand to her opened mouth, then frantically pats her mother's shoulder.

"Mama! Mama!" she cries. "Nikan! Kuaikan ya!"

Look.

But of course, there's nothing for her mother to see. I've stuffed the map deep into my pocket and leaped out of bed, erasing all evidence that I might still be in the compartment.

Qiqi's mother makes a small noise of exasperation. "Look at what? I told you not to interrupt me when I'm having a conversation, Qiqi."

"Ta—ta shizong le!" Qiqi insists, pointing at the spot I was in just now.

She disappeared.

"Yes, I know, the other girl left the room," Qiqi's mother says impatiently, then shoots Chanel an apologetic look. "Sorry, my daughter likes to talk a lot when she's bored. Says all sorts of nonsense."

Qiqi's face scrunches up, her frustration rivaling her mother's. "Mama, ta zhende… Qiqi meiyou hushuo…"

I can still hear her arguing with her mother as I creep out of the compartment, into the crowded corridor.

Passengers are pacing back and forth, grabbing packets of instant noodles and chocolate pie from the train vendors or filling up their water kettles. After a woman trips over my foot and nearly spills boiling water all over me, it becomes quite apparent that I can't just hang around here until my invisibility turns off again.

Without consciously making a decision about where to go next, I end up outside Henry's compartment.

To save the teachers time and energy, our train compartments and hotel roommates have been arranged based on our dorms, which means Henry is in there, alone.

The thought scares me a little.

But when another passenger barges right into me from behind, swearing and yanking at my hair with excruciating force as they try to regain their balance, my nerves quickly still. I slide the door wide open and step in.

I was wrong, in a way—Henry is the only Airington student here, but he isn't *alone* alone. There are two businessmen snoring on the upper bunks, one using their suit as a blanket, the other half propped up against the wall, his head lolling back and forth every time the train jolts.

Beneath them, Henry is sitting upright, hands folded in his lap, gaze fixed on the opposite wall. It's strange seeing him like this: out of his school uniform and in a plain white V-necked shirt instead, his dark hair falling over his brows in soft, unbrushed waves.

He looks really, infuriatingly good.

He also looks...tense.

As I draw closer, I notice the uneven rhythm in his breathing, the muscle straining in his arms, as if ready for combat or to jump out of the train at a moment's notice.

Then he turns toward me, some emotion I can't quite decipher flickering in his eyes. "Alice?"

He says my name like a question.

"You can see me?" I ask in surprise.

"No. I sensed your presence."

I frown. "Well, that's not good. If people can sense when I'm here, I'll need to fix that before tomorrow. Work on masking my steps better, or moving more slowly, or..."

But he's shaking his head before I've even finished my sentence. "That's not what I meant," he says, then pauses, seemingly searching for the right words. "It—it's only because... I'm around you so often. I highly doubt anyone else would be able to."

"Ah," I say, though I'm still unsure what he really means. All I know is that if Henry's being this ineloquent, maybe he's even more stressed than I realized—but about *what*, I have no clue either. "Well, then. Seeing as I came all the way here from my carriage, are you going to be a gentleman and offer me a seat or what?"

"Oh—yes. Of course."

He moves over to make room at once, and I sit, but alarm flashes through me. I've never known him to be this compliant before. Something's definitely wrong.

Still, we are both silent for a while, listening to the steady snores of the two businessmen and the creak of the train tracks below, before I finally muster the courage to point out the obvious. "Not to sound like the school counselor or whatever, but you don't seem like your usual self today."

"My usual self?" he repeats, eyebrows rising.

"You know—your superpretentious, unnecessarily formal, annoyingly arrogant, walking-advertisement-for-SYS self." The intended insult comes out sounding much more affectionate than I wanted, so I add for good measure, "You even stumbled over your words when you were talking just now."

Horror clips his tone. "I did *not*."

"You did," I say, mock-serious. Then, with sincerity: "So. Do you see my cause for concern now?"

"I suppose. I just..." He smooths out a nonexistent crease in his shirt, then says, with all the tones of someone making a terrible, humiliating admission: "I'm...not exactly a big fan of enclosed spaces."

"Okay," I say slowly, trying hard to think of what to say next. Because if this really is an admission, it means he's trusting me with something private, something precious. And god help me, for whatever reason, the last thing I want is to ruin it. "Okay," I repeat. "Do you want to talk about why...?"

"Not in particular, no."

"Oh." I clear my throat. "Well, all right then."

A long, awkward silence ensues, and I'm starting to worry this conversation is over—not that I enjoy talking to Henry Li or anything, it's more the principle of the matter—when he sucks in a tight breath, the way you would before ripping off a Band-Aid, and says, "It's...quite silly, really. And it was a very long time ago—I couldn't have been more than four or five. But..."

I wait.

"At our old house in Shunyi, there was this room in the basement—well, not so much a room as a closet. There were no windows, nothing except a door you could only open from the outside. I remember... I just remember it was always cold in there, and dark, like the mouth of a cave. My mother wanted to leave it for the ayi to store her cleaning supplies, but Father thought it'd be put to better use as a... study space." His jaw tightens. "So every day, at precisely five in the morning, he'd leave me in there with only a book of practice questions and a pencil for hours."

He pauses, rubs the back of his head. Forces out a hollow laugh. "Of course, it wasn't *quite* as terrible as it must sound. Not at first. Hannah—my older sister—would sneak me snacks and books when my father was busy working, or simply sit outside the door to keep me company... But then her own grades started slipping, and she was sent off to school in America, and it was—it was just me in that room for hours on end..." His voice grows quieter and quieter with every word, until it's swallowed completely by the rattle of the train and the shrieks of a baby in another compartment.

And I know I should say something at this point. I know. But all that comes out of my mouth is, "Oh my god."

"Yes." He shifts position slightly, so I can no longer see his face. Only the pale curve of his neck. "Indeed."

"I'm so sorry," I whisper. "I honestly—I can't imagine how hard that must've been..."

I mean this as more than just a phrase. Despite what everyone likes to assume based on my scores and general personality, Mama and Baba have never pressured me to study. If anything, they're always the ones to tell me to relax, to put the textbook down and watch some TV, go outside more.

And when *I* was five, Mama made it clear that she only ever wanted two things from me: for me to be a good person, and for me to be happy. That was also why she and Baba decided to sell their car, their old apartment, and use all their savings to send me to Airington, even if they knew I'd resist the idea at first—they hoped to protect me from the intense pressure of the gaokao.

"It's fine now. Really," he says, voice rough. "And I wouldn't be where I am without—"

"*No.*" Anger cuts through me like a knife: anger at his father, for doing this to him; anger at the universe, for letting it happen; anger at myself, for assuming his competence was rooted in an easy childhood, a painless childhood. "I hate that. I *hate* when people justify a clearly inhumane process and use it as some kind of model for success just because the results are to their liking—"

"Is that not what you're doing, though? With Beijing Ghost?"

"I—" I falter, caught off guard not just by the question, but the truth of it. My stomach twists. "I guess you're right. But the thing is... I don't know any other way to live."

Quietly, he says, "I don't either."

Then he turns back to me, the space between us narrowing to only a few dangerous inches. His eyes lock on mine, and something else locks into place in my chest. "You're visible again."

"Really," I say, but neither of us move.

We're sitting close, I realize. Too close.

Not close enough.

I draw in a shaky breath. He smells expensive, like the unopened boxes of designer shoes Chanel keeps piled up in our dorm. But beneath it there's another scent, something crisp and faintly sweet, like fresh-cut grass in spring or clean sheets warmed by sun.

We could kiss like this. The treacherous thought floats, unbidden, to the surface of my consciousness. I know, of course, that we won't. That he's too disciplined, and I'm too stubborn. But the possibility still hangs thick in the air, in the spaces we do not touch, the thought written all over his face, his half-parted lips, his black, burning gaze.

"Alice," he says, and his accent—

God, his accent. His voice.

Him.

And I'm about to say something clever, something that will not betray the mad fluttering in my chest or how distracted I am by the beads of sweat on his neck but still make him want me, when a heavy hand slaps my shoulder. Hard.

I jerk back with a startled yelp and look up.

The businessman still snoring away above us has shifted position in his sleep, one arm now dangling innocently over the bed rails.

"Are you quite all right?" Henry asks, sounding a little choked up—not out of concern, but badly suppressed laughter. It's incredible how fast I can vacillate between wanting to kiss this guy and kill him.

I shoot him a withering glare, rubbing the sore spot on my shoulder. "Could you maybe act a little more concerned? I could've gotten hit in the head. I could've been *concussed*."

"Fine, fine, I'm sorry," he says, though the corners of his lips continue to twitch upward. "Let me rephrase: Would you like me to fetch some ice for your potentially mortal wound? Perhaps some painkillers? Give you a massage?"

"Shut up," I grumble.

He grins at me then, and despite my annoyance, despite my throbbing shoulder, I am relieved. I would rather spend the rest of this train ride fighting with him than let him be trapped alone with his thoughts and fears again.

14

After we arrive in Suzhou, sleep deprived and starving from the long train ride, the first thing the teachers do is take us out to eat.

It's warmer here in the south, humid, like the inside of a sauna, and most of us are sweating by the time our rented bus pulls up outside some fancy restaurant that ranked first on Dazhong Dianping. As the only teacher here who can speak Chinese, Wei Laoshi quickly assumes the role of tour guide. We watch through the tinted windows as he approaches the waitress out front, gesturing to his school ID and then to us (a few students in the front seats wave; the waitress frowns).

Then the waitress and Wei Laoshi seem to get into a heated argument, both of them shaking their heads and fanning their faces, and even though we can't hear a single word they're saying, the message is clear: there aren't enough tables in the restaurant for all of us.

"Well, fuck me," Jake Nguyen grumbles from the row behind me. "I'm starving."

"Language, Mr. Nguyen," Julie Walsh says sharply.

"Shit—my bad," Jake says.

"Language!"

"Right, got it, Mrs. Walsh."

"It's Dr. Walsh."

"Yeah, whatever," he mutters.

Someone snorts.

"Didn't the school think to reserve us a few baojian?" Vanessa demands, standing up suddenly in her seat. Her long French braid almost whacks me in the face.

"Not all restaurants have private rooms, you know," someone else—it sounds like Peter Oh—points out.

"What?" Vanessa whips her head around with a look of genuine shock. Even her cheeks go pink. "You're kidding."

"Don't be such a snob."

"I'm not—"

Beside me, Henry sighs. It's a soft sound, barely audible over Vanessa's complaints and Jake's cursing, but—I kid you not—everyone quietens down at once.

Then Henry asks, "The restaurant's name is Dijunhao, right?"

"Yeah," I say, squinting at the golden calligraphy written backward over the restaurant's double door. "Why?"

But Henry doesn't respond; he's already on the phone. I listen to him greet whoever he's calling in flawless Chinese, ask politely if they've eaten lunch yet, rattle off his father's name, two other names I don't recognize, confirm the location of the restaurant, and hang up.

A few minutes later, the manager himself comes out to greet us with a smile so wide it looks physically painful.

"*Of course* there's space for you! You're our most honored guests," he says, when Wei Laoshi questions the sudden change. He shoots the waitress a pointed look, and the waitress scurries off as if her life depends on it, returning with menus and five more waitresses who ask to help carry our bags.

We're given the best tables with the fancy chopstick holders and red tablecloth and stunning window view of the lakes outside, and offered free jasmine tea (*handpicked from the mountains*, the manager tells us) and prawn crackers, and even the teachers are looking at Henry in openmouthed awe, like he's glowing.

"I wonder how that feels," I murmur, when Henry comes over to sit down beside me and Chanel.

"Pardon?" Henry says.

"Nothing." I take a long swig of tea, letting the hot liquid scorch my tongue. "Never mind."

Chanel, who doesn't look quite as impressed as the others—probably because she's used to receiving similar treatment herself—pokes her head between us and asks, "How was the train ride Henry? Did you sleep well?"

"I did, thank you," Henry replies mildly, with a stiff half smile. I'm so used to seeing the side of Henry that laughs aloud, that teases me and challenges me and listens to Taylor Swift on repeat that I keep forgetting how distant he is with everyone else, even people he knows.

"Mmm, that's what I figured," Chanel says. There's a glint in her eyes. "Since Alice never returned to our compartment."

I almost choke on my tea.

"We didn't—I wasn't—" I splutter, so loud that the conversation at the neighboring table stalls, and the waiters stop setting down dishes to look at me. I flush and continue in a whisper, "We were only going over business details. *Seriously*."

Chanel just winks at me, while Henry stares down with extreme focus at the single sesame bun on his plate, the tips of his ears pink.

More waiters soon step forward bearing trays of popular local dishes: deep-fried fish glazed with a thick tomato sauce, the meat so tender it slides off naturally from the bones; delicate red date paste cakes cut into the shape of diamonds; round wontons floating in bowls of golden broth.

It's all mouthwatering, but across the table, Julie Walsh wrinkles her nose at the fish and asks, very slowly, "What... *is* that?"

A pause. No one seems to want to answer, but when the silence drags on too long, Chanel rolls her eyes and says, "It's Mandarin Squirrel Fish."

Julie's hand flies to her chest. *"Squirrel—"*

"Not actual squirrel," I can't help interrupting. "It's just the name."

"Oh. Well, good," Julie says, though she still makes no move to touch the dish. Instead, to my utter disbelief, she retrieves a packet of trail mix from her handbag and dumps the contents out onto her plate.

Irritation flares up inside me, and I realize that Henry was right the other day: my anger does make me brave.

"Excuse me, *Dr.* Walsh," I say, raising my voice a little. "I thought this was an Experiencing China trip?"

Julie blinks at me, a salted almond half lifted to her painted lips. "Yes?"

"Then surely eating the local cuisine is part of the experience, is it not? Especially when the teachers are expected to lead by example?" Without giving her a chance to protest, I go on, "And weren't you saying just the other day, in our social ethics class, that world harmony could be achieved *if only* people were willing to practice empathy and explore new cultures?"

The almond drops soundlessly and rolls over the tablecloth. Julie doesn't pick it up; she's too busy staring at me like I'm a bug she wants to squash.

I don't think a teacher has ever looked at me with anything other than affection or concern before. Then again, I can't recall ever talking to a teacher like this before either.

Then Mr. Murphy stands up at the next table and claps twice to get everyone's attention, snapping the thread of tension—and conveniently saving Julie from having to respond.

"Listen up, guys," he booms, using his presenter-at-assembly voice. "Since we have a very full afternoon planned out, and won't be in the Autumn Dragon Hotel until late evening, we've decided to save some hassle and give you your hotel room numbers and cards now, all right?" He peers around at us as if we're really all sitting down before a stage. "Is that something I can trust you guys to keep safe for eight hours?"

He receives only a few lackluster nods in response, but seems to deem this good enough.

"Great." He takes out a crumpled paper folder not unlike the one I stole the history exam answers from. Guilt lifts its head, and I quickly stomp it back down. "I'll call your names one by one, and if you or your roommate can just come up in an orderly fashion… Let's see… Scott An."

There's an evident discrepancy between Mr. Murphy's idea of "orderly fashion" and our interpretation of the words, because soon everyone's standing up and jostling each other trying to get to the front.

"Orderly!" Mr. Murphy cries over the squeak of chairs and the countless voices talking at the same time. "I said *orderly!*"

In the chaos, I manage to squeeze close enough to get a view of the paper in Mr. Murphy's outstretched hand, the tens of names printed in tidy rows across it. But it's not my name I'm searching for.

PETER OH AND KEVIN NGUYEN: ROOM 902.

I carve the number into my memory. If everything goes well, this is the room I'll end up in tonight.

Once we're all back in our seats and our plates are scraped clean, Wei Laoshi takes over, leading us out to the bus again. I think he's really starting to embrace his tourist guide role, because he puts on a red bucket hat, waves a little flag with the school logo on it high over his head and says, with sincere enthusiasm, "Now—who's ready for some sightseeing?"

The old districts of Suzhou are beautiful.

Like a magical secret kept safe and hidden from the outside world. A soft, milky fog spills across the winding waterways, the crooked, crowded alleys and faded white houses, blurring the lines between land and sky. There are women wringing out their laundry by the banks, leathery-skinned men hauling nets of fish from the murky green canals, college-aged girls posing and snapping photos by the willow trees, pretty oil paper umbrellas rested over their shoulders.

"Oh—oh, it's like the Chinese version of Venice!" Julie Walsh gasps when we step out of the bus, her high heels clacking against the century-old pavement.

But the place doesn't look like Venice to me. It doesn't look like anywhere else in the world.

We start walking down the side of a canal, with Wei Laoshi leading the way. Every now and then, he stops to point at things—a statue of a solemn-looking official, a slanted inn, a boat drifting atop the waters—and call out random facts, saying how the Qianlong emperor once stayed in Suzhou for ten days and couldn't bear to leave, even reciting a few lines of the emperor's poetry.

I'm sure Qianlong's poem is great, but all I can get out of it is something about a bird and a mountain and blood—no, snow—no—

"Wait, Wei Laoshi," Chanel ventures. "I keep forgetting— which one was Qianlong and which one was Qin Shihuang again? Like, who was the dude that buried scholars alive?"

Wei Laoshi halts in his tracks and turns, fixing Chanel with a look that quite clearly implies: *you uncultured swine.*

"What?" Chanel says, defensive. "I used to go to school in Australia. It's not like they teach you much about Chinese history there."

Wei Laoshi just sighs and casts his eyes heavenward, like he might be apologizing to the spirit of the Qianlong emperor himself.

The bus ride took twice as long as the teachers predicted,

thanks to peak-time traffic, and soon everyone's hungry again. Wei Laoshi's tour is cut short as a result, and with another long-suffering look, he abandons his lecture on the history of paper umbrellas to take us all on a spontaneous trip to the night market.

The market teems with life, and everything feels sharper here. Brighter.

Children chase each other over the steep steps and arched bridges, skirt around the canal edge, flirting with the danger and thrill of it all while their parents yell at them to be careful. A woman lifts the lid off a giant wok, white steam rising from the braised meats and sizzling fried buns. Neon lights flicker over endless displays of food, some laid out in bamboo baskets and others in deep, sauce-filled trays: grilled lamb and quail egg skewers, green sticky rice cake stuffed with sweet bean paste and glazed, flaking mooncakes stamped with red characters. Little discount labels and QR codes are printed beneath them, likely for people using WeChat Pay.

"*Pe-ter*, what are you *doing*?"

Wei Laoshi's voice cuts through the vendors' calls and the distant splash of oars in water.

I whirl around.

A beggar who looks at least seventy years old has latched onto Peter Oh, her wrinkled hands seizing the fabric of his new Supreme hoodie. I would've expected Peter to shake her off—Baba's always warning me about how some beggars are really just scammers hiding iPhones under their rags—but to my surprise, he's holding out a crisp 100 RMB note. I search his expression; there's no trace of mockery or malice in his eyes, only sincerity. Even a hint of shyness.

The old woman's eyes widen, like she can't believe what she's seeing either. It makes my heart hurt. But before she can take the money from him, Wei Laoshi steps in between them and drags Peter away by the sleeve, ignoring his spluttered protests.

"Don't be so naive," Wei Laoshi scolds, grabbing the shiny pink note and tucking it firmly into Peter's pocket.

"It's not naive," Vanessa says as she paces forward suddenly, matching her steps to Peter's. Somehow, that girl manages to appear everywhere. Or maybe I've just been noticing her a lot more ever since the art scandal. "He was just being nice. Right, Peter?"

I don't stick around to hear the rest of their conversation. I don't *want* to hear it, to start thinking of Peter as the nice boy who trusts strangers and gives money to those who need it. He is a target for tonight, and nothing else.

My heart cannot soften.

"You all right?" Henry asks, slowing down near a small bridge. I realize then that the whole time I was watching Peter and Wei Laoshi, Henry was watching me.

"Sure," I say. Try to smile. "I guess… I just want to get it over with, you know?"

There's no need to elaborate; he nods.

Wei Laoshi calls for everyone to stop, tells us we're free to wander around and buy whatever snacks we want, but we'll be meeting back here in two hours so please be punctual and don't get kidnapped in the meantime. Everyone laughs at that, but my throat seizes up, and it takes three attempts before I can remember how to swallow again.

When the crowd disperses, Henry and I stay near the

bridge, eventually finding an old bench to sit on. For a while, we simply look out at the canals and crowded alleys in silence. Then he shifts closer toward me—only by an inch, maybe less, yet it somehow makes all the difference in the world— and the silence changes, crackles with electricity, demanding to be filled. His lashes lower. His eyes flicker to my lips...

I panic and blurt out the first thing I can think of: "Your dad."

He pulls back with a frown. "I beg your pardon?"

"Your dad," I repeat slowly. Too late to go back now. "Um... you never finished your story. On the train. About how things turned out with him."

Even as I'm saying the words, I want to kick myself. What kind of person ruins a potentially romantic moment by bringing up childhood trauma?

But Henry looks more surprised than offended. "You really want to know?"

"Yeah," I tell him, and even though this isn't the conversation I expected to have with him tonight, I mean it.

He doesn't reply at first. His gaze travels to a rowboat gliding out from under the bridge, a family of four huddled together on the seats, the youngest child squealing every time they bounce over a small wave. Then he sighs. Says, "I told you about how things were when I was around five. But shortly after I turned ten, during another long study session, I sort of..." He tilts his head, like he's recalling vocabulary from a foreign language. "What's that term again? When your emotions overpower rational thought and all regard for etiquette?"

"Exploded?" I offer, struggling to picture Henry doing such a thing. "Snapped? Totally lost your shit?"

He gives me a small, sheepish smile that makes my heartbeat spike. "Well, yes. Something to that effect. My father was shocked, of course, but he actually ended up apologizing. Promised he would never use such...extreme measures again." He glances back down at the family in the boat, their faces bright with moonshine and laughter. "And he never did."

"Wow." I shake my head. "Just like that?"

"It probably helped that I was doing so well at school, and that I already showed interest in running the company. But I also imagine that he simply hadn't realized there were alternative ways of effective parenting. *His* father had been even stricter with him about his studies, and so when he got into Harvard and founded SYS and became successful—"

"The results seemed to validate the process," I finish for him, remembering our earlier conversation.

"Exactly."

Henry rubs his eyes, and for one bizarre moment, I think he's crying. But then he lets his hands fall back down in his lap, the lantern light from the shops around us throwing his features into sharp relief, and the truth dawns on me, so simple I almost laugh—he's *tired*.

He had been lying today, when Chanel asked him if he'd slept well. Neither of us had slept at all on the train; we'd stayed up finalizing our plans, then the backup plans, and then one of us—I can't remember who—got sidetracked and we just...talked. About school, about his brief time in England, about the games his sister used to invent when they were kids, the Shanghainese dishes his mother made him whenever he was sick. About everything and nothing all at once, laughter and half-coherent thoughts spilling out of my lips before I could stop them. I don't think either of us had been expecting the night to go as it did.

"You can sleep now, you know," I tell Henry.

"What?" Bemusement draws his eyebrows together, and he juts his chin out—a familiar movement I'd once mistaken for arrogance, but have come to recognize as only a trick to mask his confusion.

"I mean it—you should get some rest," I say. "You're obviously exhausted, and who knows when we'll be able to sleep at the hotel?" *If we can fall asleep at all*, I add silently, a bolt of guilt striking through me.

Henry searches my face for a beat, his eyes narrowed. "You're being too nice," he says finally. "It's suspicious."

"I'm being practical. I need you alert and awake for the job tonight."

Still, he hesitates. "You're absolutely certain this is not part of some elaborate scheme to take unflattering photos of me sleeping and blackmail me with them?"

"If I wanted to do that," I point out, "I could literally just sneak into your bedroom when I'm invisible and snap as many photos of you as I want."

"That's very comforting."

But he does close his eyes, though his head remains propped up in such an uncomfortable position I offer him my shoulder as a pillow. Within only a few minutes, his breathing slows. The muscles in his body relax.

I smile and look up. Streaks of dark, wet pink and glistening blue seep through the sky like spilled watercolor, while floating lanterns rise gently over the horizon like ghosts. A soft breeze drifts over my skin, carrying with it the fragrance of chrysanthemums and fresh-baked pastries from the snack stalls below.

Then there's Henry.

Henry, whose head is resting against my shoulder, the soft curls of his hair brushing my cheek, his features smooth and unguarded in sleep. And everything about this moment is so lovely and so fragile in its loveliness that I'm almost afraid to hold it. Afraid that the spell will break.

If not for the kidnapping, I think to myself, *today might've been a perfect day.*

15

We reach the hotel by 10:30 p.m.

By 10:48 p.m., I've unpacked all my luggage and told Chanel I'll be going over to Henry's. She winks at me and makes a not-so-subtle remark about protection. I let her believe what she likes; besides, in the worst-case scenario, at least I'll have a decent alibi.

By 11:00 p.m., I've visited both the twentieth and ninth floor, taking the stairs to double-check for any hidden security cameras and measuring precisely how long it takes to get from one place to the other.

By 11:15 p.m., I've sought out Henry's room, still fully visible, and slipped through the door when no one's around.

By 11:21 p.m., I've officially started panicking.

"Am I invisible yet?" I demand as I pace in front of Henry, even though I know it's unlikely. I haven't suffered through that telltale rush of cold yet, and if anything, I feel too hot, my skin burning, the room stuffy and suffocating despite its vast size.

"You are most decidedly not," Henry says, crossing his legs over the plush bedside sofa, the gesture so casual I want to scream. How does he manage to maintain such *calm* in a time like this?

"What about now?"

"No."

"Now?"

"No."

"How about—"

"Do you intend to keep this up for the rest of the night?" Henry interrupts, lifting an eyebrow.

"Well, what else are we supposed to do?" I snap. "Netflix and chill?"

His brows rise higher.

And suddenly my face is burning too. Hastily, I add, "I meant in the literal sense, of course."

"Of course."

The conversation settles into silence for a moment, save for my frantic footsteps on the carpeted floor and the low, persistent hum of the mini fridge. Then—

"Okay, fine, That's it." I press a hand to my throbbing temples. This is the third stress headache I've had since we left the night market. "If you can think of any way to distract me from my sense of impending doom, go right ahead. Entertain me."

Henry seems to take this as a challenge. He sits up impossibly straighter, dark eyes pensive, and says, "There's actually something I've been meaning to ask for a while now..."

"No, I wasn't the one who sabotaged your science project in Year Nine," I tell him automatically. "Though, if we're being honest here, I did consider it for a while—only because you were acting so smug about getting advice from Jack Ma himself."

"That...is not at all what I was going to ask, but good to know," Henry says. Clears his throat. "What I'd really like to understand, though, is why you hate me so much."

I blink at him in surprise.

"For the record," I begin slowly, my mind struggling to assemble a proper response. "I don't hate you anymore."

A flash of a smile, so quick I almost miss it. Still, he doesn't let the question go. "But you did before."

I nod once. Sigh. "Do you remember that Scholars Cup competition we both entered in Year Eight? The one they held in front of the whole school?"

"Vaguely."

"Well, I remember it vividly." The press of the warm auditorium lights against my eyelids, the weight of everyone's gazes on me, the loud buzzing in my ears as I fumbled over my last question. The triumphant look on Henry's face when he answered his; the look of someone born and destined to win. "After I lost the final round to you...after you went to collect your trophy and soak in all the teachers' praise, and I was ushered away offstage... I fled to my room and just—just *sobbed*. I didn't even eat anything that day, I was so angry with myself..."

I swallow, hard. The memory still brings a lump of shame to my throat.

"And I know it sounds ridiculous because it was—I mean,

let's be honest, it was *Year Eight*, and the competition wasn't even compulsory. But there was a cash prize, 500 RMB, and I'd spent months preparing for that thing. Yet right before we got on stage, I overheard you talking about how you'd entered it last minute, on a whim, how you had more important things to do than study for it anyway and—I don't know. Everything was always so *easy* for you." I draw in a tight breath. "Being around you just made me feel awful. It made me hate myself, and over time... I guess that hate grew so big it had nowhere to go but—"

"—toward me," Henry finishes, a strain in his voice. "Right?"

"But I don't feel that way anymore," I say, feeling an inexplicable, overwhelming need to make this very clear. "I promise. Swear on my heart."

Some emotion I can't name passes over his face. He reaches out, his fingers forming a warm circle around my wrist, and I stop walking. Stop everything. "Then tell me," he says, very quietly. "What exactly do you feel toward me now?"

"I—" Confusion tangles my tongue, speeds up my pulse. Dimly, I think: *He really is good at this whole distraction thing.* "Why does it matter?"

"You really don't know?"

I stare at him. Something is happening, I can sense it, but just like his expression, it's impossible for me to decipher. "Know... Know what?"

He lets go of my wrist, dragging a hand through his hair instead. "Good god," he says with a little laugh. Shakes his head. "For one of the most intelligent people I've ever met, you can really be quite oblivious sometimes."

And maybe it's the way he's gazing up at me, somehow tormented and tender at the same time, or maybe it's the weird half compliment, or maybe it's every small, subtle moment I've missed along the way, now catching up to me in an adrenaline-induced burst of clarity, but all of a sudden—

"*Oh,*" I breathe.

Oh. Wow.

I sit down on the carpet, dizzy with comprehension.

After a few minutes of pure, unadulterated silence, I realize Henry's watching me, sharp-eyed and tight jawed, waiting for my response. This might be the most nervous I've ever seen him.

"Good," I manage at last. "It's good. For me as well."

I don't expect him to get anything out of my ridiculous jumble of words, but he does.

He moves so our knees are close to touching, and I ask without thinking, "Is this the part where you kiss me?"

He leans closer, and even in the dim hotel lights, I can make out the silent laughter in his eyes. "That was not my intention." A pause, teasing. "Why? Did you want me to?"

"What? N-no, of course not," I stammer, twisting away at once. Then, because I'm physically incapable of keeping my mouth shut, I babble on, "It's just—you know, in the movies…when it gets to this kind of scene, with this kind of lighting—"

There's a sharp rap on the door.

We both freeze.

It almost gives me whiplash, how quickly the mood changes, like having your emotional, family-friendly farm animal movie interrupted by a cheery ad from McDonald's.

Another knock. Even louder than the first.

The irrational, already terrified part of my brain is convinced the police have found us somehow, that they're waiting to arrest us right this second, that it's over, my life is ruined—

But then I hear a girl's giggle. Someone else whispers something I can't quite catch, and the giggle turns into a muffled shriek of laughter.

Henry and I exchange a quick, silent look, and from the grim set of his jaw, I know we've arrived at the same conclusion. The room's lights are on; there's no point pretending he isn't inside.

"Who is it?" Henry calls.

"Guess!" a voice that's obviously Rainie's replies.

Henry moves toward the door in slow, careful strides, hands held up, the way you're meant to approach an animal in the wild. "Er... Rainie? What are you doing here?"

"To see you, of course," she says, the same time another person shouts:

"We heard you got the best suite, dude! Let us in—we want to check it out!"

At this rate, they're going to wake up the entire hotel.

And to make everything so much worse, at least two others—god, how many people *are there* outside the door right now?—start chanting: *"Let us in! Let us in! Let us in!"*

Henry glances at me in a there's-nothing-we-can-do kind of way, and despite the stone in my stomach, I nod.

"Okay—just be quiet you lot," Henry says as he pulls the door open. Immediately, Rainie Lam, Bobby Yu, Vanessa Liu, and Mina Huang stumble into the room in a giggling heap, bringing with them the strong, unmistakeable scent of alcohol.

"Wonderful," Henry mutters under his breath.

But even in their intoxicated state, our four unwelcome guests stop and stare when they realize I'm here as well. Vanessa almost drops the half-empty bottle of Jack Daniel's in her hands. Bobby's mouth opens so wide I'm tempted to ask if his jaw hurts.

Rainie actually gasps. *"Alice?"*

"Hi," I say.

After the four of them have recovered from their initial shock and voiced their suspicions that Henry and I are secretly dating, they make themselves at home, lounging on the plum-colored sofa and the king-sized bed. They show zero sign of planning to go back to their rooms anytime tonight.

I want to vomit.

I want to scream and shove them all back out the door.

But instead I just smile and smile as Vanessa fumbles through the mini fridge for a packet of Pringles chips and Rainie pulls out a speaker and starts playing one of her mother's hit singles, swaying and belting out the lyrics as if we're in a karaoke bar, and Bobby Yu starts doing pushups on the carpet.

The smile remains frozen on my face. Only my eyes move, checking my reflection in the window, tracking the time. The neon alarm beside Henry's bed flashes: 11:59 PM.

I'm still not invisible yet.

At some point, Rainie gets tired of singing and turns the music down, and starts bitching about Julie Walsh instead. Everyone joins in enthusiastically, even Mina, who hardly ever talks, and Rainie does an impression of Julie that's so accurate Vanessa falls back on the floor and cries real tears of laughter.

Then the conversation turns to who they think might hook up by the end of this trip, then how much of an asshole Jake Nguyen is ("I can't believe I used to like, *like* him," Rainie laments, and Bobby complains that most girls have bad taste while Mina gives her a few sympathetic pats on the shoulder), then about what Drunk Henry would look like.

"It's just funny to imagine," Rainie says between giggles. She points to Henry, who's been standing stiffly in the corner of the room beside me this whole time. "Because you're so—so—what's the word?"

"Aloof?" Vanessa suggests.

"Composed?" Mina offers.

"Hot?" Bobby says, and we all turn to stare at him. "What?" He scowls. "The dude is objectively good-looking. Don't judge me for saying it aloud."

But *perfect* is the term Rainie settles on.

"God, you're so perfect," she says with a little hiccup. Then, to my surprise, her eyes flicker to me as well. "And you, Alice. Both of you. King Henry and the Study Machine. Our perfect model students."

I force myself to laugh along with them, but everything sounds off. The compliment burns on its way down like acid.

If only you knew what Airington's two model students were up to tonight.

But beneath the panic, beneath all the guilt, there's another emotion clawing at my chest. Resentment. Because if it weren't for the school fees and Beijing Ghost and the terrible task waiting ahead, this night would be...everything.

I would be able to join in their silly gossip and laugh with Rainie and maybe work up the nerve to sit close to Henry, continue right where we left off, snake my fingers through his. I would be just a teenager, giddy in a fancy hotel in a beautiful new city, with old classmates and potential new friends: Rainie, who gave too much of herself to a boy who took too much; Mina, whose parents recently got back together after a messy divorce, and are working to patch everything up; Bobby, whose older sister ran away three years ago, but you'd never know it from looking at him now.

I would actually be *happy* with these people, carefree—not checking the cursed clock every two seconds and waiting for a strange wave of cold to soak through my body.

It makes me almost dizzy, thinking about the stark differences in realities, what will be and what could've been. But that's the kind of difference wealth creates.

By the time I tune back into the conversation, the topic's moved on to Beijing Ghost.

"...wonder who's behind it," Vanessa is saying. "Oh, come on, Alice, don't act as if you haven't heard of the app," she adds irritably, misreading my stunned expression.

"I have heard of Beijing Ghost," I say, choosing my words with care. My heart is pounding so hard I wouldn't be surprised if they could all hear. "But I don't know who's behind it."

"Well, *obviously*," Vanessa says, rolling her eyes, and relief washes over me. "No one does. Though there's plenty of theories going around."

Bobby nods, then winces, as though the movement makes his head hurt. "Some people think the app's run by, like, a top government spy who just wants to make a quick buck.

Sorta makes sense, if you really consider it—they'd have all the right connections and the technology to make it work."

"Bobby," Rainie says, with the air of an adult speaking to a very naive child. "Top government spies don't need to build their own illegal school app to get rich quick. That's what bribery is for."

"Who d'you reckon it is, then?" Bobby challenges.

"I don't know," Rainie says, grabbing the whiskey bottle from Vanessa and gulping down the rest of the brown liquid in one go. Then she wipes her mouth roughly with the back of her sleeve. "But whoever it is—they're a hero."

Hero.

Another compliment, and from Rainie Lam, out of all people, but the word only chafes my conscience. I can't bring myself to meet her gaze.

"I'm going to do it," Vanessa says abruptly, pushing herself onto her feet with surprising steadiness. Even though she's had more alcohol than the rest of the bunch, she also seems the most sober—which, considering the fact that Bobby is now balancing the room service menu on his head like a hat, isn't saying much.

"Do what?" Mina asks.

"Confess," Vanessa says, and maybe she's drunker than I think she is, because I have no idea what she means.

Rainie does, though. "Let her go," she tells all of us as Vanessa staggers toward the door, fumbling twice to turn the knob. "She's been crushing hard on this guy for ages."

The menu slides off Bobby's head with a loud flapping sound as he turns, eyes wide. "Who?"

But whatever the answer is, I don't hear it. A chill has

started creeping up my spine, and before I'm forced to prove Bobby's government conspiracy theory incorrect firsthand, I leap up, mumble something about checking to see if Vanessa's okay, and run.

16

I knock once on Peter's door and try to steady my erratic breathing.

Taking the lift was too risky—there are always security cameras on those things, and it'd be impossible to explain a button lighting up on its own if someone else were inside—so I ran all the way up the stairs instead. The entire back of my shirt is soaked through with sweat, but it's hard to tell if that's because of the physical exertion, or the worry chewing a hole through my stomach.

After what feels like a lifetime, I hear the metallic click of the lock, and the door swings open.

Jake Nguyen squints into the hallway light, his hair a mess, one of those white hotel bathrobes draped over his bare shoulders like a villain's cape. The room behind him is dark, the curtains drawn. Beside the empty single bed by the window, I can make out Peter Oh's sleeping figure.

"What the hell," Jake grumbles, staring straight through me. He scratches his head. "Is anyone there?"

He waits a full two seconds before moving to close the door again, and I duck inside just in time. But as I fumble my way further into the room, I trip over something hard—Jake's foot. He tenses, the faint bathroom light outlining the crease between his brows.

My heart stops.

"Who was that?" Peter grumbles, his voice thick with sleep and muffled by the pillow.

Jake glances over again at the spot where I tripped, then shakes his head. "No one. Probably the cleaning lady or some dude who got the wrong door."

I stay completely still as he shuffles back to bed in his slippers, falling onto the covers with a loud yawn.

Only when he starts snoring do I creep over to Peter's bed.

He's curled up on his side like a little boy, the corner of his blanket covering his stomach, an arm resting under his head. He looks peaceful. Unsuspecting.

Undeserving of what's about to happen.

I'm so sorry, Peter, I think, as I set the prepared note down on his pillow, inches away from his nose.

It's been typed out on glossy, business card–like paper, containing only the lines:

Peter.
Please come and visit me in
Room 2005 as soon as you see this.
I have something important
I want to tell you in person.

Andrew wanted to make sure that the message couldn't possibly be traced back to him, so there are no digital receipts, none of his fingerprints, none of his handwriting. Deciding on what to actually say in the message was the other issue. I'd gone back and forth on a mock note from one of the teachers, or something with a more romantic tone, or mentioning someone he cared about.

But in the end I decided to go with something vague. Something that will hopefully pique his interest enough for him to follow the instructions.

Now Peter just needs to read it.

I take a deep breath. Flex my trembling fingers. Realize that this is my last chance to turn back, to retract everything, but I'm already here and the note has been arranged and I've never quit anything halfway before, not if I can control it—

So instead I shake Peter's shoulders gently and wait for him to wake.

He opens his eyes slowly.

Blinks around in the darkness, disorientation washing over his face like the shadows from the curtains.

I watch him rub a sleepy hand over his cheek. Watch him turn just an inch on the pillow and freeze, his gaze landing on the note. Watch him pick it up carefully, still a little disorientated, and read through the lines.

He pauses. Clicks on the night-light.

Instinctively, I crouch down to conceal myself from view, even though of course he can't see me anyway.

"Jake?" Peter calls, voice hoarse. "Did you... Did you see anyone come in here?"

But Jake is still snoring. He hasn't moved an inch.

Peter glances down at the note in his hands again, turning it over and over as if to make sure it's real, and my heart is racing so loudly I'm convinced it's going to give me away. He doesn't hear it, though. He studies the note a beat longer, then stands up, shrugging on the denim jacket laid out on his bedside table. His eyes are more alert now, his body tensed.

The air feels impossibly still.

I don't dare breathe until Peter slides his phone and the note into his pocket and heads out the door.

I follow close behind him.

Out in the bright hotel hallway, Peter heads straight for the elevators. I knew he would, but it's still inconvenient. As soon as he presses the glowing square button to go up, I press it too, turning it back off. For everything to go smoothly, Peter has to use the stairs. After my inspection of the area earlier tonight, that's the only place I know for certain where there won't be any security cameras to catch his movements.

Peter frowns. Tries again.

And again, I hit the button right after him, careful not to brush against his hand in the process.

His frown deepens. He moves to the lift on the other end of the hall, where I repeat the motion the same number of times he does, until eventually he gives up and swears under his breath.

"Stairs it is then," he mutters.

Henry was supposed to patrol the area to make sure no student or teacher sees Peter, but he's clearly still stuck in his room with Rainie and the others. *Never mind*, I tell myself as I follow Peter around the corner. I just have to avoid Vanessa, wherever she is now, and hope no one comes out for a midnight stroll through the corridors.

Though the rest of the hotel is all spotless marble surfaces, elaborate flower decorations and well-lit carpeted halls, the stairs are dark and steep and slightly uneven, everything coated in a thin layer of dust. The shadowy corners reek of garbage and disinfectant.

Peter climbs up the steps with surprising, enviable ease; I have to hurry just to keep up with him, but soon I have an awful stitch in my side and a thousand small, protesting aches in my legs and lungs.

Times like this almost make me wish I'd devoted as much effort to PE class as my academic subjects.

Then again, I doubt any number of burpees and torturous basketball warm-up exercises could've prepared me for a covert kidnapping operation in one of Suzhou's tallest hotels.

By the time we've reached the twentieth floor, an obscene amount of sweat has dripped down my back, plastering my shirt to my skin, and I can't quite tell if it's from the sheer physical exertion of the climb or my nerves.

We're so very close now. The door is just up ahead of us, down the first corridor—I can see it. And Peter doesn't have the faintest clue what's about to happen—

No.

I give myself a mental shake. This isn't so different from a prank. Just a higher-stakes version...with corporate executives involved.

Besides, Andrew She's men aren't *actually* going to lock him up forever or abuse and murder him. Andrew even promised me Peter would be well-fed and cared for until the promotions were announced, which should be in less than a week from now.

It'll be fine. Peter will be fine. I'm doing the right thing. Right?

Peter's stopped outside the room now, the numbers *2005* gleaming bright gold in the light, like some kind of sign. An invitation. Andrew She's men are waiting for him on the other side of the door.

And one million RMB is waiting for me. A future at Airington. A better future, period.

All I have to do is see Peter through it.

He clears his throat softly, adjusts the collar of his jacket, and I wonder if he can sense that something's wrong. If he's thinking about turning around, running away to the safety of his own hotel room.

I don't realize just how much I want him to do exactly that until he raps the door once, shoulders braced.

And everything happens very quickly.

Too quickly—so quick that it's almost anticlimactic.

The door swings open and I think I catch a glimpse of a gloved hand reaching out, pulling him in, and I manage to grab Peter's phone from his pocket just in time for the door to slam shut again, with Peter trapped behind it.

There's a rustling sound from inside, a series of *thuds*, and Peter's voice, more confused than afraid: "What are you—"

Then it cuts off into silence. Just like that.

It isn't violent. It isn't anything.

If I weren't gripping Peter's phone so tight my knuckles bled white, I'd think he was never here at all.

I stare at the door for a long time, as though in a dream, a nightmare, until a small voice in the back of my head urges: *Leave.*

Get out of here. Your job is done.

I tear my eyes away and move, but the second I turn the corner, my legs give way beneath me.

I sink straight to the floor as if someone's removed all the bones from my body. I gasp for air that doesn't seem to be there, wait for the sick feeling in the pit of my stomach to go away because I'm safe—I did what I had to—I succeeded—

But the sick sensation only grows. Nausea rises up my throat, filling my mouth with saliva, the sour taste of regret.

God, I must be the worst criminal in the world.

I should be celebrating. I should be thinking about all the money that'll be added to my bank account. *One million RMB.* Enough for me to never have to stress about being sent off to Maine or a local school again. I won't even have to stress about college.

But instead, all I can focus on is whatever's happening on the other side of that door. Peter had stopped talking midsentence. Does that mean they'd gagged him? Hit him? Surely I would've heard it if they did…

Peter's phone beeps.

I almost jump out of my skin. My hands are shaking as I hold up the screen, expecting to see some kind of criminal alert or imposter warning or a message from the police.

But it's none of that. It's worse.

It's a Kakao message from his mom.

Are u having a good time in Suzhou??

U must already be sleeping (if not, go to bed right now!!! your body still growing), but your father and I miss u very much. He wanted to call u earlier, but you know how busy work has been for him... It'll all be worth it when he wins the campaign.

Oh! We made some yummy fish today. Here is a pic.

There's a somewhat blurry photo of a half-eaten grilled fish dish below, a pair of chopsticks lying casually beside the plate, and the hunched-over silhouette of a man in the back-ground. Peter's father, most likely.

My chest tightens, tightens until I can't breathe. The back of my eyes burn.

But more messages are coming in.

It's a new recipe, and your father says it's very good. I'll make some for u as soon as u get home (and your favorite black bean noodles too)

Take care, my son. Make sure you eat well and stay safe and wear a lot of warm clothes! I checked the weather and it says it's going to be cold in Suzhou tomorrow. Remember your health matters more than "fashion"

Your father is scolding me for nagging you now, so I will stop here

We love you always. Give us a call when you can!

I turn the screen down, my stomach in knots.

I should throw Peter's phone away. Now. Crush it and destroy all the evidence, make sure no one can track him or contact him, just like I was told to do. This is the last stage of our plan. Once I'm rid of his phone, I'll be able to go back to my room and forget about this whole task for good. But—

God, his parents are going to be so worried. And they have every reason to be.

The worst part is that I've *met* his parents before. They'd volunteered to help out at the Global Community Day festival a year ago. His father had bragged to everyone who came within a five-foot radius of him about his genius, hardworking son, beaming so wide the entire time it must've hurt his face, and his mother, with her sharp tongue and small frame, the way she'd scolded Peter for not wearing a warm-enough jacket, had reminded me of Mama.

And if someone were to call Mama up in the middle of the night to tell her I'd disappeared in a city far away from home—

No.

Stop it.

It's too late. I just have to get up. Move. Put as much distance between me and this place—this memory—as possible.

After who knows how long, I finally manage to pull myself back up into a standing position. My feet move obediently toward the stairs, in the same direction I came from. I take one step. Then another. Somehow, it's more exhausting than climbing up a mountain.

I can't stop thinking about Peter in that room.

About his mother, who's still waiting to welcome him home with his favorite dish. Who won't be able to sleep once she finds out he's gone.

Whatever you do, do not turn around, I command myself, even as my feet drag against the carpet. *Do not turn around. Do not fucking turn arou—*

I turn around.

Without even fully realizing what I'm doing, I run back to Room 2005 and pound on the door.

"R-room service for two." My voice is a terrible, breathless squeak. It occurs to me too late how utterly unprepared I am. My own phone's battery is running low, and Henry has no idea what I'm planning to do, and the only weapon I have on me is a fruit knife I took from my hotel room. But it's also too late to go back now. "Club sandwich with truffle fries." This is the code Andrew and I agreed upon in case I needed to speak to his men directly. I can only pray it works.

At first, there's nothing but deafening silence on the other end. Then footsteps approach, slow and cautious. After a few seconds of just-audible murmuring and shuffling around, the door creaks open.

I glance up.

Three men tower over me. They're dressed in identical business suits, their striped ties straight and well ironed, all wearing dark pollution masks that cover most of their faces and fitted, surgical gloves. They don't look anything like the kidnappers I'd been imagining. In fact, if I didn't know any better, I'd think I had accidentally stumbled into a private business meeting.

The tallest of the three stares into the space behind me. "Hello?" He cranes his neck, opens the door wider. "Anyone there?"

I creep in past him.

The first thing I notice is that the TV is on, the sound turned off, and the other men's eyes are glued to a basketball game playing over the large flat screen. I guess holding a kid hostage can get pretty boring after a while.

The next thing I notice is Peter, and my heart drops to the pit of my stomach.

He's been pushed into the farthest corner of the room, blindfolded and gagged, the ropes still secured firmly around his wrists, feet, and waist. Andrew She had made it sound like Peter would be resting in a nice little resort until the company campaign was over, but this—this is too much.

There's no way in hell I can leave him here like this.

As I rush toward him, I hear the tall man mutter, "So strange." Then: "Who did She Zong's son hire for the job again?"

The man standing closest to the TV shrugs. "Person from some kind of black market app. Apparently it's built a solid reputation around their school for doing whatever people want."

"But no one knows who it is? Or how they managed to drop this kid"—the tall one jerks a finger at Peter, and I freeze, careful not to give my presence away—"right off at our door?"

"Nope."

When the three of them have turned back to the TV, I crawl forward, shaking violently all over. My fingers fumble for the ropes behind the chair, and I feel Peter stiffen.

Please act normal. I'm trying to help you, I think desperately.

If only my powers included telepathy as well.

As Peter twists his head around, I yank hard at the final knot, ignoring the burn of the ropes against my skin.

Please, please—

The ropes drop to the floor with a soft *thud*, like a dead

snake, and I've barely had time to breathe out in relief when three things happen at roughly the same time:

One, Peter rips off the blindfold, stumbles out of the chair and looks wildly around before staring at me. *Right at me.* His mouth drops open, then closes over the unspoken word: *Alice?*

Two, Andrew She's men spin toward me and Peter with varying expressions of shock. The tall one moves first, leaping over the bed and yelling at us to stay right where we are—

Three, I throw the closest thing I can find to stop him. Which, unfortunately, happens to be a pillow.

A fucking pillow.

The pillow bounces off the seven-foot kidnapper's shoulder as he growls and swipes at us, undeterred. I shove Peter in front of me and try to run after him to the door, but I'm too slow. A rough hand closes over my wrist, yanking me back so hard I wouldn't be surprised if my arm's been dislocated.

I gasp. Tears jump to my eyes.

"Where did you come from, little girl?" the man demands. His grip tightens, crushing my bones to dust. The pain is unbearable, but still I pull against him, my feet kicking out wildly, my eyes darting over the room.

In my blurred, peripheral vision, I see Peter duck past the two other men, unlatch the lock with shocking speed and fling the door open—just as they tackle him from behind. There's a terrible *crack* as his head hits the wall.

The world seems to flip upside down, my stomach flipping with it.

"*No!*" I scream.

The tall man follows my gaze, and in the split second he's distracted, I sink my teeth into his hand.

He releases me with a high-pitched cry and I bolt. The two others still have their attention fastened on Peter, who's slouched against the wall, and I'm panicking about how the hell I'm meant to get around them when I remember—

The knife.

My fingers dig into my pockets, finding the cool, smooth hilt at once.

"Stand back or—or I'll cut you," I warn the men as I step forward, brandishing the fruit knife before me like a proper sword, praying they can't see how badly my hands are trembling. How much I feel like a little kid playing pretend.

The two men falter—more out of surprise than fear, it seems, but whatever works.

I seize the opportunity to grab Peter and shake him. His face has gone scarily pale, and his hairline is wet with blood, but his eyes—his eyes are open. With a low groan, he rises back to his feet, and I don't think I've ever felt such acute relief in my life.

"A-Alice," he chokes out. "Weren't you—what—"

This kid can't seriously think now is the time for a conversation.

"Talk later," I snap, gripping his sleeve and pulling as hard as I can. God, he's heavy. "Get up. *Come on.*"

But before Peter can stand, I notice a flash of movement out of the corner of my eye. I'm too slow to react. With a grunt, the first kidnapper lunges at me, knocking me headfirst to the ground.

Pain explodes over my body.

I try to move, to fight, but a sharp knee digs into my back, the kidnapper's full weight pinning me into place. The knife is ripped from my hand.

No, no, no.

This can't be happening.

A shrill ringing sound fills my ears, so loud I can barely hear what the kidnapper is barking at the two other men. Something about taking Peter. The car. Transferring…

The men obey immediately. Together, they trap Peter between them and roughly hoist him up by the arms. Peter doesn't even resist; he seems to have gone into shock, his eyes wide and his jaw hanging open as they drag him toward the door.

This cannot be happening. This *can't be*—

But it is.

All I can do is watch in horror, the hotel carpet scratching the side of my cheek.

And just when I think things couldn't possibly get any worse, the first kidnapper starts to tie up my hands, with the same kind of rope he must've used to tie Peter up earlier. Fuck, how much rope do these people *have*? He's fumbling with the ends—he probably knows he doesn't have much time left—and he's distracted, but he's also strong. I feel him wrap the rope once, twice, pulling it hard enough to cut my circulation off.

My arms go numb.

Then the pressure eases off my back, and the kidnapper's leaving. He's leaving with the two masked men and Peter, who's bleeding, and I'm still here on the floor with my hands tied, and everything hurts, and I can't believe I landed myself in this situation.

I count the kidnapper's footsteps as they get farther and farther away from me.

One. Two. Three.

The door whines open, then shuts, leaving me alone in total darkness.

There's no time to panic.

As soon as the kidnappers are gone, I'm half rolling, half wriggling across the floor until I bump into something hard. A desk corner, maybe.

Good enough.

I turn around awkwardly, blindly, so that my bound hands are pressed tight against whatever the sharp edge is. Then I begin to move them back and forth like a saw, praying for the ropes to snag.

"Come on," I mutter, and the sound of my own voice, low and much steadier than I feel inside, helps ground me a little. "Come on, *come on*."

It's working, I think. I hope. Already, it feels like the ropes aren't digging into my skin as much as before. Maybe if I just apply more pressure here, and twist my wrists this way—

Yes.

The ropes come loose after the ninth try; some combination of finding the right angle, the disgusting amount of sweat slicking my hands, and the lucky fact that the kidnapper didn't have time to double knot.

I toss the ropes aside and scramble toward the door, ignoring the weakness in my knees, the tingling in my fingers. The tightness in my lungs.

Save Peter. That's all that matters right now.

As I flip the lock and burst through the doorway, squinting into the sudden light, I try to figure out where the kidnappers would go.

It seems unlikely they'd hang around an area where Peter could easily be recognized. And they'd mentioned something about transferring Peter, about a car—

The parking lot.

But not just any parking lot. A secluded spot, connected to the stairs instead of the lift, a place without security cameras to catch suspicious activity.

I run down the stairs, taking two steps at a time, my mind reeling. I've spent so long committing the map of the hotel to memory that I can see it as clearly as if someone's holding it in front of me: all the labels marking out cameras and exits, the lines intersecting at corridors and staircases...and the diagram of the abandoned lot two levels underground.

That's where they're taking Peter. It must be.

Now I just have to find them before they leave.

I move faster. My feet slam over the concrete, my heart beating so hard I'm scared it'll explode. I wish I were an athlete. I wish I had been quicker to unfasten the ropes, or to escape with Peter when I had the chance. I wish I'd never agreed to kidnap Peter in the first place.

Numbers flash by me as I make my way down flight after flight of stairs.

Level Fifteen.

Level Twelve.

Ten.

Seven.

"Alice!"

I stumble to a stop. Whip my head around, half certain I'm hallucinating.

But there's Henry, standing only a few steps above me, the neon exit sign casting a red glow over his features. His eyes are dark with concern.

"I was looking everywhere for you," he says, coming down toward me, his footsteps light and swift. "I managed to get away from Rainie and..." He pauses, his gaze raking over my face. "What happened? Did they hurt you?"

I shake my head, too winded to speak at first.

My lungs and legs feel like lead, and there's an awful knife-sharp stitch in my side. It takes everything I have not to double over.

"They—they took Peter—" I finally manage, my voice a dry croak. "We have to—save him—"

I wait for the barrage of questions, the moment of disbelief, but Henry doesn't even look surprised at this dramatic turn of events. He simply rolls up his sleeves and says, "Okay. Let's go."

I can't believe I ever wanted to push this boy off a stage.

Somehow, with Henry by my side, it's a little easier to run down the remaining stairs. And by easier, I mean it doesn't feel *quite* like I'm dying a slow, excruciating death. Still, white dots have started to dance over my vision by the time we reach the entrance to the parking lot.

The air is colder underground, wet and dense with the stench of petrol fumes. I try not to choke as we hide behind a half-open door, our backs to the wall, and listen. I try not to entertain the possibility that we might be too late.

But then I hear it—

The angry squeak of shoes, of rubber against concrete. Male voices bouncing off the walls, amplified by the open space. The loud slam of a car trunk.

Henry and I exchange a quick look.

We've pulled off enough Beijing Ghost tasks together to know what needs to happen next.

I watch as Henry adjusts his posture, straightening so that he looks even taller than usual, fixes his shirt collar, and smooths his hair with one hand. In an instant, he's no longer just Henry, but *Henry Li*, son of a self-made billionaire, someone who wears their privileged upbringing and powerful connections like a badge. Someone untouchable.

But that doesn't stop my stomach from knotting over and over with worry when he strides out the door.

"Hey," he calls in flawless Mandarin. Even his voice sounds deeper, older, which is good. If the kidnappers don't take him seriously, we're pretty much screwed.

His appearance is met with abrupt silence.

The tension makes my skin itch.

I hold my breath and count to fourteen before someone grunts, "Who are you?" They sound closer than I expected— no more than twenty feet away from the door.

"I should be asking you that," comes Henry's smooth reply. "What are you wearing masks for?"

"None of your business."

"It is my business, actually," Henry says, and I imagine him tilting his head to the side, his brows raised, condescension written all over his face. "My father owns this hotel, see, and I'm sure he'd like to know why there are three strange, masked men sneaking around our unused parking lot in the middle of the night. If you don't want to tell *me,* maybe I can invite him or the hotel manager over to—"

"*Fine,*" the man snaps. "If you *must know,* we're headed to a nightclub, that's all. Didn't want our wives catching us."

Despite myself, I almost roll my eyes. Even their excuses make them sound like complete assholes.

"Can we go now?" another one of the kidnappers demands.

"No, you cannot," Henry says. "Since your car is here, you need to pay for parking."

"But—"

"Payment is nonnegotiable. Of course, you can use We-Chat Pay if you'd prefer, or scan this QR code on my phone, or get a discount by signing into your hotel account, then registering through one of our five affiliates…"

While Henry rambles on about hotel policies and bank sponsors and viable memberships, I sneak out through the door. The scene that greets me looks like something out of a low-budget action film: the parking lot is empty, save for an old dust-covered van rotting away in the far corner and a sleek black vehicle that's surrounded by three men. All of them have their backs toward me, their attention on Henry.

Henry, who's positioned his body directly in front of the car, has rested both hands on the hood, so they'd have to run over him just to drive away.

It's a good strategy, I reason with myself, fighting the strong compulsion to push Henry out of the way, to protect him. *They wouldn't want to—wouldn't dare—kill the son of the hotel owner. It'd get far too messy.*

I just have to rescue Peter before the kidnappers lose their patience, and their ability to think rationally.

Careful not to make a sound, I duck my head and creep closer to the car trunk, heart pounding in my throat. Then I get a good look at the license plate: N150Q4. Sear it into my brain.

Henry is still talking. "...Bank of China is actually offering a limited-time promotion on the app—"

"Wait," the man at the front interrupts, and the shift in his tone—from annoyance to something else, something like suspicion—leaves my mouth dry. I glance up.

Henry doesn't move, though his eyes are wary. "What?"

"I think I recognize you," the man says, and everything seems to freeze. Blur at the edges. The lights overhead flicker and the low parking lot ceiling threatens to collapse on me. "You—you were in that magazine article. And that *China Insider* interview... You're the son of the SYS founder, aren't you?"

For a split second, panic flashes over Henry's features.

Only a second. But it's enough.

"Who sent you?" the kidnapper growls, stepping around the car's blazing headlights, his shadow stretching out menacingly over the concrete. He advances on Henry. *"Who?"*

Before I can react, Henry raises a fist and swings it into the man's face. *Hard.* I swear I hear the crack of bone as the man hisses and stumbles backward, hands covering his nose, and all my thoughts fracture—

Henry punched somebody.

Henry punched somebody.

Henry Li just punched somebody.

Nothing about this night feels real.

Henry looks almost as stunned as I am; he stares at the

hunched-over man, then at his own clenched fist, as if some unknown force might have possessed him. Which would honestly make more sense than what just happened; I doubt Henry has even given anyone a fist bump before.

But then the two other men rush over, and Henry tackles the first kidnapper to the ground with a resounding *thud*, and everything descends into utter chaos.

I can't see what's going on from where I'm hiding, can only hear the muffled grunts of pain and repeated collision of limbs, of bodies pushed onto the floor, and Henry's voice when he yells—

"*Catch*."

Something small and silver flies through the air in a perfect arc. I don't even think; I just spring up and reach for it, my fingers closing over the metallic object. Car keys.

Of course.

Pulse speeding, I unlock the car and yank open the car door.

Peter's curled up in the back seat, next to an opened pack of bottled water. Horror and relief crash through my chest at the sight of him. *He's alive.* He's alive and awake and staring at me like I might be a ghost as I free his arms, help pull him out. His knees wobble violently, but he manages to stand.

Ahead of us, the sounds of the struggle intensify.

Henry.

"Go inside," I order Peter. "Wait for us by the door."

He doesn't protest.

While he hurries off, I seize one of the water bottles from the trunk and hold it like a baton, feeling its weight in my hand. *It's not heavy enough to kill someone*, I decide, which is all I need to know before stalking forward.

The men don't notice me. They're too busy forming a kind of human sandwich: Henry's got two of the kidnappers pinned under him, but he's been held down by the tallest one. The same one who tied me up.

I'm more pissed off than terrified now, and I let my anger guide my aim...

The plastic bottle smashes into the back of the man's head with a satisfying *thunk*.

As the man lurches sideways, I bend down and grab Henry's hand. His knuckles are dark red, a thin bloody cut running down his thumb. My heart twists, but I know it's not the time to apologize, or to thank him, or to voice the million other things I'm feeling in this moment.

"Run," is all Henry says as he jumps to his feet.

And we do. We sprint through the narrow exit, where Peter's waiting, and bolt the door behind us, then race up the stairs in a mad blur of pounding hearts and feet. Henry reaches his floor first, and then it's just Peter and me, my hand secured around his wrist to keep him from falling. We keep going. We have to keep going. I don't know if Andrew's men have found their way inside or alerted someone else or if we'll ever make it out of this mess okay. All I can do is urge my legs to move faster, faster still, mouth parched and knees sore, my lungs aching, dying for air as I cut the corner, pull Peter into the open hall of the ninth floor—

And crash straight into Mr. Murphy.

17

For the first time in forty years of Airington school history, our Experiencing China trip is cut short.

All because of me.

Well, *technically* speaking, Vanessa Liu is responsible for the abrupt change in schedule too. Of all the guys in our year level, it turns out she'd been harbouring a secret crush on Peter, so when she'd gone to his room to confess—only to find Jake half-asleep and Peter's bed empty—she'd feared the worst and notified Mr. Murphy.

The timing couldn't have been worse, really. If Vanessa hadn't been so drunk, she would never have stumbled into Peter's room *after* I'd already kidnapped him, nor would Mr. Murphy have shown up in a bathrobe to search for him the exact moment Peter and I hurtled up the stairs.

Everything unraveled pretty quickly after that.

Mr. Murphy had taken one look at my expression, then Peter's stunned face and the thin trail of blood trickling from

his hairline, and sent him to the hospital for a suspected con-
cussion. Then he'd informed Peter's parents, who'd screamed
so loud into the phone I could hear the whole conversation
from six feet away. After they finished threatening to sue the
school and the hotel for gross negligence, they'd sent out a
private jet to bring Peter home—presumably to be treated at
a better hospital.

The rest of the year level was ordered to pack their bags
and check out before sunrise, so we could catch the earliest
train back to Beijing. No explanation was provided.

But by now, I'm sure everyone's come up with their own
theories on what happened; the cause behind Mr. Murphy's
frantic calls at 4:00 a.m., the shriek of the ambulance siren
cutting through the night, the terrible look on Wei Laoshi's
face ever since...

And, of course, the reason I've been separated from my cohort, forbidden from speaking to anyone and forced to sit in
the teachers' train compartment instead. I haven't even had a
chance to check on Henry. To see if he's okay. None of the
teachers have brought up his name so far, which means he's at
least evaded suspicion, but I can't stop thinking about the fight
last night: all his potential injuries, the thin cut on his fist.

I can't stop worrying about him.

"Alice, I'd like to give you a chance to explain," Mr. Murphy says. He's sitting directly across from me, hunched over
awkwardly to avoid bumping his head on the upper bunk.

I'm hunched over too, but it's fear that keeps my spine bent,
my eyes down, rather than a lack of space.

"Explain what?" I mumble, stalling for time.

"I spoke with Peter before he was taken to the hospital, and he said you were there in the hotel room with him."

I clench my teeth. It's too hot in here, the walls threatening to close in, the low ceiling lights blinding like a policeman's torch. A drop of sweat rolls down my neck.

"He also said," Mr. Murphy continues, with some uncertainty, "that you almost seemed to...appear out of nowhere. That he isn't sure how you got into the room in the first place." He pauses. "Does that sound right?"

A choked, gurgling noise escapes my lips when I open my mouth to protest. I swallow, try again. "He was *concussed*, Mr. Murphy," I say finally. "He couldn't—I mean, have you ever heard of anyone appearing out of thin air before? Outside of movies and comic books? It—it's ridiculous."

Mr. Murphy shakes his head. "While the idea itself does appear far-fetched, and quite obviously defies the basic laws of physics, I'm afraid to say that the other parts of his story do add up." His expression grows stern, and my heart seizes. "For example, when I asked Vanessa Liu about you, she recalls you being in Henry Li's room at around midnight. But Mina Huang tells me you left shortly after Vanessa—at a time that coincides with a mysterious knock Jake Nguyen received on his door—and did not return at any point. As another example," he goes on, listing each point off with his fingers, "I've contacted the hotel for security footage, and they noticed something rather...peculiar. That is, there's no record of you entering Room 2005 at all, yet somehow, you were seen *leaving* the room with Peter."

If I wasn't so concerned about being expelled or sent to

jail, I might actually be impressed by Mr. Murphy's detective work right now.

He sighs. "See, I don't believe in supernatural abilities, Alice, and I don't want to believe that you would be the type of person to commit such a crime. There is also something to be said about the fact that, regardless of what happened prior, you did help Peter escape in the end…"

There's a *but* in his tone. I can sense it.

I steel myself.

"…but the evidence we have so far doesn't look good. Even if we were to ignore the anomalies, the fact stands that Peter was taken against his will, injured, and—judging from the marks on his wrists—tied up, and you were missing the same time he was. If Peter's parents decide to investigate further, to file a lawsuit…"

I was prepared for this. But still, my throat constricts. A loud ringing fills my ears.

"Of course," Mr. Murphy adds, "it would be a different matter if someone had set you up for the ta—"

"No," I blurt out. Too quickly.

His eyebrows draw together. "Are you sure, Alice?"

"I—I'm sure."

And I am. I'd weighed out the pros and cons of telling the teachers or police about Andrew all night, and it became clear, even in my distressed state, that the cost would simply be too great. I can't offer them any proof of correspondence without exposing Beijing Ghost, and everything that comes with it—Henry's involvement, my classmates' secrets, the private bank account, the stolen exam answers.

If anything, confessing would only increase my chances of being punished by law.

Not to mention all the questions it would raise about a power I can't even explain myself.

In my prolonged silence, Mr. Murphy's face sags with disappointment. He seems to sink deeper in his seat.

"Very well," he says, rubbing a weary hand over his eyes. "I suppose we'll discuss this in more depth when I meet your parents—"

"Wait. My parents?"

He stares at me like I've missed something obvious. "Yes. I called them as soon as I got off the phone with Peter's father. I told them to wait for us in my office."

And just like that, all the air leaves my lungs. Whatever semblance of composure I've managed to maintain cracks down the middle like an egg, my anxiety spilling out in an uncontrollable, ugly mess.

"You—you called—" My voice cracks too, and I have trouble finishing my sentence. "You called—"

"I had to, Alice," Mr. Murphy says. Another sigh. "It's important that they know. You're only a kid, after all."

The words sound oddly familiar, and it takes me a moment to recall the last time I heard them: Mr. Chen, after praising my English exam, telling me with such sincerity that I deserved to dream, to carve out a future of my own.

Now the memory feels a million years old.

Apart from orientation and my scholarship interview, my parents have never set foot on school campus before. They always say it's because the public transport is too inconvenient, which is true—most students have private drivers, so the school has never bothered to invest in anything more accessible—but I suspect it's really because they're afraid of embarrassing me. Because they don't want to stand out for all the wrong reasons when they appear beside the typical Airington parental crowd of company owners, IT executives, and national stars.

Whatever the reason, I can't imagine them navigating their way through the five floors of the humanities building, to the tiny office at the very end of the hall, having never even come close to the place before.

So when I race out of the bus, past the other students taking their time to unload their bags in the courtyard and waiting for their drivers to pick them up, and into Mr. Murphy's office, I'm not entirely surprised to find it empty.

But that doesn't stop me from panicking.

"They—they must've gotten lost," I babble to Mr. Murphy, my chest tightening at the thought of my parents wandering around campus in a daze, looking for me. "I have to go find them—they don't know English that well—"

God, it's like America all over again.

"They're grown adults, Alice," Mr. Murphy says with a confused look, like I'm overreacting for no reason. He doesn't understand. "I'm sure they don't need a tour guide just to find—"

Someone knocks on the door, and I whip around.

My mouth goes dry.

A senior student I recognize but have never spoken to before is leaning against the door frame, my parents standing close behind him, their expressions equally pinched and closed off. With a pang, I notice that Baba's wearing his blue work overalls, that Mama's wearing the same faded floral shirt I last saw her in at the restaurant.

Both of them look older than I remember. Frailer.

"Found these folks walking around the primary school. Say they're looking for a Sun Yan in Mr. Murphy's office," the boy tells us, shooting me a glance that's at once pitying and curious.

"Great. Thanks for bringing them here, Chen." Mr. Murphy smiles.

"No probs."

The boy glances at me one last time before disappearing behind the door.

The second we're alone, Baba stalks over.

I'm still holding on to one last straw of hope that he and Mama won't react as badly as I feared—not without hearing my side of the story first, at least—but then I see the fury in his eyes.

"What were you *thinking*?" Baba shouts, spittle flying from his lips, a dark vein bulging at his temple. He's shaking, he's so mad. I've never seen him this angry before, not even that time I accidentally spilled water over the laptop he'd spent years saving up for. His voice is deafening in the closed space, and I know from the sudden hush that falls over the courtyard outside that everyone must be listening. That all my classmates and teachers can hear every single word. Chanel. Mr. Chen. Rainie. Vanessa.

Henry.

For the first time I find myself praying that I can turn invisible permanently. Disappear right this instant, sink into a void deep beneath the hideous office carpet and never resurface again.

"Are you trying to rebel?" Baba continues, his voice getting louder and louder. "How could you even— Your Mama and I don't believe it at first when the school call us, not for award, but say you're a *criminal*—"

Mr. Murphy keeps his gaze leveled at a random spot on the wall, looking terribly uncomfortable. When Baba takes a short break from his yelling to breathe, I muster all the courage I have left and whisper, "Baba, can we please—*please*—talk about this somewhere else? Everyone's listening—"

But this is the wrong thing to say.

An awful, unforgiving look flashes over Baba's face. "Do you only live for other people?" he demands. "Why do you care so much what they think?"

I don't know how to reply without enraging him further, so I keep quiet. Pray this will all be over soon.

"Sun Yan. I'm *talking to you.*"

Then he reaches down for his shoe, and I recoil, certain it's going to come flying my way, but Mama quickly intervenes.

"Laogong, now's probably not the best time for this," she murmurs to Baba in Mandarin, with a pointed look at Mr. Murphy.

"Fine." Baba grabs my wrist—not hard enough to leave a mark, but hard enough to hurt. "Let's go."

I dig my heels in, wrenching my arm away with difficulty. "W-Where are you taking me?" I blurt out. There's a low buzz building in my ears, a painful pressure rising up my chest and throat like bile. "I still have class—"

Baba barks out a laugh. "Class?" Without warning, he

slams his hand down on the desk with a hard *thud*. Everyone jumps, including Mr. Murphy. Then Baba switches abruptly to English, and his already-disjointed words jumble together further in his rage. "Do you know what education for, huh? Why school charge 350,000 RMB—"

Mr. Murphy clears his throat. "Well, actually, it's 360,000 RMB now—a reasonable price, if you consider our new state-of-the-art facilities—"

Baba ignores him. "It help you grow, form connection, see the world, one day give back to society. Not worship money. What your Mama always say? If you not good person, you're nothing. *Nothing*."

Heavy silence falls in the wake of his words like the drop of an axe. I'm trembling uncontrollably, my teeth chattering in a loud staccato. I think I'm going to die, or throw up, or both.

Then Baba shakes his head, eyes fluttering closed. Heaves a sigh. When he looks back up at me, he seems to have aged ten years in the span of ten seconds. It's in Mandarin that he says, "No matter what happened, your Mama and I always felt so proud to have raised a daughter like you. But now..." He trails off.

My skin burns with shame.

"I—I'm sorry," I choke out, and once the words have left my lips, I can't stop repeating them. "I'm so, so sorry, Baba— I really am—I didn't want it to be like this either..."

But Baba's expression doesn't soften. "We are leaving."

Mr. Murphy chooses this moment to speak up. "Actually, given the current circumstances...a short break from school may be best for Alice." He catches my look of horror, and quickly adds, "Not saying that she's expelled, of course—it'll likely be a while until Peter's parents and the school board reach a decision. But until then…well." His eyes flicker to the window, as if he, too, knows the entire Year Twelve cohort is eavesdropping on our conversation. He sighs. "I believe some distance would be beneficial. Give us all time to reflect and potentially make amends. What do you think, Alice?"

All three adults turn to me, and I realize it doesn't matter what I think. The decision has already been made.

I swallow. "Can I at least go grab my stuff? From the dorm?"

Mr. Murphy looks visibly relieved. I guess it'd cause him a lot of trouble if I were to resist. Or maybe he just doesn't want Baba to start yelling again.

It's Mama who answers first.

"Yes," she says quietly. Her voice is so distant she could be talking to a complete stranger—and just when I thought I couldn't possibly feel any worse. "Go. Be quick." She folds her hands together, the white scar peeking out from under her fingertips. "We still have to catch the subway."

The short walk from Mr. Murphy's office to my dorm is torture.

Everyone scatters the second I step outside, but I still sense their eyes trained on the back of my head, glimpse the suspicion and worry and judgment written all over their faces. My stomach squeezes. I've always hated negative attention.

I wonder how many of the people watching have pieced together that last night had something to do with Beijing Ghost. And how many more of them figured out that Beijing Ghost is me.

The walk starts to feel like a death march.

My eyes ache with tears as I climb up the steps to Confucius Hall, but I refuse to cry. To show weakness. I hold my head up high and throw back my shoulders, staring straight ahead, as if I'm not one wrong move away from breaking down in front of the whole year level.

A bitter wind picks up, howling in my ears, and over the noise I hear a faint voice—

"Alice!" someone calls after me.

I ignore them and move faster. I don't want to talk to anyone right now, whether they're well-intentioned or not. I have no idea what I'd say.

When I reach my dorm room, I stuff everything I own into a sad-looking duffel bag. There's not much for me to pack, really; a stack of certificates and a few trophies, some toiletries, and a school uniform I might never have the chance to wear again...

"Oh my god. *Alice.*"

I jump and look up. It's Chanel, her eyes wide as she takes in the opened wardrobe, the unzipped bag lying at my feet.

Then, without another word, she crosses the room and pulls me into a crushing hug. I stiffen at first, taken aback by the sudden gesture of affection, then rest my head tentatively on her bony shoulder, letting her hair tickle my cheek. For a moment, all the terror and uncertainty and guilt of the past few days catch up to me.

You can't cry, I remind myself, as hot tears threaten to spill over.

"Dude. I was so worried," Chanel whispers. She steps back to look me in the eyes. "What *happened*? I thought you were with Henry last night, but then—then I heard the ambulance sirens, and Mr. Murphy started calling all of us to pack at like, four, and he sounded scared shitless, and the teachers wouldn't let any of us speak to you on the train… And now this?" She jerks a finger toward the duffel bag, its meager contents exposed. "What the hell is going on?"

"I'm leaving," I say numbly.

She stares at me. "*Leaving?* Where? How long?"

All I can do is shake my head. If I speak another word, I'm scared I'll fall apart.

But Chanel won't let it rest. "Is the school making you leave?" she demands, angry now, two spots of color rising to her cheeks. "Because whatever you did, it can't be *that* bad. And besides, you're one of the best students they have. No— they can't. I won't let them." She spins away from me, already reaching for her phone.

With enormous effort, I manage to find my voice again. "What—what are you doing?" I croak.

"I'm telling my dad," she says. Her mouth twists into a grimace that's half bitter, half smug. "He's been extra nice to me ever since I found out about—*you know.*" The corners of her lips pull down further, but she continues, "I bet if I ask, he can pull some strings, get the school to reconsider—"

"No." I grab her by the shoulders, force her to put her phone away. "No—Chanel, don't. Please. I mean, I'm so grateful you'd even want to—but it's not the school. Well, not *only* the school. I just. I can't be here right now." My voice cracks on the last word, and Chanel's eyes darken with concern.

We're both silent for a while: me trying to breathe through

clenched teeth and shove my emotions down; her standing completely still, gaze trained on the ground.

Then she sighs. "God, this sucks."

The massive understatement draws a shaky, slightly hysterical laugh from my lips, and I nod.

"Can I help you pack, at least?" she asks, glancing at my bag again. "Or I could help you get a Didi? My driver's probably coming soon, too—he could give you and your parents a lift."

Her kindness is overwhelming, like the fierce blast of a heater in winter. I give her hand a light squeeze, too choked up to speak for a minute. "No, no, it's fine. I'm pretty much done anyway," I finally manage, gathering the last of my things. "And my house is almost a two-hour drive from here. It'd be too far for your driver."

Before she can protest, I throw my arms around her small frame, hoping it can convey everything—all the guilt and gratitude—I don't know how to say.

Then I turn and walk out the door, pushing aside the awful thought that this may be the last time I'll ever see these halls.

Mama and Baba do not speak a single word to me the whole subway ride home. It's better, I suppose, than being screamed at in public again. But not by much.

When we finally reach their flat—*our flat*, I keep reminding myself—it's even smaller than I remember. The ceilings scrape Baba's head. The walls are stained yellow. There's barely enough room for all of us to stand in the living room without bumping into the dinner table or the cabinets.

Silently, Mama picks up my bag and suitcase, and for one terrible second I think she's going to throw them and me out of the house. Force me to go live on the streets. Disown me for good.

But then she dumps my stuff in her and Baba's bedroom—the only bedroom in the flat.

"You sleep there," she instructs, without looking at me.

"Where will you and Baba sleep?" I ask.

"On couch."

"But—"

"Not for discussion," she says firmly, such finality in her tone that I can only swallow my protests and comply.

"Thank you, Mama," I whisper, but she's already turned away. If she heard me, she doesn't show it.

I swallow the lump in my throat. All I want is for her to hug me, reassure me the way she did when I was a child, but I know that's impossible. For now, at least. So instead I unpack my bags, change the sheets, shower, going through all the motions like a machine. Disciplined. Unfeeling.

And only when I'm alone in their bedroom, the door shut tight, do I pull the thin covers over my head and let myself cry.

18

The next morning, I wake up with a pounding headache and the pattern of my pillow pressed into my cheek. For a few short, blissful seconds, I forget I'm back at home. I forget why my throat feels so dry, like I haven't drunk any water in days. Why my eyes are almost swollen shut.

Then I hear the clatter of pots, the *click-click-click* of the stove turning on in the kitchen—the *kitchen*—and everything comes flooding back to me in one sweeping, nauseating wave—

Fuck.

My lungs seize up as I'm assaulted by memory after painful memory, forced to relive every second of yesterday's meeting, the look of profound disappointment on Baba's face, the way Mama kept her lips pursed on the long subway ride home, as if she was trying to hold back tears.

I can't remember the last time I messed up on such a catastrophic scale. I've never even been *grounded* before; whenever I did something wrong as a child, like accidentally scribble on the walls or shatter a plate, I'd be so harsh on myself that Mama and Baba would end up comforting me instead of handing down punishments.

But this is different. What I did was completely, undeniably wrong on every conceivable level. You can always fix or replace a broken plate, but when you hurt *people*—there's no going back from that.

And that's not even considering the legal implications. If Peter's family decides to sue—which, let's face it, they probably will because he's their only child and I'm powerless and they're used to having their way... If the school decides to expel me, put "criminal activity" into my permanent academic records... Or worse, if this ends up going to court... I'm not even sure how much lawyers cost, but I do know they're expensive, a thousand times more expensive than we could ever afford, and if any of the court dramas I've watched are grounded in truth, a legal case like this could drag on for years. But what would the alternatives even be? Prison? Would they force my parents into jail in my place, because I'm underage? Or would they send me to some kind of juvenile detention center, where kids hide knives under their pillows and attack the physically weak like me?

A terrible wheezing sound fills the room, like that of a dying animal caught in a snare, and it takes me a moment to realize it's coming from me. I'm curled up on the bed in a fetal position, panic threatening to crush my very bones.

I don't know how much time I spend like this, trying and failing to remember how to breathe and hating myself, hating everything—

Then Mama's voice cuts through the closed bedroom door:

"Sun Yan. Come eat."

My heart stutters a beat. I cling onto the tone of her voice, try to dissect her every word. Mama only ever calls me by my full Chinese name when she's angry, but at least she's still willing to feed me. To *speak* to me.

Maybe I haven't been disowned just yet.

I rub the sleep from my eyes, take a deep breath, and tip-toe out into the tiny living room, feeling like a criminal in my own house. I half expect to find a lawyer or the police or maybe one of Peter's parents' assistants sitting on our worn sofa, ready to take me away at a moment's notice, but the room is empty except for me and Mama.

Mama doesn't look up from her seat at the dining table when I move to join her. Just pushes my breakfast closer toward me.

It's the sort of food she used to make me when I was in primary school: a bowl of steaming soybean milk—not that silky, supersweet stuff you can buy in cartons at the supermarket, but the homemade kind you need to filter through a sieve—an already peeled hard-boiled egg, two platters of Laoganma chili sauce and pickled vegetables, and half a chunk of white mantou.

Though I don't have much of an appetite, hunger pinches my stomach. I realize I haven't eaten anything in the past twenty-four hours.

I rip off a small piece of the mantou and chew. It's still warm, the bread soft and faintly sweet. If only I wasn't having difficulty swallowing.

"Is Baba joining us for breakfast?" I ask quietly, cautiously, wincing as the words scrape their way up my throat.

Mama doesn't reply for a long time, the room deadly silent save for the soft crunch of peeled eggshells and the clink of her spoon against her bowl. Then at last she says, still not looking my way, "He already go to work."

My heart sinks to my feet.

"I'm really sorry, Mama," I whisper, staring down at a stain on the table. "I just— I wish—" My throat closes up, and I go quiet, fighting back the sudden press of tears. Deep down, I know there's nothing I can say to change the situation; even if I'm sick with regret, even if I apologize a thousand times, in a thousand different ways, it's too late. The past is permanent.

"We're out of duck eggs."

I jerk my head up, certain I've misheard. It's not as if I expected Mama to respond to my apology, but... "What?"

"I need to go to market before work."

Mama downs her bowl of soybean milk, wipes her mouth with the back of her hand, and rises to her feet. Then, for the first time in months, she looks at me. Her gaze is gentler than I would've dared imagine, more tired than angry. "You coming or no?"

It's been years since I last visited the local grocery store with Mama. After I moved into the dorms at Airington, I was simply too far away to visit home on a regular basis. But even during the summer holidays, I'd turn down Mama's offers to go shopping—if trying to find the biggest possible cabbage for the cheapest price can even be called that—choosing instead to get a head start on coursework for the next year or polish up my holiday homework.

But not a lot has changed around here since I was twelve or thirteen.

There are still the same clustered shelves of ripe fruit: round nashi pears wrapped in white foam netting, sliced watermelon quarters and whole dragon fruits; the same overflowing trays of recognizable candy usually distributed at weddings: sticky peanut sweets wrapped in shiny red foil, tiny plastic cups of translucent jelly, thick marshmallows with strawberry swirls; the same glass displays at the Asian bakery, showcasing the freshly made sausage rolls and glazed egg tarts and purple taro buns stuffed with whipped cream.

Even the people seem the same: the little girl staring longingly at the row of fruit cakes, the old nainais squinting at the different brands of soy sauce.

And as I drift from aisle to aisle like a fish in freshwater, trailing behind Mama as she slaps a watermelon to check if it's sweet, weighs out a bag of roasted sunflower seeds with expert precision, a strange feeling washes over me.

Peace.

Because it hasn't just been years since I last visited the grocery store. It's been years since I did anything that wasn't for school, or, more recently, for Beijing Ghost. Years since I wasn't so busy—always hustling, always striving to get further, do better—I could barely breathe.

The sudden freedom is dizzying. It makes me feel…well, *human* again.

All this time, I'd thought the nickname Study Machine was a compliment of sorts. That it meant productivity, above-human levels of discipline, that I was programmed for success.

Now I wonder if it describes someone devoted to doing at the expense of feeling. Something barely alive.

Mr. Chen's words resurface in my mind—

What is it that you want?

The answer had seemed so obvious to me then: I want whatever other people want, whatever they assign the most worth to. But standing here in the middle of a crowded supermarket, like some scene from a childhood dream, the first thing I think of is the English program Mr. Chen recommended to me. Well, not so much that specific program, but the idea of just getting to *write* for two whole months, or even longer, of having that be what I'm best at…

"Ready to leave?" Mama asks, pulling me from my thoughts. Her basket is only half filled with vegetables and fruit, her hands pale and chapped over the handle. The winter always makes her skin dry, the scar more noticeable.

I'm about to tell her *yes*, when my eyes fall on the little pharmacy store next to the seasoning section.

"Wait right here," I say, ducking around the nearest shelf. "There's something I want to see first…"

Over the course of the next week, I do everything I can to distract myself.

I catch up on all the popular costume dramas from the past few years, the kind that stretch on for over seventy episodes and involve such complicated relationships you'd need a diagram to sort them out. I read books that aren't *Macbeth* or dry classics or compulsory texts for IB, but fun fantasy novels with magic and mythology. I help Mama cook when she's working, help Baba fold his clothes even though he's still not speaking to me. I make long to-do lists, SMART goals, Five Year Plans, then toss them in the trash, knowing how pointless it all is when my future now hangs on such a thin thread.

And no matter what, I try not to think about Peter, or Andrew She, or the fact that the school should be calling any day now to announce what exactly my punishment will be.

I try not to think about Henry Li.

But then one afternoon, when Baba's still at work and I'm watching the last episode of *Yanxi Palace* alone in my bedroom, a knock sounds on our front door.

"Alice," Mama calls from outside, and I know right away that something is wrong. She's using her fake polite voice, usually reserved for chats with the neighbors at the local park or large family gatherings.

I bolt upright from bed, pulse already racing, and call back, "What is it?"

"Someone's here to see you."

Henry Li is standing in our living room.

There's something so surreal about the scene that I'm half convinced it's a hallucination. Henry—with his perfect posture and ironed button-down shirt and polished shoes, the very image of wealth and privilege—next to our battered sofa, our yellow-stained walls with bits of old newspaper pasted over the holes.

He seems too big for the room. Too bright.

It's like one of those *"Which of these things is out of place?"* games, except the answer is painfully obvious.

Then Henry's eyes land on me, and I realize how *I* must look. I'm wearing Mama's baggy plaid pajamas—the ones that have a wide tear in the sleeves—my eyes are still single-lidded and puffy from crying, and I haven't washed my hair in four days.

A hot, sticky sensation fills my stomach, humiliation turning into anger and back again, and suddenly I want to crawl out of my skin.

"Hi, Alice," he says, his voice overwhelmingly soft.

"Bye," I blurt out.

And I flee.

Our flat is so small that it takes only seconds for me to sprint back into my room, slamming the door shut behind me with such force the walls tremble. I haven't felt this kind of panic, this mad, heart-pounding, nauseating rush of adrenaline, since the last Beijing Ghost task. Since everything fell apart.

My mind whirs as I fall onto the bed, pulling the blankets high over my head as if I can somehow pretend this nightmare scenario away. I have no idea why Henry's here, but I need him to leave. Now.

Maybe I'll tell him I've developed a rare but very serious allergy to other humans, I think desperately. *One that will cause intense choking and potential death if anyone comes within three feet of me. Or maybe I'll say I have a dog in here who's terrified of strangers. Or maybe—*

"Alice?" He knocks on the door once. Twice. I hear the faint rustle of fabric, and imagine him sliding his hands into his pockets, cocking his head to the side. The image is so vivid, so terribly familiar it makes my chest hurt. "Can I come in?"

I open my mouth to give him one of my very flimsy excuses, but I choke on the words. After all that's happened, I'm still a terrible liar. Maybe it's for the best.

"Um—wait a second," I tell him, scrambling out of bed. In one sweeping motion, I clear the dirty laundry and empty snack packets and wads of tissue off the sheets and stuff them all into a basket, cringing at the thought of Henry witnessing such a mess. When I'm absolutely certain there are no more unwashed bras or socks lying around, I open the door.

"Thank you," Henry says, his tone and expression so formal I'm almost tempted to laugh.

Then he steps inside and examines the tiny bedroom carefully, as if trying hard to come up with a compliment. Him and his manners. At last, he points to a plastic tiger statue by the bed that was a Lunar Festival gift from Xiaoyi to Mama—the only object in the room that isn't a necessity.

"This is really nice," he says.

"Thanks. It's my mum's."

He quickly drops his hand.

I debate offering him a seat out of courtesy, but there's barely enough room for him to stand as it is. "Sorry this place is so small," I mumble, then realize who I'm talking to. Remember how he usually acts in such cramped spaces. "Wait. Aren't you afraid of—"

"I'm fine," he says, but he doesn't *look* fine. Now that he's this close, I can make out the familiar lines of tension in his shoulder and jaw.

God. As if I needed another reason for this arrangement to be a bad idea.

"You should get out," I tell him. "I mean, not as in I want to kick you out or anything, but if you're not comfortable—"

"I *want* to be here," he says, like that settles everything. Then he adds, quietly, "It's been ages since we last saw each other. I..." He clears his throat. "I've missed fighting with you at school."

My heart stutters.

"Same." I allow myself just two more seconds to fully indulge in those last words, the look on his face when he said them, before moving on to business. "Speaking of school... How are things there?"

"Well, Peter still hasn't been discharged from the hospital yet."

All remaining thoughts of Henry's dark gaze and parted lips vanish in a crushing wave of nausea. I can't help picturing Peter's pale, almost lifeless face, lying completely still while strapped to a heart monitor and IV, his parents weeping beside him. "Oh, god. Is he—"

"No," Henry says quickly. "No, it's not that bad. He's lightly concussed, but he should technically be able to go about his life as usual by now. His parents are the ones keeping him there—they're somewhat paranoid about him getting injured again. Understandably, of course."

"Of course," I echo, hugging a pillow to my chest. My pulse still hasn't returned to normal yet.

"You know, if I'm being honest," Henry says suddenly, "part of me was expecting you to go back for Peter."

"You...were?"

I lean back, unsure how to respond. Unsure if I want to keep talking about this at all.

But Henry continues, "Because deep down—"

I glare at him.

"Deep, deep, *deep* down," he amends, "you're hardly as terrible as you try to be."

"And look where I ended up," I say bitterly, even though I don't mean it, not *really*. I've had time to regret plenty of things—but somehow, going back for Peter isn't one of them.

"See." Henry gestures in my direction, eyebrows raised. "That's precisely what I'm talking about." A pause. "I never entirely understood why you'd insist on creating such an app—on forcing yourself to be someone you're not—"

"It's not that simple—"

"But I—"

"You don't get it," I say. I want to sound angry, to push him away, but my voice comes out thin and fragile as eggshells. "You—you and all the kids at Airington... All you have is light. Light and glory and power and the whole world laid out for you, just waiting for you to take whatever you like." I draw in a shaky breath, wrap my arms tighter around myself, bury my chin into the pillow. "Is it really too much to ask? For people like me to want a bit of that light for ourselves?"

He's silent for a long time. I watch the faint movement in his throat, the tension bunching in his shoulders. His eyes lock on mine. "No," he says softly. "Of course not."

"Then why..." My voice trembles. I inhale, try again. "Why do I feel so fucking tired all the time?"

He opens his mouth. Closes it.

And despite myself, I choke out a laugh. "I've never seen you so lost for words before."

"Yes, well..." He looks away. "I'll admit I really don't know what to say."

"Look, you don't have to say anything—"

"But I do." He shifts position slightly, his attention going to the plastic tiger again, then back to me. His expression is pained. "I wasn't even aware that your family was living like this. I mean, I suspected, but..."

"Yeah," I mutter, forcing down that same awful, itchy feeling from earlier: the desire to run, to hide, to turn into someone else—*anyone* else but me.

The desire grows even stronger when Henry asks, with the air of one who's just grasped something incredibly obvious and can't believe it's taken them this long, "Is *that* why you came up with the idea for Beijing Ghost? To pay—to pay bills?"

No point denying it now, I guess.

"Not bills." I dig my nails deeper into the pillow. At this rate, I'm probably going to tear a hole through the fabric. "Just...school fees and stuff."

"If I'd known—Alice, you realize I don't care about my cut of the profits, right? It was never really about the money for me."

"Well, good, because you're definitely not getting any of it now," I tell him, only half-joking.

"It's just not fair," Henry says after a pause, and I'm surprised by the burr of anger in his voice. "You're indisputably the smartest person in our entire year level—no, the entire school. You shouldn't have to resort to monetizing your supernatural powers just to stay at Airington with the rest of us. It's honestly..." He rakes an agitated hand through his hair. "It's ridiculous, that's what it is. You deserve to be there more than people like Andrew She. You deserve to be there more than I do."

I stare at him. "Henry... Did you just admit that I'm smarter than you?"

He shoots me a half exasperated, half affectionate look. "Don't make me say it again."

I feel the corners of my lips twitch, and the tension between us seems to thaw a little.

"Really, though. I'm sorry I didn't notice anything earlier," Henry says after a beat. He's speaking slowly, like he's weighing out every word in his head first. "You shouldn't be in this mess, and you certainly shouldn't be the only one shouldering the blame for what happened."

"I shouldn't, but I am," I remind him. "That's just how the system works. I don't have the right connections, or the money to hire a good lawyer, or parents who've donated millions to the school—"

"But you have me," Henry says, eyes blazing. "I'm responsible for Beijing Ghost too, and I'm going to do everything I can to help you. In fact, that's part of the reason I came here today."

"What do you mean?"

He pulls his phone out of his pocket and holds it up for me to see. The familiar Beijing Ghost logo blinks back at me. "I figured it would be safest for everyone involved if we were to shut down the app—before Peter's parents or the police decide to investigate further."

I'd considered this before, too, but...it still feels very sudden. "Shut it down...right now?"

"Would you prefer to hold an elaborate farewell party first? Take time to write out a touching eulogy?" Henry says drily, much more like his normal self. "Or perhaps wait until the tenth day of the Lunar calendar, when the sun and the moon align?"

"Fine," I grumble, shifting position so I can see his phone screen more clearly. "What do we need to do?"

"Lucky for you, I've already set everything up." He clicks away from the app, and a black page appears, crammed with tiny, multicolored lines of code I can't possibly comprehend. "All I need is your permission, and the app will be gone. Erased, forever. Permanently rem—"

"Okay, I get it," I snap. I know Henry was kidding about the farewell party, and that the app's caused me more pain than anything these past few months, but I still feel a small jolt of grief. We've been through a lot together. And at the end of the day, Beijing Ghost did make me a hundred thousand RMB richer—if the police don't get involved and force me to give the money back, that is. "Just—start already."

He brings his finger to the screen. Glances back at me. "You sure?"

I roll my eyes, but nod.

"Three…"

I hug the pillow tighter. Lick my chapped lips.

"Two…"

This is for the best, I remind myself. The less evidence, the lighter the punishment.

"Wait," Henry says, frowning.

A notification has popped up over the page: *Mobile network not available.*

"Well, that was anticlimactic," I mutter, taking the phone from him and holding it up at different angles. "Sorry about that. I should've warned you—sometimes the connection's really shitty around here."

"Maybe I can try one of my other phones," he suggests.

"I don't know, it usually doesn't…" I trail off as an idea sparks in my mind. I drop the phone and turn to face him, my heart pounding at the possibility. If it works… "Actually, let's not shut the app down."

"Pardon?"

I smile. "I have a better idea."

Four hours later, Henry and I are staring down at a five-page-long, just-completed article, a draft email, and the Beijing Ghost app.

Though the cartoon ghost logo and the name are still the same, everything else about the app has changed. The home page no longer promises complete confidentiality and anonymity, or advises the preferred method of payment, but instead encourages students of Airington to "get on top of their studies."

All my previous private messages have been erased too, replaced by innocuous questions from different accounts—thanks to Henry and Chanel's many phones—about exam results and the recent chemistry assignment and different interpretations of *Macbeth*.

Well, not *all* messages. Andrew She's long instructions for kidnapping Peter are still there, in bold, as well his original offer of one million RMB in exchange for the task.

"Okay, let's go over our story one more time," I tell Henry, who's now sitting cross-legged on the bed beside me. "How did I end up accepting Andrew's offer on Beijing Ghost?"

Henry nods and straightens like we're about to take an exam, then rattles off the answer with impressive speed. "At the start of the school year, I decided to create a study app for some user experience design practice. The main idea behind it was that through the app, anyone at Airington could help each other answer school-related questions, while also earning some extra cash as an incentive. All the accounts are anonymous, but there's a point system that awards extra points to those who've offered the most help, and thus have the most credibility. And since you were, by far, the highest-ranked account, with a reputation for taking on whatever problems came up, regardless of subject or difficulty..."

"Andrew figured that I actually needed the cash, which made me the person most likely to accept his offer and get the job done," I finish, clapping my hands together. "That sounds plausible, right? Like, specific but not too specific?"

"Right," Henry says. "And if that doesn't fully convince the school, your article will."

I hope so, I think to myself. Writing the article was weirdly cathartic; I'd poured everything I had—everything I've experienced in the past five years, every great injustice and minor disappointment, all my loud fears and quiet hopes, all my time spent both on the inside and outside of Airington's elite circle—into those words. Now I just want to make them count.

"So." Henry's finger hovers over the send button on the screen. "Shall we?"

I gnaw on the inside of my cheek and try to act like I don't feel nauseated at the very thought of emailing the school board. "We shall."

Before I have time to regret this whole plan, the email leaves my inbox with a loud whooshing sound.

No going back now.

In the silence that follows, I hear loud footsteps, mixed with Baba and Xiaoyi's voices; something about taking their shoes off. They must've just gotten here.

Henry hears them too. He quickly combs his hair with both hands, as if it doesn't already look perfect, adjusts his shirt collar, and springs to his feet. Then he catches me staring. "What?"

"Where—where exactly do you think you're going?" I splutter.

"To introduce myself to your father, of course," he says, now heading for the door. "It's the polite thing to do—"

I grab his shirt and yank him back toward me. "No. No, no, no, no. You can't."

"Why not?"

"I'm barely on speaking terms with my dad right now," I hiss, refusing to release my grip on his sleeve. "If he sees me coming out of the room with you, he's going to think—he'll think—"

"Yes?" Henry arches one brow, testing. Teasing. "What will he think?"

God help me. *"You know,"* I snap. My whole face burns. "Point is, it's a very bad idea."

But instead of being discouraged, he just offers me one of those smug, terribly attractive smiles that used to get under my skin so much. It still kind of does—just in a way that makes me focus far too long on his lips. "Don't worry. All parents love me; I'll be sure to make a good impression."

As I consider the potential risks of hiding Henry under the bed versus introducing him to my family, Xiaoyi's voice travels through the door. "...Yan Yan inside?"

"She's with someone right now," comes Mama's reply.

Well, I guess my decision's been made for me.

With a quick warning glare at Henry, I let go of his shirt and enter the living room.

Xiaoyi, Mama, and Baba are all sitting on the couch, a plate of skinned and diced apple set out before them, complete with a set of toothpicks on the side.

"Yan Yan!" Xiaoyi greets me brightly, standing up and shuffling over in her slippers. "I hear you're a criminal now!"

Both Baba and Mama make a series of deeply disapproving noises.

"Please don't encourage her," Mama mutters in Chinese.

But Xiaoyi's already turned her attention to Henry beside me. I'm not exaggerating when I say that her eyes literally light up, her jaw dropping all the way to her feet. You'd think she's never seen me with a tall, good-looking, well-dressed boy my age before.

Okay, fine. She hasn't.

Still, she doesn't have to look *that* surprised.

"Oh!" she exclaims, looking Henry up and down at least five times. "*Oh!* Who's this?"

"It's lovely to meet you," Henry says before I can reply, slipping smoothly into Mandarin to address both Baba and Xiaoyi. His smile is bright and earnest, his head bent at a respectful angle. "I'm Henry Li—I go to the same school as Alice. I just wanted to see how she was doing."

Xiaoyi positively melts.

Baba looks less enthusiastic about Henry's presence. His brows furrow. "You came all the way from school just to see our Alice?"

Henry nods. "Yes, shushu."

It's the polite, appropriate term to use, but Baba's frown only deepens. He gets up and walks closer so that he and Henry are standing face-to-face and asks, very slowly, "Are you…dating my daughter?"

Oh. God. I definitely should've made Henry hide under the bed.

"No, no, of course not," I hurry to tell Baba, the same time Henry says, "Yes."

I whip my head around so fast I hear my neck crack, my heart flying into a frenzy. *No way.* Henry meets my disbelieving gaze with a grin, and I don't know if I want to strangle him or throw my arms around him.

This is all very confusing.

"Not officially though," Henry adds, turning back to Baba. "Since we're still high school students, we obviously need to focus on our studies first. But I'm happy to wait, and I hope that in the future—"

"Alice's future is very uncertain right now," Baba cuts him off, his expression stern. "It's not something to joke about."

Henry doesn't falter. Doesn't even blink. "I know, and I'm being one hundred percent serious. Whatever happens, she's more than smart enough to get through it, and I'll be there to support her."

There's a long pause as Baba stares Henry down.

My heart keeps skipping beats.

"Hmph," Baba says at last, which is actually a much better

response than I expected. Coming from him, that's almost an invitation to join the family.

I let out a small, silent breath. Henry winks at me.

"Wait!" Xiaoyi suddenly slaps her thigh like she's just had a major epiphany, making everyone except Henry jump. "Is this *the* Henry Li? The boy you've been talking about since Year Eight? Your"—she makes large air quotes with both hands—"*biggest academic rival?* The one you keep having to share the award with?"

I flush. "Uh…"

Henry leans in with great interest. "Oh? So she talks about me a lot?"

"*A lot,*" Xiaoyi confirms generously, and I contemplate fleeing the city.

"What else has she said?" Henry asks, a gleam in his eyes. "Did she mention anything about—"

"You know what?" I step between them, piercing a chunk of apple with a toothpick and stuffing it into Henry's mouth. "Maybe we should just eat first. And…you know. Not talk for the next three hours. Or ever."

Xiaoyi glances at me, amused. "Yan Yan. Your face is very red."

"I… Thank you so much for pointing that out."

Henry makes a sound that strongly resembles a muffled laugh. I scowl and force-feed him another piece of apple, doing my best not to react when his lips brush my fingers, not to notice how warm his skin is.

The room is quiet for a blissful three seconds before Xiaoyi starts talking again.

"Tell me. What's your shengchen bazi?" she asks Henry casually.

Shengchen bazi: The Four Pillars of Destiny. As in, the exact time of a person's birth used to calculate their destiny—and their suitability for marriage. And judging from Henry's expression, he knows exactly what Xiaoyi means.

While I scramble for some way to dissuade Xiaoyi from planning out any future weddings, my phone buzzes. I pick it up at once. Refresh my inbox: *One New Message.* I click on it and—

My stomach flips.

Even though this is what I planned for, it's still slightly unnerving to receive a vague, passive-aggressive email from the Airington school board agreeing to meet as soon as possible.

"What happened?"

I start at Mama's voice and look up to see everyone staring at me: Henry, with a grim, knowing sort of expression; Baba and Mama, with concern; and Xiaoyi, with bright curiosity. If I were to give her my shengchen bazi now, I wonder what destiny she'd predict for me. Where the events of today might lead.

"It's the school," I tell them, glad I don't technically have to lie about it. Then I turn to Henry. "We have to leave immediately."

19

"Andrew. Glad you got my message."

Andrew She almost falls out of his chair when he sees me enter the school conference room. He's seated at a giant oval table meant for at least eight people, but right now, it's only the two of us in here. Just like I wanted. The place is perfect for private conversation; we're far away from the classrooms, the door is shut, the entire room windowless, and the overhead heater is blasting loud enough to mask what should be a very interesting conversation.

"Alice," Andrew croaks. Licks his lips. "What—what are you doing here? I thought you'd left the school."

I don't say anything. I grab the chair opposite him, cross my arms over my chest, and wait for my sentence to register. Watch him as he squirms.

One, two, three—

"Hang on." His brows pull together until they've practically formed a single line, a dark slash over his forehead. "*You* were the one who messaged me? But I thought Henry—"

"Well, obviously you wouldn't have come if you knew that I wanted to see you." My words hang heavy in the air between us, and I'm both surprised and kind of thrilled by how threatening I sound. I'm not even acting, really; the anger comes easily. All I need is to think about Andrew's kidnapping request and the fact that he's been hanging out at school as if everything's normal, as if he's *innocent*, while I've been sobbing alone in my room. "Did you get an email from the school, too?"

Andrew's eyes go very round—then they narrow. "Yeah. I did. The school told me all about your accusations." He shakes his head. "I—I can't believe you lied about the app."

"It wasn't exactly a lie," I reason, leaning forward and propping both elbows on the table. I may or may not have Googled *best power stances* on the car ride here with Henry, and he may or may not have laughed at me. But it seems to be working. "You literally hired me to kidnap Peter."

"You—you were the one who kidnapped him."

"Only under your orders," I shoot back. "I may be complicit, but you're the one who's guilty."

"As if. My family lawyer will be the judge of that."

"No. They won't be."

Andrew blinks at me, his face going slack for a second. Clearly, he was expecting the fancy lawyer card alone to shut me up. Rich people can be so predictable sometimes.

"I have the right to sue you for false accusations," he insists, though he already sounds more uncertain than he was earlier. "We could launch an in-depth investigation."

"You *could*," I agree, shifting into another one of the Top Ten Most Effective Power Stances of All Time, "but I personally wouldn't."

"What..."

With two fingers, I pull out the BMW keys I've been keeping in my pocket and hold them up in plain view, letting the shiny metal catch the artificial lights. Andrew's face pales. The heater above us roars louder.

"Your men dropped these the other night," I say pleasantly.

His mouth opens and closes like a goldfish. "Where did you—" He cuts himself off. Taps his nails on the polished table surface, eyes flicking away. "Whatever. It doesn't matter. You can't really prove the car—"

"Can't I? What if I matched up the keys to the license plate N150Q4?" I speak over him, savouring the look on Andrew's face when he recognizes the number. Wow, this feels even better than answering a Kahoot question correctly in front of the class. "Between that, the message you sent me on Beijing Ghost, and the lawyer Henry's going to lend me, the evidence is kind of stacked against you."

"Whoa, wait—he's going to lend you a lawyer? *Henry Li? You?*" Andrew looks like he's only just now realizing the nature of my relationship with Henry, and hates himself for the oversight.

I shrug. "Well, Henry's company has twelve lawyers. All graduates from Harvard, Tsinghua, or Peking University. He can definitely spare one if things get messy for me."

A dark vein jumps in Andrew's forehead. He's sweating profusely—from the heat or nerves, I can't tell. Maybe both. Either way, I seize the chance to keep talking. "Look,

Andrew, I'm short on time, so I'll just spell it out for you. If you take this to court, or sue me—if you dare try to absolve yourself of this crime—you're most definitely going to lose. You're also definitely going to waste time and money and resources—"

"So would you," Andrew interjects.

"I know," I say, keeping my voice level. "But I don't have an important company position to worry about. If this case were to blow up, and news were to get out that you and your father hired someone to kidnap a child just to secure a promotion... Well, it wouldn't look too good for you, would it?"

"No." He shakes his head. More sweat forms along his hairline, trickles down his cheek. "No. *No.* That's not..." He trails off and stills, as if something's just occurred to him. Looks up at me. "You had other clients for Beijing Ghost, didn't you?"

"What of it?"

"They'd be able to prove you're lying. Beijing Ghost wasn't a study app—it was a *criminal app.* With them backing me up—"

"Do you know how much dirt I have on the kids in our year level?" I raise my eyebrows. *Did you seriously think I wouldn't have thought of this beforehand?* I add in my head. "Even if I didn't blackmail them, do you expect them to willingly reveal to the school or the police the sort of things they hired me for?"

His nostrils flare, lips setting into a sullen line. I'm right, and he knows it. He looks so defeated, so helpless, with his massive frame hunched over the low table, that for a moment I almost feel bad for him.

Almost.

"Fine, fine, fine. You've made your point," he finally mutters. "What do you want me to do?"

I try not to show how weird this new dynamic is to me; *I'm* always the one doing what others want, the one desperate enough to agree to pretty much anything.

"Just go along with my story," I instruct. My mouth feels dry all of a sudden, likely in anticipation of what's to come. I wish I'd remembered to bring a bottle of water. There were so many in the back of Henry's company car. "A representative from the school board will be meeting with us soon."

He frowns. "*Soon?* How soon?"

I grab my phone and fire a quick text at Henry: All done. He responds immediately with a thumbs-up. "As in...now."

Right on cue, the conference room doors swing wide open, and Henry and Chanel stride in like characters from a movie scene. Seriously. I wouldn't be surprised if they were moving toward me in slow motion, and dramatic music started swelling in the background. Since school has technically ended by this hour, they're both wearing their own clothes, instead of uniforms. Henry looks distractingly attractive, dressed in the kind of crisp, tailored black suit that wouldn't make him seem out of place on Wall Street, and Chanel has on this elaborate, shoulder-padded blazer with gold buttons.

Next to them, my discount supermarket sweater must look even cheaper and sadder than usual—which is the whole point. When I messaged Chanel today about helping out at this meeting, I'd asked her to dress as nicely as she could, and made the same request of Henry.

For my plan to work, I need to swallow my pride and really lean into the desperate-student-attempted-crime-just-to-survive look.

On the heels of Henry and Chanel, a woman who can only be Madam Yao, representative of the school board, makes her entrance. She doesn't so much walk as *glide* into the conference room, her movements streamlined like a shark in water. Everything about her is elegant, unnervingly precise—from the string of delicate pearls arranged around her neck and her silver-streaked gravity-defying bob, to the hard angles and creases of her unsmiling face.

Even in heels, she's shorter than I am, yet she manages to tower over everyone as she moves to take her seat at the head of the table, barely even reacting when Henry helps pull out the chair for her like the gentleman he is.

For a long time, she doesn't speak. Just fixes each of us with her cold black gaze—first Andrew, then Chanel and Henry, who are both now standing close by my side, then finally...me.

Despite the hot air blasting through the vents at full force, my teeth chatter violently.

"Sun Yan, was it?" she says, breaking the silence at last. Her accent is part British, part Malaysian, and something else I can't quite identify. All I know is that she looks and sounds like old money, and that she probably already hates me. "I believe we corresponded over email."

"Yes." I try to match her formal tone. "Thank you for your prompt response."

She ignores me.

"And this..." She turns to Andrew, who immediately stiffens in his seat. "This is Andrew She? The student who reached out via the study application named Beijing Ghost, and offered money in exchange for the execution of the kidnapping?"

I shoot Andrew a quick, warning look.

He pouts, but nods once. "Y-yeah. That's me."

"Well." Madam Yao sniffs. "I do wish we didn't have to meet in these unfortunate circumstances. The school board is deeply disappointed in both of you, you know. It is difficult enough running one of the top schools in Beijing without having to deal with a major potential lawsuit. Peter's parents are still *very* angry, as I'm sure you can imagine, and *someone* is going to have to take full responsibility. After all, Airington would never condone such lowly criminal behavior."

I doubt it's a coincidence that her eyes land on me. The easy target. The only one who isn't paying full school fees, who doesn't have the ability to donate entire school buildings. Despite Andrew's confession, it's still more convenient for the school if *I'm* guilty, rather than him.

I grit my teeth. If I'm honest, part of me had been hoping to settle all of this in a polite, nonconfrontational fashion, but I guess that's off the table. Madam Yao can't even look at me without looking down on me.

Time to go on the offensive.

"Someone should take responsibility," I agree with forced calm. "Which reminds me—did you read the article I sent you?"

Her voice is cold. "I don't see how that's relevant right now."

"Don't you?" It goes against my every instinct to talk to an authority figure like this, but I plough on. "Because the article should offer a vastly different perspective on the events leading up to the kidnapping. *My* perspective. If it were published, who do you think the public would side with? The working-class girl who resorted to helping her rich classmate pull off a crime just to pay for school, or the classmate who devised the whole thing for personal gain, and yet was still given the benefit of the doubt by everyone in charge?"

Madam Yao's thin lips press together until they're almost white. Yeah, she definitely hates me.

"I bet people would also find it interesting," I continue, "that I was put in such a difficult position to begin with. I mean, Airington's second main school objective is that it's accessible for all, right? That it welcomes students from different backgrounds? Yet you have a twenty-million-RMB mini golf course and only one scholarship offer for the entire student body. And it's not even a *full* scholarship. Do you even realize how much money 150,000 RMB is? How long it'd take for anyone below the upper middle class to earn that?"

The more I speak, the angrier I get, and the steadier my voice grows. I think of all the people like me, like Lucy Goh or Evie Wu or even the young woman from the restaurant with Chanel's father. The neglected ones, the unlucky ones, the ones who want more than they've been given. The ones who have to crawl and scrape and fight their way up from the very bottom, who have to game a system designed for them to lose. Always the first to be punished and blamed when things go wrong. Always the last to be seen, to be saved.

And I know that's not going to change within a matter of days or even years, but maybe it can start with something like this: with me, sitting across from Madam Yao, Henry and

Chanel positioned by my side, wrestling back power from the powerful bit by bit by bit.

"You believe that someone should take responsibility," Madam Yao says stiffly, when I pause to take a breath. "But based on what I'm hearing now, and what I've read, you don't think that someone should be you, correct?"

I lay my palms flat on the table. "Look, I'm not saying that I'm completely innocent, or that I'm the victim here. I made some wrong choices, and I'm genuinely sorry Peter's injured. It should never have gone that far. *However*," I add, before she can try to twist my words again, "I *am* saying that this case should be handled fairly, and that the consequences should be proportionate to our actions, not our places in society."

"Of course we'd handle it fairly," Madam Yao says, in such a dismissive way she might as well outright state she's lying. "But even if we didn't, do you really expect a single unpublished article to sway our opinion?"

Chanel snorts.

Madam Yao's eyes flicker up to her. "Is there something funny, Ms. Cao?"

All things considered, I guess it shouldn't surprise me that Madam Yao has no problem identifying Chanel right away, but it still makes my fingers curl.

"Oh, nothing, really," Chanel replies, her voice breezy. "But I wouldn't underestimate the power of a *single article* if I were you. Don't you know how easy it is for things to go viral these days? Especially when they're posted onto a platform with twenty million active followers?"

At last, a small crack in Madam Yao's stony mask. "I'm

afraid you will have to be more specific. What is this...platform you are speaking of?"

Henry steps in, his arm resting deliberately on the back of my chair: a casual reminder to everyone that he's on my side. "Well, as you may know, Madam Yao, my father runs the biggest tech start-up in all of China." For once, I don't correct him with *second biggest*. "We have a mass following across our many apps, as well as various social media accounts. Connections to the media. Resources we could access in an instant..."

"And not to brag, but we're both kind of popular in our social circles," Chanel chimes in, smiling sweetly. "I know like, forty international kids from my school in Australia who are thinking of coming back to Beijing to study. I *was* planning on recommending Airington to them and their families, but now, seeing the way you're treating my dear friend Alice... I'm not so sure."

"I'm not so sure, either," Henry says, all solemn, and I have to swallow back a bubble of hysterical laughter at the look on Madam Yao's face. Her lips are almost invisible. "My father and I may be forced to reconsider whether Airington even deserves all those donated buildings. In fact, I don't know if I want to stay at a school that favors some students over others."

"I'm also not sure," Andrew offers. Everyone turns to stare at him. "What?" he says defensively, sliding lower in his seat. "I thought we were doing a thing."

"Yeah, and you just ruined the thing, Andrew." Chanel rolls her eyes. "You're not part of this."

Andrew scowls. "I'm never part of anything."

"Well, maybe if you stopped hiring people to kidnap your classmates..." Chanel mutters.

"I obviously wouldn't have had to *hire* anyone if I were in like, a squad," Andrew protests. "I bet the members of BTS could just call each other to help out with that kind of stuff."

"Andrew," Henry says on an exasperated sigh. "You have grossly misunderstood the point Chanel was trying to make."

"As well as like, the general situation," Chanel adds.

Madam Yao clears her throat loudly.

"Right. *So sorry*, Madame Yao," Chanel says, applying just enough sarcasm to her voice to get away with it. "Back to what we were saying—"

Madam Yao raises one pale manicured hand in the air. A ridiculously large emerald ring gleams on her middle finger, beneath a thin band of sparkling diamonds. "You've said quite enough, Ms. Cao. All of you have."

"And?" Chanel prompts, totally unfazed. "What do you think?"

I hold my breath, my heart punching my ribs.

I'm only around seventy-eight percent certain how Madam Yao will respond, which, statistically speaking, isn't the best odds. But if there's anything I've learned from my time running Beijing Ghost, it's that the people here care about reputation above all else. Reputation is currency, a source of power. The same way that money is only valuable because everyone deems it so, Airington is only considered *elite* and *exclusive* because rich parents keep wanting to send their kids here.

That would change pretty quickly if we made good on our threats.

"I think," Madam Yao begins, her words laced with equal parts venom and resignation, "that Sun Yan here has proven just how...important she is to the Airington student body, and how much she has to say on the subject. The school board will review her and Andrew's involvement in the kidnapping accordingly. Now, if you'll excuse me..." The chair squeaks as she pushes back her seat and rises, straightening her already-immaculate silk blouse with a grimace. "It appears I have a few calls to make."

And just like that, she's off, her kitten heels clacking every step of the way to the door.

Once she leaves, the temperature in the room seems to warm by a few degrees. I stretch in my seat and exhale a long, tired breath. I hadn't realized how tense my muscles were until now.

Andrew looks around at us hopefully. "So, uh, do you guys want to hang out for a bit or—"

"Andrew, again, *you're not part of this*," Chanel interrupts, hands on her hips. "And shouldn't you be, like, taking this time to reflect on your actions?"

"Yeah, yeah, I know," he grumbles, his face falling. "Kidnapping is bad. Being a criminal is rough. Never hire smart people to do your dirty work for you."

Henry pinches the bridge of his nose. "Please just go."

As Andrew slides out of his chair, still sulking and muttering under his breath the whole time, I turn to Henry and Chanel.

"Thank you guys so much," I say, instantly hating how awkward I sound. "It really... It means a lot. And Chanel— I'm sorry to have messaged you so last-minute. And for kind of ghosting you these past few weeks. I swear I—"

"Alice. Oh my god." Chanel shakes her head at me with a kind of affectionate incredulity. "We barely even did anything except flex a little. *You're* the one who came up with this whole idea and wrote the article and all that. Besides," she adds, her voice growing serious, "it's pretty fucked-up how the school was treating you. If I'd known earlier…"

"You couldn't have. I didn't want you to."

She sighs. "Well, at least now we do. Henry and I have both been worried as hell about you, you know." She pauses and nudges Henry, who pointedly looks away. "*Especially* Henry. I don't think I've ever seen him so distracted in class before. He even answered wrong to a basic chemistry question that *I* knew."

I raise my brows, a slow smile rising to my face. "Really?"

Henry makes a low, noncommittal noise with the back of his throat. Busies himself adjusting the cuffs of his sleeves.

I won't lie, the suit really does look good on him. It doesn't hurt that he just threatened one of the most powerful people in Airington for my sake. And when he finally meets my gaze, crow-black curls falling just over his brows, biting his lower lip, something fills the tight space between my ribs. A lovely pain, a tender ache that feels suspiciously close to longing. Not just that, but… For the first time since our Experiencing China trip ended, I allow myself to acknowledge how much I've missed him. *God*, I've missed him. I somehow still do, even though he's standing right in front of me.

I must've zoned out of the conversation, because the next thing I know, Chanel's grinning at me like she can tell exactly what I'm thinking, and Henry's saying, "Do you want to go home now?" and I feel kind of dizzy. My whole body feels overheated, like a laptop that's been left charging for way too long. Electricity courses through my veins.

Do I want to go home now?

"No. Not yet," I say, more sharply than I mean to. Henry tenses, his expression bemused. Chanel merely winks. "Just— just come with me."

Without another word, I grab Henry by the wrist and lead him out the building, across the empty courtyard, and into the shelter of a small pavilion well concealed by the school gardens. Pale chrysanthemums bloom from the shadows like fresh snow, almost the same shade as the pagoda's five tall pillars.

I push Henry against the closest one, bracketing his body with my own.

This isn't like me at all.

My heart's beating at twice its usual rate, and I know I'm not thinking clearly, that there's too much adrenaline and euphoria left over in my bloodstream from the meeting, but right now, I don't care. I truly *don't care*, and it's kind of terrifying.

It's also kind of thrilling.

"Okay," I say, because I know Henry's waiting for me to speak. To explain. "Okay, so here's the thing: There's no guarantee what decision the school board's going to reach in the end, right? And there's no guarantee when or where we'll see each other again, or if I'll even be allowed back on school grounds, so I just think… Well, I've been thinking about it for a while now, but I guess I was in denial, or just scared…" I pause, scrambling for the right words. If the right words even exist for this strange heat inside my chest. "There's so much out of our control, but I can control what I do now, with you, or else I'll probably kick myself for it later. You know what I mean?"

We're standing so close that I can feel Henry's muscles tense as I wait for his answer, hear the subtle shift in his breathing. After what seems like an excruciatingly long pause, he replies, "I...do not have the faintest clue what you're saying."

I bite back a frustrated sigh and look at him. Really *look* at him, at the rare hints of uncertainty mixed with amusement in his elegant features, at the slight part of his lips, the scorching black of his eyes.

Dimly, I remember myself thinking not too long ago that we could never kiss. Something about stubbornness. Something about discipline. I remember thinking a month ago about how much I hated him, how I couldn't bear to even be in the same room as him.

Now I can't bear the few inches of distance between us.

"You know what? I'm just going to go ahead with it," I decide out loud.

Henry freezes and stares at me as if I'm speaking another language. "With what?"

"This."

I draw in a sharp breath. Focus on his lips.

Then, before I can lose my nerve, I seize Henry Li's collar and kiss him.

Or rather, I sort of smash my face against his, which is exactly as smooth and romantic as it sounds. I don't even have time to *register* how it feels when he jerks his head back with a muffled yelp.

I release him, mortified, and see him raising one finger to the corner of his mouth, a stunned expression on his face. Both his lips and ears are tinged red. "Alice. You just *bit* me."

Well, shit.

"I—I'm so sorry," I babble, fighting the urge to flee to the other end of the universe. Oh my god. Why did I just do that? What was I thinking? Why am I even *alive* right now? "I swear I wasn't— It didn't—"

I break off when I see Henry double over, his shoulders shaking. For one horrifying, heart-stopping moment, I'm scared I might've actually caused some severe tissue damage.

Then I realize that he's laughing.

All my concern boils into indignation.

"It's not funny," I protest, my cheeks hot, my voice coming out embarrassingly shrill. "This—this was meant to be a very serious, touching moment, and you were meant to fall desperately in love with me on the spot and discover how good I am—"

The rest of my words die on my tongue as Henry straightens, laughter still dancing in his eyes, cups my face in one hand, and presses his lips against mine.

This time, I do register the kiss, everything from the warmth of his skin to the brush of his lashes when he closes his eyes and—

Wow.

It's nothing like the way they describe it in the movies, like all the stars aligning and fireworks exploding across an ink-black sky. It feels both quieter and bigger than that, as simple as coming home and as dizzying and all-encompassing as the wind rushing in around us. It feels like a thousand banished and buried moments have been building up to this—to us alone and untethered and weak with wanting—and maybe they have.

A low, embarrassing sound escapes the base of my throat.

Henry responds by leaning deeper into the kiss, and the world goes hazy. All I can think about is his lips, so devastatingly soft on mine, and his hands, now firm around the back of my neck, tangling deep in the roots of my hair...

There's a slight chance that he's better at this than I am.

Just this once, I'll let him have it.

20

I barely remember the car ride from Airington to my apartment. I'd let Henry's chauffeur drive us, partly because I wanted to be around Henry as long as time would allow, and partly because I wasn't sure I could trust myself to take the subway without getting lost. My mind felt numb, hot, like it'd been set aflame. I couldn't think straight. I couldn't even *breathe* properly.

Worse still, I couldn't stop glancing at Henry's lips, even as he walked me to my front door and waved goodbye. This, I suppose, is one of those unexpected side effects of kissing that no one ever warned me about: after you kiss someone once, the possibilities of kissing them again are endless.

But now, sitting back down inside my cluttered living room, the idea of making out with Henry Li is the last thing on my mind.

Both Xiaoyi and Mama went out while I was still at school—Xiaoyi, to get a foot massage, and Mama, to handle something at the hospital—leaving only Baba and me in the flat.

"I just got call from your school," Baba tells me as he enters the room.

I watch him carefully from the couch, assessing his expression, his tone. I wasn't exaggerating when I told Henry that Baba and I aren't exactly on speaking terms these days; he only addresses me when necessary, and always with a heavy air of disappointment. But the near-permanent furrow between his brows appears to have smoothed out a little, and he's approaching me directly. Good signs.

"A call?" I say, feigning surprise.

"Yes." He moves to sit on the opposite end of the couch, the springs creaking under his weight. "They told me about app... What's the name... China Ghoul?"

My pulse speeds up.

"Beijing Ghost, you mean?"

He nods slowly, and continues in Mandarin, "Why didn't you tell me or the teachers earlier you were part of the study group?"

"I guess..." I fumble for the right words, for an answer as close to the truth as possible without giving everything away. "I was scared it'd seem suspicious. I mean, I *did* make a lot of money off the app—just through tutoring. Over one hundred thousand RMB. I was worried you or the school would make me give it back."

Baba's eyes widen a fraction with shock. "One *hundred thousand* RMB?"

"Yeah," I reply. "It's a lot, I know. Hence why I was worried..."

"And you earned that much only by helping your class-mates study? Nothing else?"

I have to laugh, though nothing about the question is really funny. Just ironic. "Well, you and Mama spend almost all your income on my school fees," I point out. "Is it so surprising that other kids would want to invest in their education, too?"

"Hmph," is all he says, but I can tell he believes me.

"Anyway," I continue, more quietly. Sincerely. "I'm really sorry things turned out the way they did. I just... When An-drew offered me the money, all I could think of was how you and Mama were struggling to pay for school—how you were struggling because of *me*. At the time, his offer seemed like the quickest solution to everything. Like completing the task might somehow allow me to pay you guys back." I swallow and press my hands together to keep from fidgeting. Every word feels like pulling teeth. "But I was being irrational, and greedy, and just...incredibly dumb. And I understand if—if you can't forgive me, or if you plan on being disappointed in me for all of eternity, but... I wanted to say I'm sorry, Baba. That's all."

Baba takes a deep breath, and I hold mine, anticipating yet another lecture. But it doesn't come.

Instead, he places a gentle hand on my head, briefly, the way he used to when I was a kid, whenever I was scared or injured or couldn't fall asleep at night. When I look up in surprise, all the anger is gone from his eyes.

"Alice," he says. "Your Mama and I don't work hard for you to repay us. We work hard so that you can have a bet-ter life. An easier life. And sending you to Airington—that was our choice. Spending our income on your school fees—

that was also our choice. In no way should you feel obligated to take on the burden of our decisions for us. Is that clear?"

To my embarrassment, my throat constricts, the basin of my heart overflowing, spilling into hope. There is so much stubborn hope.

I manage a small nod, and Baba smiles at me.

Maybe everything will be okay, I think.

"Speaking of Airington..." Baba pulls his hand back. Rests it on his lap. "They've already passed on the new information to Peter Oh's parents. Since you apparently play a more minor role in the incident than they initially thought, they've chosen not to press charges."

"But?" I press, sensing the shift in his tone.

"Peter's parents are not pressing charges...but they *are* pressuring the school to make you leave once this semester is over. And based on my call with them earlier, I believe the school would like that as well."

Oh.

I bite the inside of my cheek, waiting for the anger and panic to hit with full force, the questions to go off in my brain like a string of firecrackers: *What will I do next? Who will I be without Airington?*

And while I do feel all those things, dully, an unexpected calm washes over me. A kind of resignation. Deep down, I'd suspected something like this was coming; there was no way I could walk away from a crime of this magnitude *completely* unscathed.

"I understand," I say, and the steadiness of my own voice surprises me. I sound calm, confident like Chanel or Henry. In a weird way, after hitting rock bottom and confronting

Andrew and standing up to a representative of the school board, I feel ready to take on anything. Or survive anything, at least. "We'll work something out."

"What will you work out?"

Baba and I both turn at the faint rattle of keys, the low click of the front door shutting behind Mama. She's wearing the old coat she bought on sale in America, her hair pulled back into a tight bun that emphasizes the sharpness of her eyes and chin.

"It's…nothing to worry about. I'll explain over dinner," I say as she heads into the kitchen for her usual after-work routine: washing her face and scrubbing her hands for twenty seconds. After a moment's deliberation, I get up too.

When Mama reemerges, I've already laid the small paper box out on the couch, the white of the package almost blinding in contrast to the old mustard cushions. It's a silly little gift, probably a basic necessity for other families—but since gifts are so rare in our house, I'd been wondering when to give it to Mama. In light of Baba's news, now seems like as good a time as any.

"What's this?" Mama asks, eyeing the box.

"I bought it for you. With my own money, of course," I add hastily.

Mama opens the box very carefully, as if afraid she might break it with one wrong move, and a bottle of expensive hand cream falls out into her open palm. She doesn't say anything, just stares at the pretty bottle, at the delicate flower print snaking up its side, the recognizable brand name printed on top.

"I… I know your hands are always super dry from work," I explain, more because the silence makes me nervous than anything. Will she think it's a waste of money? "And when we were at the store the other day, I just thought, I might as well... It's apparently supposed to help heal scars too." I wring my hands together. "But if you don't like it, I could always return it—"

Mama throws her arms around me, pulling me close. "Sha haizi," she whispers into my hair. *Silly child.*

And as I lean against her, breathing in her familiar scent, I think, *Maybe I was right earlier.*

Maybe everything really will be okay.

Three long phone calls and countless rounds of emails later (all of which are ominously titled: *Re: Alice Incident*), I'm standing back outside the Airington school gates, a light bag in my hands.

After some negotiating, the school and Peter's parents and I came to an agreement: I'm to leave Airington this December, but I get to spend my last few days here, finishing up my coursework for the semester and saying goodbye to my friends and teachers.

"Name?"

The security guard stares at me through the iron bars, and I'm struck by a sudden, overwhelming sense of déjà vu.

"Alice Sun," I tell him, and offer a small smile. It's weird how much I'll miss everything about this place, now that I know I'm leaving—even this guy who can never seem to remember my name.

And who's now watching me suspiciously.

"Why are you smiling?"

"Nothing, just..." I gesture to the deep blue sky above us, not a single winter cloud in sight. "It's a nice day, that's all."

He glances up, then back at me, then up again, confusion shadowing his features. He looks young, maybe somewhere in his midtwenties. I wonder if he's just graduated from college, how long he's been living in Beijing, why he chose to work here. I hate that I'm only noticing these things now. "Uh, yeah, I guess it is..." He clears his throat. "Your year level?"

"Twelve."

But I'm not the one who answers.

"Hi, Mr. Chen," I greet as he draws closer to the gates, hoping he can't detect the nervous wobble in my voice. He's always been the teacher I respect the most—and the one I'm most afraid of disappointing.

Judging from his expression, the way his eyes dart to my bag and understanding flickers over them, he's well up-to-date with the whole *Alice Incident*. Yet he doesn't appear angry, exactly.

"Well, don't just stand there like a stranger," he says, waving me forward. "Come in. There's something I've been meaning to talk to you about."

"If I asked you about the main point of *Macbeth* now, what would you say?" Mr. Chen asks as we enter his office.

It's quiet here. Clean. The bookshelves stacked but tidy, the walls almost hidden beneath rows of plaques and certificates from Harvard, Peking University, TED. I'm so busy staring I almost forget he's asked me a question.

"Um..." I scramble to collect my thoughts. There's a double

meaning in there, I'm sure of it. "That…no action is without consequence? That ambition should not go unchecked?"

He nods, satisfied, and motions for me to take a seat. "Good, good. Just wanted to set my conscience at ease first—but so long as you've learned your lesson…"

"I have," I say quickly. "Really."

He nods again, then says, "I heard you'll be leaving Airington after this semester. Have you decided which school to attend next year?"

"Not yet, no. There are certain…limitations I have to work through."

Mr. Chen doesn't look surprised. After my parents visited the school, I guess most people have realized I don't come from one of the wealthier families.

"Well then." He claps his hands together suddenly, startling me from my thoughts. "I might have just the solution."

I stare at him. "You—you do?"

"Now, I probably should've checked with you beforehand about this but… A friend of mine, Dr. Alexandra Xiao, recently opened up her own international school in Chaoyang District. It's much smaller than this, of course, and they don't have student housing, so you'd have to figure out the accommodations. The environment isn't the best either—there's a fish market right next to campus, though Alex promises you get used to the smell after a while…" He laughs a little, and I get the sense I should be laughing too, except I can't. I can't do anything but grip the edge of the seat and pray he's saying what I think he's saying.

"Anyway, they still have a few spots open, and I mentioned your family situation, showed them your report card and some of your recent coursework, and told them you're one of my best students—"

My eyes widen. "You did?"

"I did, because it's true," he says simply. "And since Alex knows I never exaggerate, she might potentially be able to offer you a scholarship. You'd still have to take an entrance exam first, of course, but I'm sure you'll do well." He pauses, gives me time to let this all sink in. "So. What do you think?"

I almost trip over my own tongue to answer him. "O-of course, that's— When are the exams? Are there practice exams available? Do I need to prepare references, or—" Then I calm down a little, and a more obvious question occurs to me: "Why... Why are you helping me?"

Mr. Chen looks out the window of his office, at the students throwing their heads back in laughter, books tucked under arms, walking in groups from one class to another. Carefree. Happy. Sunlight spills everywhere around them, over them, flooding through the wutong trees. Slowly, Mr. Chen says, "You know, I was the first person in my entire village in Henan to attend college, and then I moved to the States with my mother. My father never came with us—he didn't speak a word of English, but he tried to fund my education as best as he could by selling sweet potatoes every morning..." He shakes his head. "I get it, how hard it is. And while it's important to know how to fight your way to the top... It's always nice when there are others to help lift us up, don't you think?"

Thank you, I try to say, but gratitude swells in my chest, up my throat, stealing my voice away.

He seems to get it, though.

"It's strange," he adds, his gaze drifting to the certificates on his wall. "There was once a time when no one really noticed me at all. When I was invisible to the world..." He smiles faintly, as if sharing a private joke with himself. As if recalling some distant memory that makes sense to him alone.

My heart stutters. Stops. *Could it be...?*

"So what changed?" My voice is hardly more than a whisper. "Getting into a good uni? Getting recognized?"

He shakes his head. "No. No, on the contrary, after I got into Harvard and started winning all these awards... I felt more invisible than ever. People were complimenting me, congratulating me left and right, saying my name over and over again, but none of that really mattered. It was only when I left to teach English—to do something I genuinely cared about, that made me feel like myself—that everything started getting better." He looks over at me, his eyes crinkling. "Descartes was wrong, you know, when he said, 'To live well, you must live unseen.' To live well, you must learn to see yourself first. Do you understand what I'm saying?"

And I do. I do.

Henry and I meet by the koi ponds before dawn.

I study him as he makes his way over in quick, purposeful strides. His hair is still slightly damp from the shower, hanging in dark waves over his forehead. His cheeks are pink from the early morning chill. He looks good. Familiar. Vulnerable, in the best way.

I'll miss you, I think.

"Punctual as ever," I say, closing the distance between us.

He offers me one of his rare Henry Li smiles: soft and beautiful and so startlingly sincere it takes your goddamn breath away. "Well, I wouldn't want you to miss it."

For a second, I imagine he's read my mind. "Miss what?"

He raises an eyebrow. "The midyear awards ceremony?"

"Oh." A small, surprised laugh escapes my lips. In what now feels like another lifetime, the ceremony alone would've been the highlight of my day. Maybe even one of the highlights of my life. "I guess I forgot."

"That's understandable," he says, his smile widening. "Since I'll be getting all the awards anyw—"

I elbow him, hard, and he laughs.

"Don't get too cocky," I warn him. "Just because I'm going to a different school, doesn't mean I won't beat you in our IB exams."

"We'll see," is all he says, the challenge clear in his tone.

I suppress a smile of my own. *Challenge accepted.*

We start walking around the frozen pond, breaking the easy silence with our footsteps, breathing in the crisp winter air. I bury my hands into the warmth of my blazer pockets and look toward the empty courtyard to our left, remembering the first time I turned invisible there. It's funny, but I haven't felt cold in a long time now. I'm not sure if I ever will again.

"So," I say, as we approach a stone bench and sit, his shoulder bumping lightly against mine. "Did you get my business proposal?"

"Yes. All seventy-five pages of it." His eyes gleam. "And the summary. And the summary of the summary. And the annotated diagram. And the table of contents—"

"Excuse me for being *thorough*," I huff. "I really want this app to be good, you know?"

"I know," he says, no longer teasing. He hesitates, then laces his slender fingers through mine, and I have to focus very hard on remembering how to breathe. I don't think I'll ever get used to his proximity, or the way he's currently looking at me, like he's in as much awe as I am that we can just do this now. Just sit and hold hands in the near dark and say what we mean. "Trust me, it will be. With the two of us working behind the scenes, your promotional strategy, and the template ready... It'll be perfect."

This time, I can't hold back the grin that stretches across my face.

The idea came to me around a week ago, when we first transformed Beijing Ghost into a fake study app. My plan is to make the app a legit one—one that helps connect rich, privileged kids from private international schools with low-income students like me. It's meant to work both ways; tutoring and homework help starts from a minimum rate of 400 RMB per session for those from wealthier demographics, but it's completely free for working-class students. Then there's the added bonus of allowing kids from disadvantaged backgrounds to form connections with Beijing's elite.

I've also decided to keep the point system in; the three highest-ranking working-class users at the end of each year will get a full scholarship to any school they wish, sponsored by Henry's company.

"Oh yeah—I sent the business proposal to Chanel, too," I tell Henry.

He doesn't look surprised. "Of course you did. What does she think?"

"She's in," I say, which is a massive understatement. When

I pitched the idea to Chanel over WeChat three nights ago, she'd squealed and started brainstorming slogans and making calls to her fuerdai friends right away. "I mean, her exact words were: *fuck yeah!* She also thinks the three of us should have weekly meetings to sort this out, starting with hot pot tonight. Her treat."

The corner of Henry's lips tugs up, briefly. "I suppose we'll be seeing each other quite often then. Even after you leave."

"Even after I leave," I echo, and the gravity of these words, this reality, pulls both of us back into silence once more. I don't know what else to say, so I move to nestle my head against the strong curve of his shoulder. He lets me.

"What do you imagine you'll do?" he asks, a few beats later. "In the future?"

"I don't know. I want…"

I trail off, my mind whirring. I still want so much, so badly. My heart still aches for all the bright things beyond my reach. I want to be smarter and richer and stronger and just…*better*.

But honestly? I also want to be happy. To invest in something meaningful and fulfilling, even if it is difficult, and maybe not the most practical option in the world. To spend more time with Baba and Mama and Xiaoyi, and finally hang out with Chanel, and go out on a proper date with Henry. I want to laugh until my stomach hurts, and write until I've crafted something that delights me, and learn to bask in my small, private victories. Learn to accept that these things, too, are worth wanting.

"For a start, I think I want to focus on English more," I muse, and just saying it aloud feels…right. Like my heart has been waiting for my mind to catch up this entire time.

"Maybe sign up for a journalism course over the break. I've compiled a list of suitable options already—ones that offer full merit-based scholarships..."

"That sounds great," he says, with full sincerity.

"Yeah?"

"Yeah."

"It's a deal then," I say, angling my head to look up at him. "You'll become the head of the number one tech start-up in all of China, and I'll be a renowned, award-winning journalist or English professor. Together, we'll—"

"Be the nation's greatest power couple?" he offers.

"I was going to say *conquer the world*," I admit. "But sure. I guess we can start small."

He laughs, and the sound is like bottled magic. Like birdsong.

I turn my gaze toward the sky, my fingers still intertwined with his. In the distance, the darkness has started to lift like a veil, the first light of dawn spilling over the Beijing skyline, a promise of all the beautiful and terrible and sun-soaked days to come.

★ ★ ★ ★ ★

ACKNOWLEDGMENTS

I have a small confession to make: when I was drafting this book in the dim light of my college dorm, I would often stop and daydream about one day writing the acknowledgments section. That I get to actually live out this silly daydream now is thanks to many, many people.

Thank you to my superhero of an agent, Kathleen Rushall, for believing in this book, and in me. From our very first email exchange, I knew it would be a dream to have you in my corner, and I remain in constant awe of how masterfully you handle everything. None of this would have been possible without your enthusiasm, wisdom, and guidance. Thank you also to the entire team at Andrea Brown Literary Agency for all your incredible work.

Thank you to Rebecca Kuss for seeing straight into the heart of my story and opening up the doors to the publishing world, and to Claire Stetzer for taking me in and making me feel at home. My endless thanks to the brilliant Bess Braswell, Brittany Mitchell, Laura Gianino, Justine Sha, Linette Kim, and everyone at Inkyard Press for your dedication and support. A huge thank you to Gigi Lau and Carolina Rodríguez Fuenmayor for the cover of my dreams—I still cannot believe how stunning it is, and how lucky I am.

Thank you to the extraordinary Katrina Escudero for everything you've done.

More thanks to my wonderful former teachers: Mr. Locke, who encouraged my writing all the way back when I was a very obnoxious Year Seven student. Mr. Mellen, who taught me how to craft an essay and sparked my interest in the humanities. Ms. Nuttall, who told me I was a writer and helped me believe it too. Ms. Devlin, who inspires me every day with her passion and knowledge and is a literal saint.

All my thanks to the authors I admire, both as writers and as people. To Chloe Gong, for being such a huge source of inspiration and serotonin—please know I will always be one of your biggest fangirls. To Grace Li, for being one of the very first people to read this book, and for being as incredibly kind as you are talented. To Gloria Chao, for being so welcoming and generous, and for paving the way with your words. To Zoulfa Katouh, for making me cry over your book, and also over your sweetest messages about mine—I'm so glad to know you. To Vanessa Len, for being so supportive from the beginning, and for being so patient in explaining how taxes work. To Em Liu, for seeing the heart of my book, and understanding all the little references. To Miranda Sun, for hyping me up all the way back when I first signed with my agent, and for your delightful company online. To Roselle Lim, for taking the time to read this and writing such a lovely blurb—I couldn't be more honoured.

Thank you to Sarah Brewer for being the first person to read one of my earlier, embarrassing attempts at a book, and saying such kind things. Your encouragement meant more to my teen self than I can express.

A huge thank-you to all the lovely book bloggers and librarians and early readers. To everyone who celebrated with me on Twitter when my book announcement went live, who commented the nicest things on my cringe TikTok videos and Instagram posts, who liked my excerpt in the Facebook Beta Readers and Critique Partners group, who added my book on Goodreads when there wasn't a cover or even a blurb. You're the reason I do this, and get to do this.

Thank you to Phoebe Bear and Fiona Xia for being amazing friends, and amazing in general. Phoebe—remember when I mentioned this new book idea I had at brunch and you said, "I'd read the shit out of that"? I'm infinitely grateful you did. And Fi, who's cheered for me despite still not knowing what YA is—I'll always cheer for you too in everything you do. Thank you also to the Khorovians, who are some of the warmest and most talented people I know.

Thank you to Taylor Swift for existing.

Thank you to my little sister, Alyssa Liang, for being my first and biggest fan. Thank you for your puns and your patience, your constant reassurance that the book isn't bad, and your excitement, which often exceeds even mine. Though I'd been prepared to remain an only child, I'm grateful every day that I'm not.

And finally, thank you to Mama and Baba, who are prouder

of me than I deserve, and far less strict than the parents in this book. The only reason I am able to get anywhere is because I know there will always be a home waiting for me, with warm clothes and sliced fruit and all my favorite dishes.